I0589850

Noodles for Shakespeare

Pygmalion Down Under

Cenarth Fox

Noodles for Shakespeare

Copyright © Cenarth Fox 2017
All rights reserved.

This is a work of fiction. It is based on the play *Shakespeare in Saigon*. The names, characters, businesses, settings, events, and incidents are either products of the author's imagination or are used fictitiously.

Apart from fair dealing for the purposes of research, study, criticism or review as permitted under the Copyright Act, no part of this book may be reproduced, or stored, or transmitted in any form or by any means, without the express written permission of the publisher.

Cenarth Fox has asserted his right to be identified as the author of this work in accordance with the Copyright Act 1968.

First published in 2017 by Fox Plays
www.foxplays.com
www.cenfoxbooks.com

ISBN 978 0 949175 14 4

Cover design by oliviaprodesign

Because this novel is written in English, Vietnamese names are written with the given names first and the family name last.

Dedicated to the memory of
David Small
actor, broadcaster, writer, gentleman

1

Vietnam 1975

THE AMERICAN ARMY OFFICER RAN FOR HIS LIFE. He threw open the front door, scared the life out of his wife and kids, and shouted. 'We're going, now! Come on!'

The family had a plan. One packed suitcase stood ready, and the family dog joined its new owner. The humans piled into their car, and headed straight for the Saigon airport. Their great escape began.

It did so because Dad, and thousands of others, heard a certain song on Saigon radio. Some songs have an interesting back-story. In 1942, Israel Beilin wrote a Christmas ditty. Israel was a Russian Jew, probably born in Siberia, who became a self-taught pianist in the Big Apple. His Christmas song featured snow, had eight sentences, and one version became the best-selling single ever.

Towards the end of the Vietnam War, this famous tune became a secret code advising Americans to vamoose. Harry Lillis Crosby Jr. singing *White Christmas* by Irving Berlin (bit of a name change there), became the tip-off telling thousands of Yanks and their South Vietnamese allies to hit the road, Jack; which they did.

Now in case you haven't been to Saigon, or as it is now known, Ho Chi Minh City, there's not a lot of snow in that part of monsoonal Asia. It has a sort of mad-dogs-and-Englishmen type climate, and some wag reckons there are only two seasons in Vietnam—hot and hotter.

Imagine the following scenario. It's late April 1975, and you are an American in Saigon, minding your own business, when without warning, on local radio, you hear Bing Crosby warbling Mr Berlin's popular lyrics. You cup your ear. Can you hear sleigh bells in the snow? What snow? There's no snow in stifling Saigon, and since when has Christmas ever been celebrated in April?

Then you remember—*White Christmas* is the code.

Translated, it means 150,000 Communist troops are heading south, sharpish, and right now, you'd better pack up your troubles in your old kit bag and flee, flee, flee. People fled. Thousands of Americans and their South Vietnamese allies scarpered, lickety-split.

One wonders if any North Vietnamese sympathisers, sneakily living down south, ever knew that a warbling Bing Crosby doubled as a government secret agent. Here's what happened.

President Ford and his advisors decided it was time to go. *White Christmas* appeared on Saigon radio, and the rush hour began.

There was no time to sort through family albums and underwear drawers. It was grab your cash and kids, and get the hell out of town. Stuffing bank notes in your smalls became all the rage.

But how did people escape?

Some hurried downstream, and climbed the gangway of many a ship moored in the Saigon River. Some caught a bus to Saigon's Tan Son Nhat Airport, and clambered up the portable steps of a plane. Mind you, once North Vietnamese shells began kissing the runways, that option vanished.

Some scrambled inside a Chinook helicopter, which landed in the grounds of the US Embassy. That was the final option. The choppers flew out to sea and landed on the USS Blue Ridge, command ship of the 40-vessel evacuation armada.

Many South Vietnamese pilots with their own much smaller helicopter, flew their family out to the American ships, offloaded their human cargo, then saw their chopper pushed overboard to sink in the South China Sea.

Now to get inside a Chinook, you first had to get inside the US Embassy, where high walls, barbed wire and armed marines meant most of the would-be escapees never made it past security. Bayonets and broken fingers were common.

When the last US chopper flew out on April 29, 1975, there were about 10,000 desperate South Vietnamese hopeful escapees waiting outside the US Embassy. Most who wanted to escape, didn't, couldn't.

The vast majority of Saigon residents knew nothing about Bing's code, and these folk were nowhere near the US Embassy as the escape took place. The city heaved with trapped locals, their numbers boosted by the North Vietnamese driving half a million refugees south to Saigon. Hitch a lift on an ox-cart or take Shanks' pony.

Locals had one option—they could make your own arrangements.

Some stayed and suffered. Some floated out to sea on homemade rafts and drowned. Some found a new life in a new country. Many died an unimaginable death.

By 1975, the end of the Vietnam War was expected. Locals knew that once the Americans departed, surrender by South Vietnam would be a formality. It was.

Quang Van Nguyen was born and bred in Saigon. As the War ended, he was 30, and a damn good tailor. His father once owned a Saigon clothing shop, and made shirts for French Army officers in the 1940s. Quality was a hallmark stamped on every Nguyen garment.

Son Quang lived over the shop with his wife Hoa and their four young children—daughter Thu, sons Trai and Minh, and baby daughter Thanh. The older kids played in the shop while their parents worried.

'I need to tell you what I've heard,' said Quang. Hoa knew what was coming as she fed baby Thanh. 'The Communists could be here today.'

'Everybody knows that. What we don't know is what will happen when they get here.'

Quang hand stitched a garment. What could he say? His wife nailed the issue. People in Saigon who had never fired a shot in anger faced a terrible fate. Just being from South Vietnam condemned them as an enemy of the late Ho Chi Minh and his soon-to-be victorious army.

At least the Nguyen children, aged from 6 months to 6 years, were ignorant of the potential hell their parents faced. But what would happen to these little ones if their parents were tortured, imprisoned or killed?

Baby Thanh stopped feeding, and recommenced her vocal exercises, refusing to use the volume control.

Hoa lived in hope. 'I know people who believe they will be saved by the Americans,' she said.

'Sadly, they are deluded,' replied the tailor. 'The Americans will save themselves, and only those South Vietnamese who have worked with and for them.'

'You made a suit for an American soldier last year; the one who married a Vietnamese woman. You should ask him to help us escape.'

'He is a lowly sergeant in the catering corp. He has no influence.'

'But why not try?' She raised her voice. 'We have to do something.'

The older children saw their mother crying. Her anger and fear joined forces. The children were puzzled. *Why is Má crying?*

She spoke sarcastically. 'Well perhaps you should make a suit for an American general, because without the Americans, we are at the mercy of the Communists, and they show no mercy. Remember the thousands of murdered innocent citizens in Hue and Da Nang. Some were buried alive.'

Quang made a *shhh* sound and indicated the children. Hoa continued in a soft voice.

'Doing nothing may guarantee our children become orphans.'

Quang knew his wife spoke the truth. Of course he wanted to protect his family. But how? Like so many South Vietnamese families, the Nguyens faced a horrifying future.

They had a profitable business with quality equipment, which no one would buy. They had modest savings, and a motor scooter. In this climate of fear and uncertainty, their assets were worthless.

For months, Quang and Hoa discussed their options. Their best possible plan, their only plan seemed ridiculous. It involved two adults, three children and a baby, plus whatever gold and cash they could sew into their clothes, all strapped onto a motor scooter. Their food supply would consist of noodles, nuts and rice. That was it. How far could they travel? How long could they survive?

They would abandon their shop, their home, and their extended family. They would take no furniture or belongings. What sort of a future is that? And that was their *best* plan.

Then there was the matter of their destination. They would head south but with no specific port in mind. Once they arrived, they would try to sell their scooter, find a boat, and buy a passage to a new homeland.

And all this was based on hope with no refund or security.

Would the Communists capture them en route? Could the family afford the fare on the boat? Would it be safe? Would they die at sea? Would a new country accept them? Despair dominated their thinking.

Hoa persisted. She would try anything to save her children. 'Why don't we pay an agent to get us into the American Embassy?'

Quang stayed silent.

His wife begged. 'We can't just wait here to die.'

He whispered. 'I know a family who paid an agent a lot of money to bribe an American official and get the family to safety.'

'And?'

Quang looked at his wife. 'The agent disappeared with all their money.' She despaired. 'Hoa, we cannot trust anyone, not even our own people.'

She pleaded with her husband and tears filled her eyes. She lifted the screeching Thanh's head so the baby's suckling at least quelled her cries. These were dreadful, terrifying times.

An elderly neighbour came into the shop. 'I have just heard the news,' he said. 'The Americans are gone, and the Communists are driving into Saigon.'

The parents looked at one another. Their nightmare began.

'Come and see,' said the old man, leading the couple into the street.

Hoa put the baby in her crib, told the older children to play quietly, and joined Quang in the city.

The Nguyens looked at the new Saigon. Things were strange. Yes, the pedestrians, cyclists, motor scooters, busses, trucks, the ubiquitous cyclo-pousse, and even old Renaults left behind by the French, still jostled for position. Yes, the frangipani trees still added colour and aromas.

However, the Americans and their jeeps were gone, and in their place, locals hurried by, carrying unusual objects. The Nguyens saw people going home with office chairs, tables, lamps, bookends, even a filing cabinet and potted plants. It was "loot Saigon day" with the US Embassy fair game. Anything not nailed down got nicked.

Then there were men walking home in their underwear. Why? Was this madness? Hordes of South Vietnamese soldiers stripped in public. They removed their army fatigues and hats, and pulled off their boots. Clothing and footwear littered the city.

Such actions made sense. Let's face it; if you were a South Vietnamese soldier, would you be wearing your uniform when the enemy hit town?

And hit town they did. Soviet and Chinese tanks rolled into Saigon with North Vietnamese soldiers atop their machines. The grins of the fighters were as big as their weapons. To the victor belong the spoils.

Quang and Hoa faded into the crowd and returned home. They locked their shop, and put their children to bed. Their livelihood was ruined and so too their lives. They were certainly under threat of arrest and detention, and with that, possible imprisonment, torture, even execution.

Nobody dreamt of Christmas, white or otherwise. Their future had *grim* written all over it.

For weeks, the Nguyens survived—just. Quang had few customers. Everyone feared the conquering army, and the way to survive was to keep your head down and try to become invisible.

Hoa rationed food, and despaired when her brood asked for more. Little children and hunger pains created heartache. Hoa's health suffered, and breast-feeding baby Thanh became a real struggle.

Then, finally, it happened. About a month after the war ended, a dreaded knock sounded on the shop door. Quang and Hoa looked at one another. The knocking became louder and a person shouted.

'Open the door in the name of the Socialist Republic of Vietnam.'

Three bullying officials strode in dispensing threats with the leader demanding answers. One thug helped himself to shirts Quang had lovingly created. Payment? You have to be joking.

'You have been aiding the Americans,' declared the leader. It was a statement, not a question.

'I beg to disagree, sir,' replied Quang. 'I am a humble tailor making a modest living to support my wife and children.'

'We have witnesses who saw you make clothes for the enemy. You have paid taxes to the capitalist regime. These are crimes in the new regime.'

It was pointless to protest. Being a law-abiding citizen and earning an honest living made Quang a criminal.

'You are under arrest,' said the official.

Hoa gasped. The goons tied Quang's hands behind his back and pushed him to the door.

He pleaded. 'Please, may I say goodbye to my family?'

'You have one minute,' snapped the official.

Hoa gathered her brood and held up each child for Quang to kiss. The tailor refused to cry. His wife wept enough for both of them.

'Be good for your mother,' said Quang as he kissed his children. Baby Thanh screamed. She was hungry, teething, and needed a clean nappy.

Clutching the howling infant, Hoa leant in and kissed her husband. Both parents knew this could be the last time they would ever see one another. *Helpless* didn't even come close.

The goons pushed Quang to the door. He looked back and saw his bewildered, terrified and distraught family. Then he was gone.

He travelled, cattle-class, to the Vietnamese countryside and to one of the hundreds of re-education camps. The term *re-education* became a euphemism for punishment, torture and death.

Quang was not alone. Vast numbers of South Vietnamese citizens became inmates in these camps. Many never left.

Back in Saigon, massive change swept the city. The Republic took what it wanted, calling it the expropriation of property belonging to non-communists. The State became the new owner of the Nguyen business with no such thing as compensation. Hoa and her children moved to live with her sister and parents in a cramped room where cat swinging was impossible.

Welcome to the new Socialist Republic of Vietnam.

The Nazis had concentration camps and the Soviets the Gulag. The North Vietnamese re-education camps existed to "help" their former enemies but revenge drove the conquering army. Many South Vietnamese Army officers and foot soldiers became labourers given backbreaking tasks.

Torture was commonplace. Punishment for failure to finish a job or for showing the slightest disrespect to a guard was brutal. Food rations were meagre, disease rife, and medical attention non-existent. Thousands died.

Quang Van Nguyen entered this brutal world, a tailor who never joined any army, never fought the Communists, and only wanted a peaceful life. Now he faced separation from his beloved wife and children, and years of slavery. And for what crime? Bespoke tailoring?

According to international law, the camps were illegal. So what? Amnesty International and the Red Cross can take a running jump. Yet amidst the horror of the re-education camps, there appeared a ray of sunshine; family visits might be possible.

If true, Hoa could visit her husband. They could touch and kiss, and share news of their children. The idea of such a visit fired Hoa's soul. She would make it happen despite labyrinthine obstacles.

Her first task was to locate Quang. Inmates often moved. Who would know the right camp? Discovering a government department with such knowledge seemed insurmountable.

She searched. Her perseverance triumphed. She found Quang's camp but then needed official permission to visit. Which form was required? Where can one obtain such a form?

Now it is unfair to say the Communists had a monopoly on red tape and bureaucracy, but in the World Cup of Obfuscation, the new Socialist Republic of Vietnam won gold.

Hoa kept going. Having located her husband, and obtained a visitor's pass, she still had to make the journey, arguably the toughest part of her quest. Re-education camps were often isolated. They didn't spring up beside railway stations or along bus routes. Because of their cruelty, the government wanted them out of sight.

Everyone suffered, even visitors, because visits were often restricted to a measly 15 minutes. After months of planning and hours, sometimes days of travel, you enjoyed but a fleeting greeting. Now that was sadistic.

Hoa was strong, her mental toughness extraordinary. Physically, her efforts were herculean. She raised four children while living in cramped and impoverished conditions. Now she set off to see husband Quang leaving her sister and mother to care for the children. Hoa's journey took seventeen hours.

Quang had no inkling of her arrival, and when he saw her, he thought his heart would burst. He started to move but the shock and joy made him stumble. They embraced and wept. Words were irrelevant. He looked painfully thin and her physique matched his.

Her news thrilled him. Their children were alive, and every day asked about their father. Little Thanh had taken her first steps.

But the sight of one another, being able to touch and share their news became as nothing when Hoa revealed her secret.

'I think I can bribe an official and have you released for a home visit.'

Quang froze. Words would not come.

'Do not get your hopes up,' she said, 'and be ready to leave at any time. But do not tell anyone, *anyone* about this matter. Do you understand?'

Quang still couldn't speak. Seeing her, touching her, smelling her hair, hearing her, all seemed like a bizarre fantasy and yet he wasn't dreaming; this was real. And when Hoa told him he might be released from this hellhole, even for a short time, his brain failed to function. The idea was incomprehensible.

Without warning, an insensitive guard ended their meeting. Hoa squeezed her husband's hand before she watched him being dragged from the room. Their eyes locked until he left.

Now she had a plan, and he had a dream.

2

Australia 1975

THE BIRTH CERTIFICATE listed his name as *Matthew James Cadwallader* but everyone called him Matt. Occasionally he got Matty, and one of his grandfathers invented Buster. Some of his teachers called him Matthew but later chose to go with the flow.

Matthew the baby was bonny. As a bub, he had endless reserves of laughter. His baby nickname was Cheeky. Lying on his back, he flapped his arms, kicked his legs, and grinned. His facial muscles must have ached, so often did he smile. His eyes sparkled with mischief, and matched his goo-goo sounds and dribbling. Was there ever a more contented bubba?

Parents David and Judith delighted in the happiness of their firstborn. They almost fought to change his nappy. The sprinkling of powder set off squeals of delight, and the baby made noises too.

This was the perfect family scenario. The newborn was wanted and loved. The baby was healthy, and adored the company of his parents. It was impossible to tell who got the better deal. Mother and father worshipped the infant, and the little tacker produced a permanent purr.

How then could things go so wrong?

No two teenagers are the same. Some from a rough, even dangerous upbringing become sensible, model citizens. Some from a stable, loving and nurturing family go right off the rails, only to crash and burn.

Why is this so?

No idea; ask an expert.

Matthew's parents were normal, whatever that means. They married for love, and raised two children in a caring and respectful household. Matthew had a younger sister, Rosie Elizabeth, and life was fine and dandy for the clan Cadwallader. During his childhood years, Matt

9

blossomed. He was healthy, inquisitive and kind, but as he grew older, things changed, and not always for the good.

It was Matthew's Year 10 report, which shocked his parents. It came out of nowhere. His early years in high school were brilliant but overnight, Matt's results went south. David and Judith went to their son's parent-teacher meeting and spoke with Matthew's teachers.

'Have you noticed any change in his behaviour at home,' asked his form teacher?

David and Judith looked at one another, and shook their heads.

'He gets moody at times,' said Judith. 'But we put that down to normal teenage behaviour.'

'I can't believe he's got such low grades,' said David.

'That's why I asked about life at home,' added the teacher. 'We are just as shocked as you.'

David and Judith had that same conversation with all of Matthew's teachers. Each reported a drop in his interest and application.

Driving home, the parents discussed their son.

'He couldn't be on drugs,' said David. 'We'd notice that sort of thing.'

'Would we?'

David looked at his wife.

'Watch the road,' snapped Judith.

They drove in silence.

'Perhaps we introduced him to wine when he was too young,' said Judith.

'Oh for God's sake, he's 16. Every kid his age has tried smoking and drinking.'

'I don't like his new friends.'

'What new friends?'

'He talks about that Jefferson boy and his older brother. The parents run their own business and are never home, so the brothers have no adult supervision.'

'I haven't been in his room for a while.'

'Shows how much you care.'

David shook his head. That was below the belt. He tried again.

'What's it like? That could be a pointer to his attitude.'

'Bad,' said Judith. 'It was never tidy but now it's a tip.'

More silence. More worry. A troubled teen might mean strife.

David pinpointed a possible cause. 'I blame his injury. He was a bloody good footballer; he could have made it. I mean at the highest level.'

Indeed Matthew was good at most sports, but a cruciate ligament injury stopped his sporting career overnight. And so from an active and healthy lifestyle with excellent grades at school, he dropped out of sport, and started spending time alone in his room. He mixed with the wrong crowd, and his education copped a hammering.

'You need to read him the riot act,' said his mother.

'Oh please, Judith, if I've learnt anything from decades of teaching, it's that lecturing teenagers never works.'

'So what, you do nothing?'

'Now you're being silly.'

Sarcasm filled the car.

'Wonderful. It's my fault our son failed at school.'

David tried deep breathing. He and Judith had been arguing a lot of late.

'Let's not argue. I'll have a chat with him, and follow the golden rule when dealing with teenagers.'

There was a pause. 'Which is?'

'If you have a teenager, you must get a dog.'

'A dog?'

'Yes, because that way, when you come home, someone'll be glad to see you.'

Judith shook her head. 'Always the bloody comedian; you can't discuss anything without cracking some pathetic joke.'

Under his breath, David quoted Groucho Marx.

Humour is reason gone mad.

The rest of the trip home took place in silence.

David didn't rush his father-son chat. He waited until the weekend when Judith took daughter Rosie shopping to buy clothes.

It was late Saturday afternoon, and Matthew was ensconced in his room. David listened to the football then wandered upstairs, and tapped on his son's bedroom door.

'Oi oi,' said David, opening the door. Matthew didn't see or hear his father. The teen leant out the window blowing smoke from his spliff. Headphones on his ears pumped heavy rock music to his brain until he sensed movement and turned.

The cannabis landed on the roses below. Matthew closed his window and removed his headphones.

'What's up?' he asked his father.

'Bombers had a good win.'

Matthew flopped on the unmade bed. 'Couldn't care less.'

The uneasy atmosphere drifted towards confrontation. David worked hard at keeping things low-key.

'So what's happening at school?'

Matthew shrugged. 'Same old, same old.'

This conversation was never in danger of becoming loquacious.

David chose the direct approach. 'How long have you been smoking dope?'

The teen gave a no-big-deal shrug. 'Once in a while.' There was a long pause. 'Just don't tell Mum, all right?'

It was David's turn to shrug. 'Do I look like a snitch?'

Matthew trusted his father. They had an understanding rather than an intimate and loving relationship. Then Matthew dropped a bombshell.

'I'm thinking of leaving school.'

That shocked the parent. 'You're kidding?'

'I'm a businessman, Dad. I'm gunna start my own business.'

'Right,' said David and paused. 'What happened to choosing maths and science, and aiming for engineering?'

'That's garbage. Complete waste of time. You work for some company for years for peanuts. Entrepreneurs are the megastars today. I'm gunna start a business from scratch, watch it grow, and make a mint.'

David knew that to argue or preach would be counterproductive.

'Sounds good. So where will you get the finance to launch this brilliant new business?'

'I've got a few contacts.'

'I see.' The pauses grew ever longer. 'I hope you aren't thinking of asking your old man for money?'

Matthew laughed. 'I'm serious, Dad. You think I'm joking.'

'No, not at all, I'm sure you're serious.'

'And when I start coining it big-time, I won't forget my dear old boring parents.'

David grinned. 'Too kind,' he said, and headed for the door.

Matthew called. 'Chill out, Dad. I'm okay. No need to worry about your son and heir.'

'It's not you I'm worried about. How am I going to explain this new career move to your mother?' Softly, David added, 'and survive?'

He forced a smile, and paused in the doorway. 'And I'd rescue that spliff before your mother starts her Sunday gardening session.'

Matthew froze then relaxed and gave his father a thumbs-up sign.

The old man's mind got busy.

What the hell is happening to my son?

David was spot on about his wife's reaction. Judith went ballistic.

'Drop out of school? That is insane. And please tell me you told him to forget such nonsense and put his head down and pass those bloody exams.'

David said nothing so Judith continued to glare at him.

'You didn't did you? God, you're a weak bastard.'

'To climb steep hills requires a slow pace at first.'

Judith nodded. 'That'd be right. Get Shakespeare to fix the problems of the world.' She stormed out of the room.

Mind you, Judith knew better than to tackle her son herself. He was a lot like her; not afraid to speak his mind. She would get as good as she gave.

At least Matthew's situation was now in the public domain. His parents dispensed with their rose-coloured glasses. His cavalier attitude to dope, unsuitable internet sites and alcohol consumption with the Jefferson brothers, now needed planning and sneakiness. He'd been sprung, and if he planned to continue this hedonistic lifestyle, his ability to tell lies would need to improve.

David knew threats were useless, and Judith knew if her son wanted to rebel, he'd find a way. Locks existed to keep out honest folk.

Matthew finished Year 10, just. Before his parents could ask about his choice of Year 11 subjects, he made an announcement.

'The Jeffersons have offered me a vacation job.'

'Great,' said David.

'Doing what,' asked Judith?

'They have contracts with estate agents. Every property up for sale or lease needs to be cleaned and decorated. I'll be doing the lot.'

'Cleaning,' sneered Judith? 'You're going to be a cleaner?'

'It's only a vacation job,' said David. 'And well done, mate. Good to see you using your initiative.'

'So the teenager with the world's messiest bedroom will soon create pristine boudoirs,' said Judith.

'And get paid for it,' replied her grinning son.

'How about I pay you to clean your room?'

'You couldn't afford me, Mum.' He winked and started to leave. 'See ya. Oh, and I won't be in for tea. I'll eat with the Jeffersons.'

He left with his parents in disarray.

'Well, from engineering to cleaning toilets; that's a smart move,' said Judith.

'He told you. It's only a vacation job.'

'And what's he going to do with the money?'

David shrugged. 'What millions of teenage boys spend their money on—clothes, music, and girls. Live and let live, Judith.'

'He'll spend it on drugs.'

That stopped the conversation. David wanted to leave the room.

'Do you know he's smoking marijuana?' David said nowt. He needed think music.

Judith continued. 'Now either you know and are covering for him, or you don't know, and have been shocked into silence.' She looked at him. 'So which is it?'

David shrugged. 'He asked me not to tell you.'

'Oh wonderful. And of course you told him that smoking dope is often the first step towards serious drug addiction.'

'Look, he's not stupid. He wants to be an entrepreneur. He's not like his boring parents with our 9 to 5 jobs. He's got ambition.'

'And a drug habit.'

'Oh for God's sake, woman. I smoked dope when I was at uni. It's a rite of passage.'

The temperature of the argument increased. Their relationship drifted from robust discussion to minor skirmish. Sporadic small arms fire began. Before heavy artillery entered the fray, the phone rang. David answered it.

'Hello.'

It was Robert, his wife's brother.

'Oh mate, I'm sorry. Are you there now?'

David had agreed to meet financial advisor Robert in a local pub for a chat about superannuation.

'Look, I'll leave now. See you in 15.'

He hung up and started to leave.

''That was your dear brother. I promised to have a drink with him. I won't be late.' He left.

Judith called. 'I've only got one thing to say, David.' He re-appeared. 'Let the buyer beware.'

He gave a weak smile and departed.

Robert was a smooth talker. He was a smooth everything, and oozed plastic sincerity. His sole goal in life was to extract money from people. It didn't matter who but the amount extracted was seriously important. Too much was never enough, and everyone was a potential client, especially family and friends.

David found Robert at a corner table with a beer awaiting the brother-in-law cum victim. They toasted one another.

'Cheers,' said David.

Robert asked his usual question. 'So how are the wife and kids?'

'All well.'

'That wasn't said with a great deal of conviction.'

David grimaced. 'Matthew wants to drop out of school and start his own business.'

'Fantastic—good luck to the lad.'

'That's not exactly what his mother said.'

'He'll need income protection. I can get him a great deal. Tell him to give me a call. There's something wrong with the world if you can't take care of your own family.'

Don't look now, Robert, but your insincerity's showing.

David nodded. He decided to spell out some ground rules.

'Listen, mate, you know I'm Mister Boring. You know I've had the same government super scheme for yonks, and I'm not interested in risking my quaint little nest egg.'

'I do know that, but you just said the magic word—*little*. The super laws have changed, and you can do much, much better with your own scheme.'

Robert put a glossy brochure on the table. David looked at it and felt uncomfortable. He and Robert were chalk and cheese. David was flashy watch, flashy car and flashy wife number #3 (or was it #4?). David had worn the same corduroy jacket with scuffed leather arm patches since Captain Cook went surfing in Hawaii. Change was not a part of Dave's DNA.

'I know you want security, mate,' said Robert. 'I know you hate risk, and cling to old-fashioned bricks and mortar. Well this deal gives you all of that but with a much higher return.'

David hated arguing full stop, and his major dislike of his brother-in-law was that Robert had an answer to everything. He was programmed to never accept the word "no".

'All I'm asking,' said Robert, 'is that you read the brochure; nothing else. No commitment, no obligation, just read with an open mind.'

If contrived friendship and fake sincerity could be bottled, Robert was on a winner.

'Fair enough,' said David, who changed the subject.

Not far from the pub, Matthew Cadwallader copied his father and uncle in consuming alcohol. It was against the law for a 16 year old to purchase grog, and to consume same in a public place such as a park or beach. However, there was no law against 16-year-olds drinking liquor in private.

Matthew drank with the brothers Jefferson in their home; well, the home of their never-at-home parents. Tom was 17 and Matt's mate from school. Big brother Tony was 20 and a criminal in waiting.

They were sampling the homeowners' whisky, and went into the garden to smoke pot.

'Great to have you working for the family, Matt,' said Tony passing the visitor the spliff.

'I tell you, mate,' said Tom, 'you do the right thing by the old man and you'll be set for life.'

Matthew discovered a new brand of excitement. This family had wealth. They were successful. He wanted that lifestyle, and right now his mates offered it to him on a plate. However, something else was on offer.

Tony produced a small tin of tablets, and opened it, showing the contents to his brother and Matthew.

'Here you go, boys. Give yourself a real high.'

Matthew Cadwallader delved into the world of Class A drugs.

3

Vietnam 1976

MONEY CAN WORK MIRACLES. Hoa became acquainted with a low-ranking Communist official and explained Quang's situation. Her husband was never an enemy of the former North Vietnam. He did not deserve to be an inmate of a re-education camp. 'Is there anything I can do to have my husband released for a home visit?'

The official replied. 'For the right fee, something might be possible.'

Hoa hesitated. If she offered more than the official would accept, she would needlessly overspend. Would his fee be more than she could afford? The official quoted his price. Hoa felt tremendous relief. It was less than she expected.

But what about crooked agents, like the ones who took money to bribe Americans but kept the cash? This could be the same thing. She thought.

It might be a rip-off but doing nothing won't help Quang come home.

'I will pay you the money now,' she said. 'And when my husband returns to Saigon, I will pay you a bonus.'

The official liked the offer. His pay was poor. This scenario could turn into a nice little earner. He thought about doing a runner then figured that if he did the right thing, others might ask for the same favour. It could indeed become a nice little earner.

'But please, you must help me,' said Hoa. 'I do not know how to contact the camp or what I should say.'

The official explained. 'You need a reason for his release. If your husband's mother or father is seriously ill, that might persuade the camp officials to grant your husband a home visit.'

'They are dying,' said Hoa without thinking. 'Both are ill and one is near death.'

Hoa was desperate and lied or guessed. Quang's parents fled Saigon before the Vietnam War ended. They eventually arrived in Australia and, unknown to their family in Saigon, lived in the suburb of Footscray in Melbourne, in a vibrant Vietnamese community.

'You will need to pay the camp commander as well,' said the official.

Hoa felt sick.

This is a scam. I pay different people with no guarantee of success. But what else can I do?

She paid the corrupt official and did as he instructed. She wrote to the re-education camp commander enclosing bribe money but never calling it that. Then she spent her waking hours caring for her brood.

Two months later, Hoa was washing little Thanh's clothes when a strange scream erupted. Then more screams. Hoa raced to investigate.

What a sight. Her older children were squealing, crying, and clinging to their long lost father. Hoa's heart exploded. She leapt into the throng.

As with Hoa's visit to the camp some time ago, Quang's arrival in Saigon was unannounced and unexpected. It certainly provoked joy.

For the children, this occasion was better than every happy birthday they had ever enjoyed, all rolled into one. It took ages for things to settle. Hoa fussed and made the best meal she could. What a meal. What a celebration. What tears, what happiness.

The funniest scene involved baby Thanh. She was now walking, well, staggering. Quang knelt, held out his arms and called to his tiny daughter. She thought.

Who is this strange man? Why is he here? Should I go to him?

With much encouragement from Hoa and Thanh's siblings, the toddler set off to greet her father. Her wobbly legs wobbled. She almost made it but stumbled. The excitement kept building. She started again and then, just within hugging distance, Thanh tripped and fell flat on her face.

'Wah!' she bellowed, and bawled like a baby. Her father scooped her up, and everyone clapped and laughed. Thanh looked at her father, then at her family, then back at her father. She put a hand on his face and patted the tears rolling down his cheeks. Thanh laughed and the world rejoiced.

Finally, with the children asleep, Quang and Hoa lay together on a single mattress. Their breathing mingled. Their smells mingled. They mingled. At last they spoke.

'I have only three days,' said Quang. 'If I am not back in the camp by Thursday, they will arrest me and punish me like never before, and I will die there.'

Hoa said nothing.

Words were not important. Heartbeats, touching and tears were all that mattered. Then Hoa whispered.

'You have only one day.'

Quang thought he misheard; certainly, he did not understand.

'No, my darling, I have three days.'

'No, my darling,' she replied, 'tomorrow we escape from Saigon.'

Hoa had been planning the escape for months. She regarded the home visit as cruel and heartbreaking. Her plan in obtaining a home visit for her husband was so the whole family could flee Saigon, and start a new life in a new land.

Step 1 of the plan, check—√.

Quang had trouble comprehending. He believed returning to the camp was his best option. To say he was shocked at Hoa's plan would be a massive understatement. He thought of questions and asked them.

'Where will we go? How will we travel? What will we do for money?'

The more he asked, the better she answered. The only thing more impressive than Hoa's plan was her determination to make it work.

Quang couldn't sleep. He was already restless, but with Hoa's idea, he remained wide-awake.

Her plan covered travel arrangements, destination, money, food, maps, emergency rations, even a Plan B and C. It was impressive.

She had visited the local market. Farmers from down south brought their wares to Saigon in trucks. Some trucks returned empty. Here was the perfect solution. She, Quang and the children would pay a farmer to drive them south. The farmer would make money, and the family would escape.

Of course it was dangerous. If she asked the wrong farmer, he might report Hoa to the government, meaning Quang would go back to the camp, and she would join him.

She listened to farmers at the market. She spoke to people she hoped were honest, and looked for the right man. The chosen farmer mistrusted Hoa just as she mistrusted him. He thought.

Is she a stooge for the government? Is she trying to trap me?

They reached an agreement. He wanted all the money up front. She stood firm and paid only a small amount.

'When it is time to leave, I will pay you the full amount,' she said.

Preparation was the key to Hoa's plan. When Quang arrived in Saigon, she had everything ready; clothing for the children, money and gold sewn into garments, food in packages—nuts, noodles and rice—and even a map with towns and places which offered their best hope of a successful escape.

It was 5am and the children were asleep. 'Wait here,' Hoa told her husband, and headed for the market. Her thoughts were many.

What if that farmer is not there? What if he's changed his mind?

She wandered around avoiding people, pretending to be shopping. She spotted the farmer and her heart sang. He saw her approach and knew from her face that today was the day.

He led her behind some crates. 'I want the money first,' he said. She gave him the money. He counted it and grunted. Hoa worried.

'In one hour,' he said. 'Be at the meeting place or I will go without you.'

He walked away and Hoa trembled. Her plan, her dream, her greatest hope was now a reality. She hurried home.

The look on Quang's face spoke volumes. He struggled to comprehend her amazing plan.

'What has happened?'

'All is well,' she said. 'We leave in 15 minutes. I will wake and feed the children. You must eat too. And remember, wear two layers of clothes.'

Soon the children were fed, washed and dressed. They too wore an extra layer of clothes. Carrying many bags would look suspicious.

Quang felt helpless. His wife had arranged everything and her preparation was meticulous. He watched as she spoke to the three older children.

'Today we go on a trip to the country. You must be especially good. Do not ask questions, and do not speak to anyone. Do you understand?'

The children were confused but nodded. Hoa scooped up little Thanh. 'And you, little Miss, you must be as quiet as a mouse. Will you do that for your Má?'

Thanh was sleepy. She looked at her family. Quang put a finger to his lips and said, 'Shhh.' Thanh hesitated then copied her father. It was smiles all round but the tension bubbling in the breast of each adult was palpable.

'Let us wake your sister and parents to say goodbye,' said Quang.

Hoa looked at him and shook her head. He was stunned. He gasped. 'They do not know about your plan?'

20

'This is the best way. It is risky to tell anyone. I have left a note.'

Hoa wiped Thanh's runny nose, picked up the child and a bag, and walked into the Saigon dawn. Quang took a few seconds to come to grips with the situation. Then he too grabbed a bag and ushered the children.

Their escape began.

Stale cabbage leaves, broccoli stalks and squashed cucumbers littered the floor of the truck. The family Nguyen huddled beneath a filthy tarpaulin. The truck's shock absorbers died long ago. Every pothole brought agony. All the children cried with Thanh the loudest.

Whenever the truck stopped, the family held their collective breath. The children saw the "be silent" signal, and Hoa's hand hovered in front of Thanh's mouth ready to gag the toddler if she complained.

They could hear people and wondered who they were, and where they were. If the people were soldiers or government workers, and they discovered the family, the escape was over on Day 1.

Soon the sounds of traffic and people faded, and the roads became rougher. The journey seemed endless, until the truck slowed, turned and stopped. The farmer got out and banged on the side.

'This is it. Everyone out of the truck.'

Quang lifted the tarpaulin, and he and Hoa helped the children alight.

Hoa was nervous. 'Is this where you promised to take us?'

'Yes.' He climbed back inside his truck.

Thrusting Thanh at her husband, Hoa ran to the driver. 'Please, where are we?'

'A long way from Saigon,' he said, and engaged the gears.

She shouted and held up a map. 'Please, can you show me on the map?'

Annoyed, he got out of the truck and looked at her map. He stabbed a finger. 'This is where you are.'

'And please sir, which road do we take to get to this place?'

She pointed at the port she hoped gave them the best chance of escaping Vietnam. The farmer looked at the map then pointed to a road.

'That way, but you won't get there for days, and with little children, I think you are mad.'

Hoa endured misery and hopelessness. The farmer stared at her and her family. What a pathetic sight. He walked to the back of his truck, grabbed the tarpaulin, and tossed it on the ground.

'Take this, and mind out for Communists.'

He climbed into his truck, revved the engine, and drove away. The sounds of birds and running water were loud. Quang realised. His family desperately needed leadership. His wife needed support. He folded the tarp, picked it up, and his bag, and set off down the road.

'This way, children,' he called. 'It's time to find our new home.'

Hoa delighted in her husband being decisive. He doubted the plan and her ability but now he became Mr Positive. She grabbed her bag, lifted Thanh, and followed the others.

After a while, everyone needed to rest. Quang himself, after months in the re-education camp, was still desperately thin. Hoa too was weak, and the children could not continue.

Quang walked into the jungle and found a small clearing. He used branches as poles, and using the tarpaulin, made a tunnel-shaped house. The older children found it exciting. Hoa fed the family being careful to ration their supplies.

It started to rain. They were dry but as the afternoon turned to dusk, sounds of the jungle brought new fears. Quang used branches to build a wall at either end of their "house" which gave a feeling of security. Both parents knew it would be useless as protection against wild animals.

As night encroached, the birdcalls faded, replaced by other animal sounds. Monkeys screeched. Were there leopards, tigers, wild boars and more in this corner of Vietnam?

Hoa kept thinking.

Pray God, we will be safe.

The parents couldn't sleep. Restless children hardly helped, and calls of nature became a major operation. At dawn, once the birds were up, the family joined them.

They ate breakfast, and Hoa worried about her dwindling food supplies. The tarp was soaked and much heavier. Quang failed to fold and lift it. The children were irritable and for the first time in ages, the parents argued. It was hardly a slanging match but both were under serious pressure. Quang thought about their predicament.

If I had returned to the camp, my wife and children would be safe. Now we are lost in the jungle, and could die of starvation or be killed by wild animals. Why did I listen to Hoa?

A screaming Thanh stopped the parental dispute. Hoa picked up her daughter, and headed back to the road. Her children followed. Quang toiled with the tarp. In frustration, he threw it on the ground and stormed after his family.

After some time, they stopped to rest. Hoa made sure the children had plenty of water. She looked back at Quang and nearly died.

'Where is the tarpaulin? You've left it behind.'

'It was soaked. I could not even fold it, let alone carry it.'

'But that is our shelter for tonight and for the rest of our journey.'

The children were not used to their parents being upset with one another. Thu, the oldest, began to cry.

'I want to go home,' she sobbed.

This shamed her parents, and both moved to comfort their daughter. Her younger brothers were afraid, their young minds confused.

What is happening to our parents and to us?

Quang and Hoa knew their chances of escaping were slim; close to impossible. They decided to move when they heard an unusual sound.

'Listen,' said Quang. The sound grew louder.

'It's a truck,' said Hoa.

'It's heading the wrong way, going back to Saigon. Quickly,' said Quang. 'Everyone come into the jungle and hide.'

The children did as ordered. They saw their parents signal to be silent. The truck got closer. Just as it was about to pass, Hoa leapt up and ran to the road. Quang froze. The truck screeched as the driver swerved to avoid the crazy woman. She waved.

It was an army truck with soldiers. Hoa's desperate attempt to get help for her family backfired. A soldier in the back of the truck picked up his rifle and aimed at Hoa. She panicked and fled into the jungle.

The soldier fired twice, three times. His target disappeared. The soldiers argued, and then the truck drove away leaving Quang and the children crouching in terror. Quang's thoughts reeked of desperation.

Hoa is dead. Who will care for the children?

The jungle was silent. Birds took off when the rifle fired. Tears rolled down Quang's face.

'Where is Má,' asked Thu?

What could her father say? Silence settled in the jungle broken by a strange sound. A branch broke, then another. The family cowered, transfixed. The sounds got louder. A large branch moved and there stood Hoa.

The children raced to their mother. Quang found it hard to stand and hold Thanh. Scratches lined Hoa's face, her clothes were torn, but her tiny frame was bullet free.

Hugging became popular, and eventually the family resumed their journey. Tough going described it well with more and longer rests. Slow progress became slower and, as the afternoon heat attacked their bodies, the fact they had no shelter made both parents fearful.

They moved into the jungle where Quang cleared an area and made a crude shelter. The family clung to one another in their makeshift home.

The rain arrived. Heavy, driving rain penetrated the branches and leaves, and soaked their clothing, bringing misery and despair.

It was not a question of reaching their destination, a port. It was a question of surviving the night.

Son Trai made the discovery.

'Look Cha,' he said to his father and pointed. 'What is that?'

Quang peered through the rain and saw the light. He told Hoa. They discussed it then decided. No matter how dangerous the situation with the light might be, it could not be worse than staying here.

The family stood outside a small house. Quang called. The door opened and an elderly woman, holding a lantern, peered into the darkness. It was difficult for her to see but the sight of a shivering and drenched family, tugged at her heartstrings.

God, Buddha, luck or happenstance smiled on the escapees, and soon they were dry, warm and being fed. Cabbage soup never tasted so fine.

The family insisted on sleeping on the floor. This was paradise. The old woman retired and snoring became contagious.

Around midnight, Quang awoke. He heard something. Hoa stirred.

'That sounds like a car,' she whispered.

'It *is* a car,' replied Quang, moving to investigate. He ducked away from the window when headlights illuminated the house. The children stirred. The family froze as they heard a rough voice with swearing to match. Footsteps came closer, and then the door opened. The visitor stumbled in the darkness, lit a lamp, held it up, and saw six pairs of eyes.

He swore and grabbed a broom.

'Please sir,' said Quang. 'We mean no harm. The old lady invited us in out of the rain.'

More swearing as the man raised the broom, and just as he moved to smash the family, the old woman spoke.

'Chien!'

He froze then addressed the woman. 'Who are these people and what are they doing in my house?'

'They are refugees with children. They are trying to escape from our wonderful country, now ruled by your friends, the Communists.'

Quang and Hoa felt sick.

This maniac is a supporter of the new government.

The old woman took control. 'Go to your room. I will bring some food. In the morning this family will be gone.'

The brute stared at his mother, and then at the Nguyens. He threw the broom at Quang, swore, and left the room. The woman moved close to the parents and whispered.

'I'm afraid you must leave.'

'Now,' gasped Quang? 'But it's the middle of the night.'

'He has been drinking and will become violent. I cannot protect you.'

Hoa pleaded. 'But the children will not survive in the open.'

The woman looked around and found the keys. She handed them to Quang. 'Take the car. He stole it and will steal another.'

Quang was speechless.

'Quickly,' said the woman. 'When you get to the end of my road, turn right, and eventually you will come to the port. Now go.'

The family made haste. They stumbled in the dark, piled into the ancient Renault, and Quang tried to start the engine. It stalled. He tried again. It stalled.

The drunken son appeared, roared and came running. Quang tried a third time and the engine spluttered into life. The man drew closer. Quang flattened the accelerator and the car lurched forward crashing into the enraged owner.

He fell against the windscreen, rolled off the car and into the mud. Hoa screamed. The children were terrified. Quang turned the wheel and drove into the night.

Two hours later they stopped. They had to; the car had no petrol. They found it hard to sleep and, at dawn, got out of the car and walked.

At least the weather was fine. They had no idea how close they were to the port. They came around a bend in the road and saw soldiers on bicycles riding towards them. The family panicked and dived into the jungle.

'Be quiet,' whispered Quang.

'Did they see us,' asked Hoa?

'I'm not sure. We need to move deeper into the jungle,' he said and led the family away from the road. They crouched and fell silent. The soldiers dismounted, discussed their next move, and moved into the jungle.

The undergrowth was thick and it was easy for the family to hide. The soldiers kept searching. Thanh wanted to scream and did. Hoa covered her mouth but the sound caused the soldiers to change direction. They were now only a few paces from the terrified family.

Quang whispered to his wife. 'I will lead them away. You take the children deeper into the jungle and I will find you later.'

The parents knew this was a lie. If ever two humans spoke with their eyes, this was such a conversation. Their eyes said *goodbye, I love you* and *thank you*.

Quang touched each of his children then crawled away. As the soldiers were about to discover Hoa and the children, a voice called.

'Over here,' yelled a soldier, and the others moved away from the family.

With a breaking heart, Hoa led her children deeper into the jungle. She could not bear her loss. Her loving husband had given his life to save his family.

Moving through the jungle was dangerous, slow and exhausting. They stopped to rest.

'Where is Cha,' asked the children?

'He will join us later,' said Hoa. 'Now rest.'

Rest was easy, survival difficult—more like impossible. Hoa's exhaustion meant she drifted towards sleep. Suddenly her mind was awake when she again heard soldiers moving through the jungle towards them. Her sweat and tears mingled as she willed her body to stand.

Who can tell what drove this woman to pick up her youngest and lead her children away from the soldiers? They crept through the jungle then heard the sound of water, and came to a river.

Its banks were steep, its current slow. Did that mean deep water?

Hoa panicked as she heard the soldiers closing in on them. Clutching toddler Thanh, she slid down the bank and into the river. Her feet slipped into thick mud. She looked up and beckoned to her children. They followed.

Minh, who had just turned four, panicked and went under the water. His hands flailed as he started to drown. Hoa thrust baby Thanh at daughter Thu, and bobbed below the water. She could not see. She copped a kick in the face and rejoiced. It was her desperate son. Grabbing his shirt and then his hair, she stood and pulled him above the water. He gasped. She placed his hands on a plant growing in the bank.

'Hold this, hold it,' she whispered. Only when the boy settled did she let him go.

But all this was the prelude to the main event. They could hear the soldiers getting closer. Soon the men would stand above them. Talk about shooting fish in a barrel.

Clutching Thanh, Hoa bobbed low in the river and pressed herself against the bank. Her children copied her. Like Má, their instinct was to survive. The children were amazing. Even Thanh chose to remain silent.

The soldiers stood above them. One kicked some dirt. It fell on the family. Hoa refused to cry. Her husband lay dead, and now her children were about to become orphans. She held her breath.

Then it was over. The soldiers left and Hoa wanted to howl with relief. They survived the soldiers but how could they escape their watery jail? The bank was steep and slippery. Climbing was near impossible.

How can I save my children?

Hoa saw a large tree branch jammed against the bank. She looked across the river. There the bank was low. She pushed through the water, and tugged at the branch with her one free hand. It came loose.

'Come here,' she called. 'Grab this branch and do not let go.'

The three older children hugged the branch. Thanh clung to her mother. Hoa ploughed through the muddy riverbed until her feet no longer touched bottom. She launched their "boat".

'Paddle, like this,' she cried, trying to demonstrate. The three older children got the message. They headed across the river, reached the other side, and exhausted, collapsed on the grassy bank. Hoa's misery at losing her beloved husband pushed her to the brink of collapse. Then it happened.

'Look, Má,' said Thu pointing. In the distance was a bridge. On that bridge were people and vehicles. It was civilization. It was hope.

After a long rest, they limped to the port. Hoa removed a small amount of gold she had sown into her clothes. With it, she bought food and fed her children. Her joy at having reached her destination was smashed by her heartbreak. Her husband had given his life so his family might live.

She moved to the dock area. Asking different people brought her to a man whose boat sailed that day.

'How much for me and my four children?'

The man wanted too much. Hoa turned away in despair but the man wanted more passengers so dropped his price. Hoa thanked him, paid, and took her children aboard.

The fishing boat was crowded with families, refugees wanting to escape their homeland for a better life.

Hoa settled her children and waited. What else could she do? Her heart ached; she wanted to vomit but had nothing to spew. To have come this far and lost her one true love meant misery. She could touch her pain. The older children asked about their father. She lied. 'He will join us later. Now sit still and be quiet.' Then she decided. She would get off the boat. She could not leave without trying to find Quang.

She stood to tell the captain but the boat's engines came alive, and the vessel moved away from the wharf. Hoa panicked. It was too late.

Through streaming tears, she watched the land of her birth for the last time. Then she screamed. She screamed so loud and so long everyone on board stared at her. Her children were scared.

Hoa screamed at the captain. 'Stop the boat! Stop the boat!'

Running along the wharf was Quang. He ran, waved and called. His wife waved and screamed. His children waved and yelled.

Annoyed, the captain moved his boat back to the dock. Quang leapt aboard and tears of joy replaced any words.

The family Nguyen escaped from Vietnam.

4

Australia 1996

'YOU NEED TO SIT DOWN,' said Judith.

David panicked. 'What's happened? Is it Matthew? What's he done?'

'You mean apart from throwing away his life and becoming a recluse?'

'I haven't seen him this week. Do you think he's sleeping in the houses he's cleaning?'

Judith despaired. She didn't know what to think. To his parents, Matthew lurched towards being a lost cause. Alas, he was not their only concern. Judith explained.

'For once it's not Matthew; it's Rosie.'

David panicked. 'What's happened?'

'Our daughter has a boyfriend.'

David experienced massive relief. 'Is that all? I thought you were going say the world will end before we see the latest episode of *Columbo*.'

'This is serious.'

'Oh come on, she's 16. You had a boyfriend when you were 15.'

'You haven't asked who he is or what he is,' said Judith.

David got serious. 'What do you mean *what* he is? Tell me he's not a druggie.'

'Worse, he's got religion.'

David groaned. 'Oh no.'

'The boyfriend and his family belong to some heavy religious sect, and our darling daughter is a recent convert.'

Judith's news would have been a worry even if she and David enjoyed a happy marriage. They didn't. They were doing it tough, and had been for some time. Any concerns with their teenage children simply added pressure to their already shaky union.

29

For months their relation*ship* had been taking on water thanks to their son. Matthew dropped out of school and worked full-time for the Jefferson family. Judith and David felt helpless, their only consolation being he made good money and, as far as they knew, lived a relatively responsible lifestyle. Having one rebellious child was a concern, but both!

Their daughter was happy at school and behaved herself. The one thing she did without her family was attend church. She went with a girlfriend. It was one of those happy clappy congregations with guitars, straw mats and hallelujahs. David and Judith were confirmed non-believers with the motto of *live and let live*. Now, without notice, their second child started to cause them grief.

'What did Rosie say,' asked David?

'That she's happy and doesn't want her boyfriend to meet us.'

'We're not that bad looking are we?'

'Apparently she's ashamed of us.'

'That's absurd. What's the matter with the girl?'

'You mean, what's the matter with us? We've failed completely as parents. Our talented son wastes his life working as a cleaner, and our daughter believes her family are unrepentant sinners and wants nothing more to do with us.'

'Oscar was right,' said David. 'To lose one child may be regarded as a misfortune; to lose both looks like carelessness.'

Judith hated David quoting poetry or plays. This time he misquoted Mr Wilde but even so, Judith fumed.

Their marriage developed cracks with the major problem being they didn't talk about it. They discussed counselling but neither got round to making an appointment. Judith had serious doubts their marriage could survive, and David impersonated an ostrich becoming well acquainted with sand.

'So how serious is Rosie,' he asked?

'So serious she wants to move out of home.'

That stunned him. 'What? And go where?'

'She wants to live with the boyfriend's parents.'

'Right, that settles it. It's time I gave our darling daughter a good tongue lashing.'

He started to leave the room to confront his daughter but stopped when Judith spoke. She mimicked him.

'Oh please, Judith, if I've learnt anything from decades of teaching, it's that lecturing teenagers never works.'

He stopped and they stared at one another. He returned to his chair. Neither spoke. Things were not happy in the Cadwallader home.

'Perhaps it would be better coming from you,' he suggested.

The silence lingered. Judith spoke in a soft voice.

'Perhaps our children are not the only unhappy people in this house.'

He looked at her. He didn't want this conversation. Okay, he knew the hand holding had long left their marriage, but wasn't this what happened to most people? Middle-aged couples muddle through; they get by.

Why can't we do that? Darby and Joan are two of my best friends.

Judith hesitated to come straight out and tell David she wanted a divorce. With both their children vulnerable, or in a tricky situation, now was not a good time to add separated parents to the mix. Before they could discuss anything, Rosie entered the room.

'Here she is,' greeted David and quoted the Bard. 'She's beautiful, and therefore to be woo'd.'

Rosie sat facing her father. 'I suppose Mum has told you everything, but Dad, you need to understand, I won't change my mind.'

He slipped into Groucho Marx mode. 'Women should be obscene and not heard.'

'And your silly quotations are just that—silly.'

'Now that hurts,' said David. 'Groucho Marx is many things but never silly.'

Judith tried to save the situation. 'Your father means well, darling. We both want you to be happy.'

'I am happy. I've never been so happy in all my life. And it's because I've met Aaron, and given my life to the Lord.'

David groaned in silence. Judith looked at him, her eyes telling him to do something. He tried a softly-softly approach.

'So, tell us about Alan. What's he like?'

'Aaron, his name is Aaron,' she barked.

'Sorry, Aaron,' said a sheepish father. Judith despaired.

'He's wonderful, and he's given his heart to Jesus.'

That was it. That was the total description of their daughter's true love. David wanted to joke that Aaron was now heartless but wisely refrained.

'Your father and I would love to meet him,' added Judith.

''Tis truth indeed,' said David. 'I would love to shake his hand and tell him my daughter is the best girl in the whole world.'

'It's not going to happen, Dad.'

'But why,' begged Judith?

'Because you have no faith, and our Lord told us to be in the world but not of the world.'

David smiled. 'I think you'll find one of the Ten Commandments is to honour thy mother and thy father.'

'It's no good, Dad. Quoting Shakespeare will never replace the bible.'

David looked at Rosie and thought of Shakespeare.

There is nothing more frightful than ignorance in action.

He wanted to say, "That *is* the bible", but saw his daughter's hormones and blind faith running rampant through her brain and body.

Judith tried a new tack. 'Your father and I want you to know we will never stand in your way.'

'You can't. I'm 16. I can do what I want.'

Rosie's attitude and answers created a quandary. Which was worse? Was it their son mixing with the wrong crowd, dropping out of school and wasting his life, or their daughter blindly following some unknown boy and his fundamentalist beliefs?

Their conversation stalled. David thought of a circuit-breaker. 'Would you mind if your mother and I came to your church?'

That threw the teenager. Judith nearly died.

'That's typical of you,' snorted Rosie. 'The Lord has no place in your life, and now you want to mock Aaron's faith.'

Judith panicked. 'No, darling, that's not true. We just want to meet him.'

'Correct,' added David. 'We just want to meet him.'

'Well he doesn't want to meet you. And it's easy to see why. I've told him and his family that I'm ashamed to call you my parents.'

She stormed out of the room, bounded upstairs and slammed her bedroom door.

'That went well,' said Judith.

David looked bemused. 'Please tell me we only have two kids. There aren't any more, are there?'

She stood and headed for the door then stopped.

'I think I'll sleep in the spare room tonight—if you don't mind.' She looked at him. 'Goodnight.' She left.

For David, the worst thing was her politeness. Had she cursed him, called him a loser and stormed out, that might have been acceptable. But no, she added ever so politely, "If you don't mind". Her message was clear. The marriage is over but I'll remain civil.

That hurt.

He thought of a quote by Groucho.

Marriage is a wonderful institution, but who wants to live in an institution?

David sat in the dark, sipped a glass of red, and pondered his situation. Aged 64, he prepared to retire. His wife wanted out of their marriage. His children wanted out of their parents. He wanted ... he wasn't sure what he wanted.

Having taught English Literature forever, David dreamt of touring the places where Shakespeare, Dickens, Miss Austen and the Misses Brontë lived and set their tales. He dreamt of writing a book about his love for the glories of the English language. What price those dreams today?

His marriage appeared doomed. His children appeared doomed. His future appeared doomed, and he recalled the words of that feline fella, Mr Eliot. It was something about the world ending, not so much with a bang but a whimper.

That's my life to a tee.

He wandered upstairs, paused to listen at his daughter's door, heard nothing, raised his hand to knock but stopped, then walked to the master suite. For decades he would slip beneath the duvet with Judith already asleep on her side of the bed. Not tonight. Tonight, he slept alone.

But sleep wouldn't come. His mind got busy.

When is the best time to suffer hardship? Surely it's when you're young and healthy and can bounce back from adversity. The wife and kids have abandoned me. So what is my future? Can one die of despair?

He drifted to fitful sleep but jolted awake when the phone rang. He looked at the clock radio. 0208. *That's 2am.* He reached for the phone.

'Hello?'

'Is that Mr David Cadwallader?'

He sat up.

I don't know this voice and they're ringing in the middle of the night.

'Yes. Who's speaking?'

'It's Senior Constable Damien Wright from Richmond Police, sir.'

'What's happened?'

Now wide awake, David panicked. The door opened and in came a bleary-eyed Judith. She muttered a question. He mouthed the word *Police*, and held up his hand.

'We have your son Matthew in custody, sir.'

'In custody? Why?'

'He's been arrested for possession of a Class A drug.'

'Possession? I thought personal use of cannabis was not a crime.'

Judith sat on the bed beside her husband and wept in silence.

'It's not cannabis,' said the policeman. David went quiet. He put his hand over the mouthpiece and whispered to Judith.

'It's not cannabis.'

'Are you still there, Mr Cadwallader?'

'Yes, yes I'm still here.'

'Your son has asked for you, sir. Do you want to speak to him?'

'Of course. Put him on, please.'

There was a pause. David again covered the mouthpiece and spoke to his wife.

'He's at the Richmond police station having been arrested for possession of a Class A drug.'

Judith slumped against her husband. It was the first time she'd touched her spouse since ... neither could remember.

'Dad?'

'G'day mate, how are you?'

'I'm fine. Bit of a misunderstanding, that's all. No big deal.'

'What have the cops said?'

'Because I'm a cleanskin and the amount of gear was less than a gram, they've given me this big lecture and told me to prove I'm not a junkie living rough. Any chance I can grab a lift?'

'Of course, but for the usual fee.'

'How about I double it?'

'You're on. I'll see you soon. Oh, and I love you, son.'

He held the phone out from his ear because it went dead in a hurry.

Judith's anxiety bubbled. 'What did he say?'

'Nothing, he hung up.'

David moved to a wardrobe and grabbed some clothes. He spoke as he dressed.

'He's at the Richmond cop shop and asked for a lift.'

'Here? He's coming home?'

'Too bloody right he is.'

Judith moved to another wardrobe and grabbed some of her clothes, speaking as she dressed. 'I'm coming with you.'

'No, I'll be fine.'

'I'm coming with you, David, and that's final.'

'We can't leave Rosie alone. Not after what she told us. She could do anything.'

'I'll leave her a note. She may not even wake up.'

It was like old home week as the two of them argued. Both were short on sleep. Both were worried sick that their son was possibly involved in crime thanks to a serious drug habit. Judith scribbled a note in case Rosie woke, and put it on the kitchen table.

In the car their arguing continued.

'So what exactly did the police say?'

'I don't think they've charged him but it involved a class A drug.'

'Which is what?

'I'm not sure.'

'Do you mean you don't know or you don't want to upset me?'

Good question. David hesitated.

'I think you need a lot of cannabis to receive the same penalty as a gram of heroin.'

Judith gasped. 'Heroin? Did the police mention heroin?'

'They didn't specify any drug. Look, let's worry about things once we know the facts.'

Judith felt angry and sick. It broke her heart to think her son might be addicted to drugs, a drug dealer or both. David too felt wretched. There was a sharp pain in his chest.

Jesus, that's all I need—a heart attack.

The streets were empty in the wee small hours. They drove in silence. When closer to the police station, Judith spoke.

'Isn't there a serious drug problem in Richmond?'

'There are drugs in every suburb.'

David parked and they walked to the station.

'Good morning,' said a young uniformed officer on the front desk.

'We're the parents of Matthew Cadwallader. I believe you have him in custody,' said David.

'Just a moment,' said the constable who left.

A short while later, a plain clothes detective appeared and introduced himself.

'Your son was arrested for possession of a Class A drug.'

David felt sick. Judith felt faint.

'It was a small quantity and as he's got no police record, we've issued him with a warning, and will release him if you can assure us he's going to a good home.'

'Of course,' said Judith.

'The best,' added David.

'And we'll make sure he stays there.'

The detective looked at them, and gave a warning.

'It's a slippery slope when the drugs get a grip. You might want to look at some form of rehab.' The parents reacted. 'I'll get your son.'

David and Judith looked at one another in shock.

'Rehab? What's he talking about?' He smokes a bit of pot,' whispered David.

Their fears mounted, and when Matthew appeared, their shock was akin to a slap in the face. Matthew looked like a homeless person down on his luck.

Judith embraced her son. 'Oh Matt, darling, I'm so sorry.'

David made it a joint hug.

'We'll get you home, mate.' To the detective, he said, 'Can we go?'

The detective nodded and the family left. Matthew sat in the front next to his father, while Judith leaned in from the back seat and squeezed her son's shoulders.

Judith made coffee and prepared spaghetti on toast. Matthew had loved that meal since he was a kid. David sat with his son.

'You gave us a real fright, mate; don't ever do that sort of thing again.'

'Chill, Dad, everything's cool. It's no big deal.'

'Matt,' said his father who waited for his son to look at him. 'That's bullshit.'

Matthew was surprised. He rarely heard his father swear. This wasn't going to be as easy as he thought.

'When your mother comes in, it's time to tell all. And I mean all.'

Matthew felt a tinge of concern. His ability to lie convincingly would need to be perfect.

Judith came in with a tray—three coffees, and a plate of spaghetti on toast for the boy wonder. Being genuinely hungry, he ate with gusto. His parents looked at one another. Once the feast was over, David took control.

'Matt's agreed to tell us exactly what's been happening—all of it.'

'Dad, I told you, it's no big deal.'

Father and son sat toe to toe.

'Matt, listen—we are not the cops, your teachers, or some social worker or do-gooder, we're your parents. We know you smoke dope. We didn't know you took hard drugs.'

'It's nothing, hardly anything,' interrupted Matthew.

'Tell me you're not dealing.'

Matthew feigned indignation. 'Dad!'

'Let me finish,' said David, showing strength with compassion, which impressed Judith. 'We're not here to judge or punish you. There'll be no threats or ultimatums. We've always loved you and will go on loving you, and nothing you've done will change that love. Or, if it does change, it'll only grow stronger.'

This was impressive. David looked at Judith for support.

'Your father is absolutely right, darling,' she said.

'So come on, mate. Let's have the truth, the whole truth and, as they say in the classics, nothing but the truth.'

Matthew looked at his parents. His plan to lie, deny and, if necessary, even cry his way of this mess, now fell apart. He wasn't happy and wanted out of his crappy lifestyle. Maybe this was the way. He paused then dived in at the deep end.

'I dealt some drugs last night.' His parents gasped. 'It was only a tiny amount and that's why the cops let me go. It was less than a gram.'

'Why are you dealing,' asked David? 'Is it because you're using?'

Matthew couldn't escape.

'Occasionally, but it's no big deal.'

'I wish you'd stop saying that,' said Judith. 'Taking drugs is always a big deal.'

They stopped talking. This was a heavy session for everyone. David wanted the full story.

'So where are you when we don't see you for days? You told us you sleep in the houses you clean for the Jeffersons? Is that true?'

Matthew hesitated. 'I've stopped working for them.'

'They sacked you?' Matthew nodded. 'For taking drugs?'

'It's Tony and Tom who are into drugs, but their parents reckon their boys are little angels. Those bastards let me take the blame.'

David kept at his son. 'So where have you been living?'

Matthew shrugged. 'I crashed at a mate's place.'

'Would that be a mate who takes drugs?'

No answer from Matthew. Judith started to cry.

David sucked in air. 'Well, looking on the bright side, mate, I think you've had a lucky break.'

Matthew nodded. He felt safe for the first time in weeks.

Judith took control. 'Right, this is your mother speaking.'

'Here's trouble,' said David.

'Have a shower and go to bed. Tomorrow we'll get you sorted.'

Judith stood and opened her arms. Matthew hesitated then moved to his mother and they hugged.

'Great to have you home, Matt.' She kissed him several times. 'Now off to the bathroom and then your bedroom—go.'

He set off, saw his father's outstretched hand, stepped back to shake it then left. The parents flopped in their chairs and looked at one another.

'Well done, you,' said David.

'Ah no,—no, no, no—well done *you*,' she replied. 'That speech was terrific; and all without a quote from Groucho or Will, which proves what I've long believed, you can be normal if you try.' She stood. 'I'm going to bed.'

'I'll hang around till he turns in.'

'Goodnight,' she said and left.

'Goodnight,' said David to an empty room.

He relaxed, took deep breaths, and thought about his family. Maybe things weren't so bad after all. Maybe the trouble with the children will bring their parents closer together. He found himself nodding off in the armchair, but not for long.

Running footsteps jolted him awake. Judith raced into the room holding a note.

'It's Rosie. She's gone.' Judith thrust the note at David. He read aloud.

'Mum and Dad. The Lord has called me to live with Aaron and his family. Rosie.'

David's response was brief.

'Shit.'

5

A TALE OF TWO SUBURBS, as told in Melbourne, Australia. Footscray and South Yarra in the 1990s were chalk and cheese. Working-class and wealthy-class were reasonable descriptions. There are many mansions in South Yarra, whereas Footscray's mansions can be counted on the fingers of a clumsy woodcutter's hand.

Then there is the tale of two families living in these suburbs. Julia Cadwallader rattled around in her South Yarra apartment. It was bigger than most of the houses in Footscray—whereas Mr and Mrs Nguyen, formerly of Saigon, shuffled about in their pokey one-bedroom, public housing flat in Footscray.

Julia's family was old money. Her father's forebears owned vast pastoral holdings, and shrewd investments meant that today, Julia, a widow, lived high on the hog.

The Nguyens were pensioner poor. They fled Vietnam in 1974 before the Communists swept to power. The middle-aged couple landed in Malaysia, and were finally accepted as refugees in Australia. 25 years later, they were elderly, unwell, poor and sad.

For the Nguyens, Footscray turned into a home away from home as the suburb became a Vietnamese enclave. There were Vietnamese shops, restaurants and businesses—a serious plus for the refugees.

However, assimilation was never a priority, and more than two decades after settling Down Under, the Nguyens still spoke only their native tongue, Vietnamese.

Mind you, after 86 years, Julia Cadwallader too spoke only one language, with her English having an accent of whingeing and sarcasm. In South Yarra, her enclave consisted of beauty parlours, coffee shops and upmarket victuallers.

Julia Cadwallader and the Nguyens were only 9 kilometres apart but said distance could arguably be the greatest in the universe. Julia's weekly hairdressing budget far outstripped the Footscray pensioners' monthly food bill. Yet despite their totally different worlds, fate prepared an unusual collision—Footscray, say hello to South Yarra.

David Cadwallader and his mother endured a love-hate relationship. Julia hated having to love her son, and David loved to hate his mother.

He made the trip from Bentleigh to South Yarra as infrequently as possible. The main reason he did so was to keep his mother quiet. If he didn't visit, her complaints matched those of a mass protest in the city streets of Melbourne. Today was visit Mother day.

'It's me, Mother,' he said into the intercom.

'About time,' came the reply and the buzzer sounded as the door to the vestibule was unlocked. The vestibule was an art deco gem.

Julia's apartment had space. She had views over the Yarra River, and the thickness of her carpets gave most trampolines a run for their money. Her pile cost a pile.

She stood at her open front door as David climbed the stairs. He thought about his mother's first words.

What time do you call this?

'What time do you call this?' Julia was predictable, and had but one consistent and enduring characteristic; she was never happy unless she was miserable. Oh, sorry, two enduring characteristics—she never listened to anyone.

David and his mother had an understanding about expressing emotion, and particularly affection. The understanding was Don't. Osculation verboten.

He closed the door and followed his mother into her magnificent sitting room. They always sat in the same chairs.

'I called the doctor last night,' she said.

Don't ask, David. You'll only encourage her.

'They sent some locum, an Asian woman, who could hardly speak English. This country has gone to the dogs.'

'I see your roses are in bloom.'

'She wrote me a prescription which I need you to get for me.'

'There's a space ship outside in the street.'

She wandered around looking for the script. 'Where did I put it?'

'I've just farted,' he said.

She found the script and handed it to him. 'What did you say?'

'Pardon?'

'And while you're there, I need some eggs.'

'From the chemist?'

She sat and prattled on as always talking about herself and her world. Then, to David's astonishment, she asked about him.

'So you're really going to retire?'

'I have to, Mother. Old Father Time so decrees.'

'At least that will mean you can spend more time looking after your frail, elderly mother.'

Oh bliss, oh joy.

She continued. 'I had a visit from three of my grandchildren yesterday.'

David recoiled in shock. 'Geoffrey came here with his children?'

'Not Geoffrey, he's far too busy. No, they came with his wife.'

It takes a special woman to refer to her daughter-in-law as "his wife".

David was curious. 'Would that be the same wife who is desperate to impress a certain dowager in order to benefit greatly from her will?'

'I never see your children. What do they do? Study at university and bring credit to the Cadwallader name I trust.'

'Not quite, Mother. Your grandson is training to become a drug dealer, and his sister left home to become a religious weirdo.'

'Well I'm pleased to hear it. And what about your wife? I can't remember the last time I saw her.'

'It was at our wedding, Mother, 28 years ago.'

'You could be divorced for all I know, and she's run off with the milkman.'

'Well if it was the milkman, they'd probably clip clop off.' Curious, he asked a rhetorical question. 'Do they still have milkmen today?'

She looked at him as if he'd lost his mind. 'I've made coffee.'

David paused. 'Right then. Shall I be mother, Mother?'

He mused. *I know her next line. Well, it won't pour itself.*

'Well, it won't pour itself,' she said on cue.

Julia had delivered that line since kettles started whistling. David took the hint—he'd been taking the hint for 17 years ever since his father died.

Across town in working-class Footscray, Mr Nguyen and his wife ate lunch in silence. His health was poor—heart murmurs, hypertension, and rheumatoid arthritis were his known conditions. Mrs Nguyen worried about her husband. Having fled Vietnam, they lost contact with their family in Saigon. Today, they had only each other.

They often wondered about their family. When they left Saigon, their plan was to find a new country, and then send for their children and grandchildren.

Two things conspired to defeat them. They took ages to escape Malaysia and reach Australia, and in Vietnam, the Communists refused to co-operate with anyone who had abandoned their homeland. Letter writing from Australia produced a zero response.

In Vietnam, in Ho Chi Minh City, their old world had changed. The Nguyens in Australia had no working knowledge of the Socialist Republic of Vietnam. They had no idea their son Quang, his wife Hoa and their four children had made an amazing escape from Vietnam.

Ms Kim Vanh knocked on the Nguyen door. Few visitors ever came to this Footscray flat. Mrs Nguyen opened the door. She smiled whenever Halley's Comet came into view and her husband less so. Ms Vanh was Vietnamese and spoke the language fluently.

'Hello, Mrs Nguyen. May I come in?'

The women bowed and the visitor entered.

Kim Vanh worked for the local council. With such a high Vietnamese population in Footscray, the council appointed social workers who were fluent in Vietnamese. Their job was to explain to residents, especially the elderly, that the council offered a number of services. For pensioners such as Mr and Mrs Nguyen, many of these services were free.

Ms Vanh was good at her job, and took an interest in all her clients.

'How are you, Mr Nguyen?'

The old man nodded. A chatterbox he wasn't.

'Don't let me interrupt your lunch. Please continue.'

'Would you like some tea,' asked Mrs Nguyen?

'Thank you, no.'

Ms Vanh ran through the usual topics such as Mr Nguyen's medication, the fortnightly home help, and any problems understanding bills or council notices. Everything seemed fine.

But then Ms Vanh produced a document and looked serious.

'I have some news I need to share with you.'

The elderly couple worried. Was this bad news? The visitor explained.

'The government in Australia has been contacted by the government in Vietnam. A woman in Saigon—(Ms Vanh used the old name of the city so as not to upset the Nguyens)—has written to the Vietnamese government to ask about a family living in Australia. The family is called Nguyen.

If the couple were impressed, they hid their reaction.

'There are many people called Nguyen in Vietnam,' said Mrs Nguyen.

The social worker smiled. 'I understand but that is why I want to find out if this letter relates to you.'

Silence reigned. Ms Vanh paused then continued.

'The person who wrote this letter refers to Mr Trai Nguyen and Mrs Thu Nguyen.'

The elderly couple looked at one another. Their nervousness increased but still their emotions remained under lock and key.

'Am I right in saying they are your names?'

Both the Nguyens nodded.

'The letter writer says that the Nguyens in question lived in a small tailor's shop in a lane off Truong Dinh.'

Ms Vanh didn't need to say any more. The look on the faces of Mr and Mrs Nguyen spoke volumes.

'Is it possible that you might be that couple?'

Another pause and silence. Eventually Mrs Nguyen spoke. 'We are that couple.'

'I have some additional family names if that will help,' added Ms Vanh.

'We are that couple,' said Mr Nguyen. He rarely spoke and never to visitors, but now his voice was strong and unmistakably clear.

Ms Vanh didn't know how to proceed. The elderly couple were transfixed. They wanted to know who wrote the letter, and what it contained. Ms Vanh explained.

'This letter is written by a woman who knew your children and grandchildren. She says that she never met you. Her name is Quyen Nguyen.'

The Nguyens looked at one another. They would have made excellent poker players.

Mrs Nguyen spoke with confidence. 'We do not know that name.'

The visitor paused. She knew the contents of the letter, and wanted to inform the old couple in a way which caused them as little stress as possible. They wanted to know.

'What is the news,' asked Mrs Nguyen? The old couple held hands.

David started the final week of his long and illustrious teaching career. He decided to retire just short of his 65th birthday at the end of the penultimate term. It meant his students would have a new teacher for the run-in to their exams, and David felt bad about that fact. Then he told himself he needed to become selfish.

He'd taught for decades, had enough unused sick leave to cover three strokes and four broken legs, and his personal life was a mess.

Be selfish, David. Look after yourself for once.

Wife Judith still lived at home although she slept in the spare room. Son Matthew left home to make his fortune but spent whatever money he made buying drugs. Once, when things got really bad, David and Judith rescued their son and paid for Matthew to live in an expensive rehab clinic in Sydney. It was said to be the best, and Sydney was a long way from Matthew's drug contacts in Melbourne.

At first, the treatment worked but the detective in Richmond was correct. 'It's a slippery slope when the drugs get a grip.' After the rehab, David fell back into addiction and dealing.

Daughter Rosie left home to worship her God with the family of the young man she loved.

David lived on hope. Hope that his son and daughter were safe and well. Hope that his wife might rekindle the love she once had for her husband. Three times he gambled on hope for people he loved, and he wondered, what were the odds he'd pick a winner, even one? With school over for the day, and only four days of teaching remaining, he drove his battered MG into the driveway.

Does anyone ever want a miserable home life? David didn't and entered the kitchen where his wife sat nursing a full glass of wine.

'Afternoon,' he said, avoiding comment on the amount of alcohol his wife prepared to consume. She turned to him, and his stomach lurched.

Her eyes were red and her cheeks wet. If this was an act, she should be on the stage or in the movies.

'What's happened?' David hated that question. He'd asked it far too often of late. Where so many parents his age rejoiced in their children, he and Judith endured misery and fear. Had Matthew been arrested? Was he right now lying in a public toilet with a needle stuck in his arm?

Judith pushed a photo across the kitchen bench. David put down his satchel and looked at the print.

No drug addict in this scene. No misery either. It was all smiles with a double scoop of happiness. He studied a wedding photo with their daughter Rosie dressed as the bride.

Staring at the picture, David quoted the Bard. 'Though she be but little, she is fierce.' He continued studying the photo. 'She looks beautiful.'

Judith lost it. 'Oh for Chrissake, can't you ever be angry? Our only daughter has taken the biggest decision of her life and managed to wipe her parents from the whole bloody event.'

'She sent us a photo.'

Judith exploded. 'She sent us a photo? Is that all you can say? Where were you when the marriage took place? I wasn't there. A father is supposed to walk his daughter down the aisle. What, you lost the invitation? Got the date wrong?' She screamed. 'Our son steals from his parents to buy drugs, and our daughter forgets to tell us she got married last week. What the fuck have we done to deserve these children?'

She threw the wine glass into the sink. Smash! Glass fragments and wine decorated parts of the kitchen, and brought a dramatic end to their little chat as she stormed out of the room.

David picked up the photo. He studied it then kissed his daughter's image. 'Congratulations, my darling; and you too, Aaron.' He looked hard at his new son-in-law. 'Welcome to the family—son.'

Ms Vanh drove the Nguyens to Tullamarine airport. It was a month since their meeting when the letter from Saigon was revealed. The elderly couple had been worried ever since, and today were nervous.

Since leaving Vietnam and settling in Australia, they knew nothing of their children or grandchildren—nothing. Now an unexpected letter brought news. Something overpowering seemed poised to begin.

The Nguyens sat in the arrivals area. Ms Vanh had a card with a name on it, written in Vietnamese. The Nguyens sat against a wall and waited. People came from the Customs area into the public area. Families and friends greeted passengers with much happiness filling the terminal.

The wait seemed endless. The Nguyens could not see those arriving because of the throng of people. Then it happened. Ms Vanh walked towards the elderly couple escorting a newly arrived passenger. The couple stopped in front of the Nguyens, and Miss Vanh spoke.

'Mr and Mrs Nguyen, this is your granddaughter, Thanh.'

6

DAVID WOKE EARLY. He slept alone these nights. His marriage was shot, his son a druggie, and his daughter estranged thanks to her strict religious beliefs. On top of all that, today was his last day of teaching, and with so much personal trauma going on in his life, celebrating the end of his illustrious career somehow got buried.

He showered, shaved and shoe shined, before attacking a bowl of cereal in the kitchen. Judith wandered in yawning.

'Good morning,' said the husband.

'Morning,' said the wife pouring some fruit juice. 'So is this the big final day for the world's number one teacher?'

'Not sure who you're talking about but for me, I'm retiring.'

She had her back to him and spoke in a matter-of-fact way. 'David, I won't be coming to your farewell.'

This he expected, but it did boost his misery stocks, and that surprised him as he thought his reservoir of sadness was chockers.

'No problem,' he lied.

'I know you don't want to hear this on your final day, but either I've lost some money or our son has been here and helped himself—again.'

David stopped eating. 'Are you sure?' Judith shrugged. 'Are you sure?'

'No, but yesterday I had at least three fifties in my purse.'

Neither spoke. A child stealing from his or her family demoralised the parents. If the money was used to buy drugs then that way lies despair.

'We have to move on that overseas rehab offer,' said David.

'We can't afford it. It's way too expensive.'

'I'll cash in some of my super. I'm getting a much better return now, thanks to your clever brother.' She said nothing. 'Judith, we can't let our son kill himself. We have to try something.'

'We've tried many things. When do we stop trying?'

'Never.'

'He's not interested in rehab. Remember that addiction expert.'

David nodded, repeating the expert's opinion. 'Some addicts don't want to be helped.'

'Exactly,' she said, and the dark mood darkened. There were no celebrations on this, his last day at work.

The budding retiree drove to school in his much-loved MG. On his final day of teaching, David would need top acting skills to hide his aching heart. The students and staff would be full of good wishes and back-slapping bonhomie. He would be miserable inside, while cracking gags and exuding happiness.

David's satchel contained the last set of essays he would ever correct. One benefit of retirement would see his social life get a new lease of life.

What social life?

The final day celebrations started in the car park. One of the science teachers arrived at the same time as David, and started to sing.

'Why was he born so beautiful, why was he born at all?'

David appreciated the thought and headed to the staffroom. Students chatted, played and ignored him. Some knew he would finish teaching today. Nobody knew he was misery writ large. All he wanted was the day to end. He dreaded the speeches and presentations in the staffroom, and declined any after-hours event to mark his retirement. His pathetic lie went as follows.

'Judith and the kids want to take me out for a slap-up meal.'

If only the world knew. His mother, like David's fellow teachers, was unaware the Cadwallader children had no connection with their parents, or that their parents had no connection with their kids. Misery reigned.

Buck up, David. You have students to inspire.

He battled through the morning, and in the afternoon, entered the classroom to take his final Year 12 English Literature class. The students chatted. David headed for his table, speaking as he walked.

'Good afternoon, ladies and gentlemen.'

In a well-rehearsed move, the students replied in a sing-song fashion as if they were 10 years younger. 'Good afternoon, Mister Cadwallader.'

He looked at their grinning faces, and picked up their essays. 'And for the final time ...'

He stopped dead because the students rose as one and applauded. David was lost for words. His miserable home life was trampled underfoot by this sincere and genuine acknowledgement from his grateful students. They kept on clapping.

Shit, I'm going to cry.

David waved a hand and called. 'Yes, all right, enough already.'

The students were pleased. Their plan had worked. They wanted to show their appreciation, and to see that their teacher understood their respect and admiration for him. They sat, smiling and murmuring.

'As I was about to say until I was so rudely interrupted.' The students laughed. If ever an English Literature lesson promised happiness and memories, this was it. He held up the essays. 'For the final time, I return herewith thy literary contributions.'

A keen student, Juliet, waited for her work. 'Did I pass, sir, please?'

David prepared to distribute the essays. 'But soft, methinks thou art privy.'

'I really do need a good mark, sir.'

'Don't we all?' He placed the essays on the table and addressed the class. 'Now children, it has obviously not escaped your attention that today is the last lesson I shall give to you lot.'

A loud cheer rang out followed by applause. He knew they were joking.

David spoke over their reaction. 'And it's my last lesson, not just for you lot but for anyone, anywhere, ever.'

A melodramatic groan filled the room.

'Ah come on sir,' called a student, 'you're too young to retire.'

'So I'm inclined to turn today's lesson into somewhat of an insouciant ceremony.'

The students instantly became a Music Hall audience, and reacted as one. 'Oooooooh,' they responded to the big word.

One would-be thespian mocked the choice of word. 'Insouciant?'

David got serious. 'And you'll notice I said cerem'ny and not ....'

As he finished speaking, his voice rose in pitch making it a cue, which the students grabbed with fervour.

'Cera-moan-ey,' they chorused with glee.

David was big on pronunciation. Juliet, still keen to receive her essay, was quick to join the game.

'If you've taught us nothing else, sir, we know how to put the em*pha*sis on the right sy*lla*ble.' Loud laughter followed.

The lesson was soon firing on all cylinders. David's train wreck of a private life faded as his students' enthusiasm and love swamped his thinking.

'Ah,' he enquired, 'but will you ever appreciate the beauty of the writings of that doyen of wit and perspicacity ....'

'William Shakespeare,' cried a captivated student.

David looked at the student. '... that profound philosopher, Groucho Marx.' The class discovered new ways to laugh.

The student who jumped the gun, leapt back into the dialogue with liberal lashings of ham. 'Oh *that* great doyen.'

David grabbed an imaginary cigar, bent from the waist, and became Groucho Marx, his voice rising at the end. 'Who once said, those are my principles, and if you don't like them ...'

The delighted audience replied as one.

'... well I have others.'

Joy filled the room as 17 Groucho Marx impersonators made laughter contagious. The hilarity refused to settle, and David's final lesson became one to savour. He re-discovered happiness; something he lost months, maybe years ago. But throughout this frivolity, his students too experienced sadness. They didn't want their time with "sir" to end.

Juliet had a serious question. 'So who's the best, sir, Groucho or Will?'

David corrected her. 'Who is the better, young lady?' He mimicked the language of the youth of the day. 'Them's just the two like.'

Juliet twigged. 'Oh, I remember—good, better, best.'

David mimicked Henry Higgins. 'By George, I think she's got it.'

Juliet said, 'Before I took this subject, sir, I knew nothin' about ...'

'Noth*ing*, ing, ing, ing,' corrected David.

Juliet copied her teacher. 'I knew noth*ing* about William Shakespeare or Groucho Marx but now, thanks to you, sir, I know two Shakespearean sonnets, Juliet's "Wherefore art thou?" speech, and lots of Groucho gags.'

What a cue. David let fly with more of his Groucho gags. 'While hunting in Africa I shot an elephant in my pyjamas ...'

The students clutched their imaginary cigars. '... and how he got in my pyjamas I'll never know.'

David had taught them well. 'I never forget a face, but in your case ...'

'... I'll be glad to make an exception,' chorused the students.

Anyone passing the room might have laughed, believed education standards had crashed, or thought Chaucer had penned a new Canterbury Tale.

With each new gag, the laughter became warmer, and David milked the situation.

'I didn't like the play, but then I saw it under adverse conditions.'

The students fired their reply. 'The curtain was up.'

David switched from an imaginary cigar to an imaginary telephone. 'Room service? Send up a larger room.'

The laughter began to wane. This lunacy couldn't last forever. It was time for serious relief, and Juliet had a confession.

'Y'know sir, my mother reckons we get much more than we deserve from your classes.'

'Ah, thy mother is both comely and wise.'

'But sir?' Juliet spoke with a rising inflexion.

David copied her speech pattern. 'Yes?'

'My cousin's doing English Lit at her school and ...

David feigned shock. '*Doing* English Lit? Doing it? My dear young lady, one explores, discovers and savours the immortal beauty of the English language; one does not do it.'

Juliet ignored her teacher's mock indignation. 'As I was saying, they don't do no Shakespeare at all.'

'And rightly so,' replied the teacher. 'Why bother with a gent who created sublime poetry, invented hundreds of words, and explored and explained the human condition better than anyone before or since?'

A genuinely confused student spoke. 'Is that you being sarky, sir?'

David walked around the room handing out essays, even throwing the odd one to a student a row or two away from where he stood. Juliet was the last to receive her essay. David spoke as he distributed.

'Well done that man. Now, does anyone have a question about ...'

Juliet shrieked with delight. 'I passed! I passed!' She stood and hugged her teacher. 'Oh thank you, sir, thank you.'

David found it endearing but tiresome so gently rebuffed her affection. 'Take flight maiden, our revels now are ended.' Juliet sat and David addressed the class. 'As always I marked according to the golden rule of essay writing which is ...'

The students knew this answer inside out and chanted. '... answer the question being asked.'

David sat on his table. The mayhem seemed to have finished. A student asked a question. It was a sincere enquiry.

'So what will you do in your retirement, sir?' The whole class paid attention.

'Ah, methinks a multitude of wondrous things.'

Another student wanted details. 'Such as?'

David looked his students squarely in the eye. 'Hmmm, perhaps the greatest being not having to teach a generation of adolescents who reckon ignorance is not only bliss but cool.'

Some pretended to be offended, while others were amused. Juliet became defensive.

'Aw, come on sir, it's not our fault.'

'It never is,' replied David. 'Behold thy creed,' he said mimicking their attitude. 'Take no responsibility. Never mind the skills of spelling, sums and syntax, just get thyself to schoolies' week.'

Well, was that ever a cue? As one, the students stamped their feet, clapped and cried. 'Yeah, schoolies! Rah!'

This celebration took a while to die, and when it did, David continued to mimic them.

He shrugged and spoke in a drab voice. 'Whatever.' More laughter.

Juliet was up for an argument. 'But sir, that's what school's all about; exams and league tables. We regurgitate the facts and pray for a pass.'

Again David over-reacted being shocked by Juliet's comment.

'Regurgitate?' He spoke louder. 'Regurgitate?' He counted on his fingers. 'But that's … four syllables; plus philosophy.' He smiled and took pleasure in his next thought. 'Maybe all is not lost after all.'

The lesson drifted. What lesson? It had been a time of relaxation, reminiscence and frivolity. David wanted the bell to ring and the day to be over. In this new found quietness, Juliet became philosophical.

'Y'know, sir, you're one of them teachers, what makes us think.

David had one last burst of energy. 'Those teachers *who* make us think.'

'But do you agree with my father?'

'Ah yes, the parent who reckons corporal punishment should be replaced by capital punishment.'

'My Dad reckons you've gotta be real smart to go to uni.'

David showed an interest. 'Really? And does Dad know that some unis run remedial classes for first-year students who can't spell or write a half-decent sentence?'

'Well you're the teacher sir. If we can't spell or ain't never heard of Shakespeare then it's all your fault.'

David pondered her reply.

What's the point? Or rather, I think she's got a point.

He slipped into his mock dramatic persona. 'Oh, Mea culpa, Mea culpa, Mea maxima culpa.'

Juliet delivered what she thought was the coup de grâce. 'And why do you always show off like now—speaking French?'

This time David's shock was genuine. 'French!?'

Juliet shrugged. 'Whatever.'

The bell rang for the end of the lesson. The students headed for the door. David looked to the heavens. 'There is a god.'

Students stopped to shake David's hand, thank him, and wish him a happy retirement. He in turn nodded and thanked them. He checked his satchel and spoke to no-one in particular.

'Right, that's it. Parting is such sweet sorrow and all that jazz; now bugger off.' He looked up and saw Juliet was the only student in the room. She folded her arms, clutching her "pass" essay and spoke.

'I just wanted to say ... thank you, sir.'

David began with a touch of Shakespeare. 'O! she doth teach the torches to burn bright.' He switched to the vernacular. 'Now damsel, sling y'hook.'

He didn't want an emotional farewell. He didn't want any farewell. He gathered his satchel and turned to go. She remained frozen to the spot. This forced him to look at her. She had prepared for this moment.

'Your presence makes us rich, most noble Lord. And far surmounts our labour to attain it.'

David's shock was genuine. Of course he knew the quote from Richard II, but the delivery and sincerity of Juliet's speech momentarily stunned him. There was a pause, and then Juliet leant in, kissed his cheek, and almost ran from the room.

'Bloody hell,' mouthed the teacher.

He was interrupted by a member of the office staff speaking via the PA.

'Would Mr Cadwallader please go to the staffroom? Mr Cadwallader to the staffroom.'

David's shoulders slumped and his spirits joined them. 'Oh Gawd—bloody presentation.'

7

DAVID WALKED TO THE STAFFROOM with a heavy heart. It wasn't every day you retired. He knew he'd be swamped with praise and presents, and all that was wonderful but he didn't like fuss. Sadly, fuss was the least of his worries. He bemoaned his family life. It was a right royal mess and, now that his work life was about to end, that family mess was all he had left. He was the clown laughing on the outside yet wretched within.

He entered the staff room where his colleagues came alive. They whistled, applauded and shouted comments. David walked to his cluttered desk, waved and spoke, pretending to be a humble East End of London tailor.

'Yes, all right, my son; enough already.'

His colleagues laughed. David was popular. Colleagues moved to him, patted or kissed him, or both. David became the centre of attention.

The principal, Janice Lees, entered with a cane basket of beautifully wrapped goodies, and placed them on a chair in the middle of the room. Another teacher placed a second chair near the principal, and she called for order.

'Thank you all. Bit of shush, please.'

The teaching staff settled. Office staff members slipped into the room followed by some parents and the cleaner and her husband. People stood against the walls, two deep in places. It was a full house. Janice beckoned to David. 'Take a seat, kind sir.'

He moved to the empty chair speaking en route. 'Let me be boiled to death with melancholy.'

People responded to most quips uttered by David. On this his special occasion, their response was fulsome and sincere. David sat then pointed a warning finger at his boss, managing to combine both Groucho and Will.

'Brevity is the soul of wit, Mrs. Claypool.'

Janice smiled. She and David had worked together for the last 12 years, and little he could say or do would surprise her. The room fell silent with all eyes on Janice. She'd spent serious time on her speech.

'Well now, what can one say about this extraordinary man? Some of us weren't even born when David started teaching.'

He cupped an ear and spoke as a frail and elderly gent. 'Could you speak up please?'

The audience laughed with feeling. Janice was in for a friendly time. She waited for silence then continued.

'*Salt of the earth, a born teacher* and *generous to a fault,* are some of the sayings which we happily apply to our terrific colleague. How many thousands of students have had their life enriched by this dedicated and amazing man?'

David turned to those colleagues closest to him and spoke in a stage whisper, heard by the whole room. 'Who's she talking about?'

Talk about a hometown crowd. They loved him, and showed that love with their laughter at his every quip. Had Janice been an inexperienced principal or new to this school, she might have failed. But she too neared retirement and David was an old pal. She resumed her speech.

'Today we read that teaching has changed, that the so-called best teachers should be paid more, and that testing creates curriculum. But with change all around, one thing remains constant. Teaching is and always will be about skill and passion; skill in knowing how to guide and inspire students; and above all, passion for the profession and text. David Cadwallader is one of those wonderful, unsung teaching heroes with skill and passion to burn.'

David spoke out front. 'I'm not dead am I?'

That got a laugh but by now the response eased a touch. People knew this was a serious occasion. They wanted to hear the words of praise, and they wanted to hear David's speech in reply. Janice continued.

'Anyone who can help generations of teenagers understand and enjoy Shakespeare is a brilliant teacher. Anyone who can do that via the Marx Brothers is a genius.'

Unsurprisingly, David slipped into his Groucho routine. 'I've had a perfectly wonderful evening. But this wasn't it.' More laughter.

For the first time, Janice faced David and addressed him. Her sincerity was out on show.

'David, to say we're going to miss you is a serious understatement. We'll miss your irrepressible personality, your energy and enthusiasm, your passion for books; your infectious sense of lunatic humour, and of course, your wonderful friendship and love.'

A hubbub of support was heard along with cries of 'Hear, hear'.

On song, David chimed in with, 'You left out my modesty.'

Laughter rippled around the room as Janice sorted the gifts in the basket.

'Now choosing a gift for the man who has everything was one hell of a task.' She held up the first gift. 'Knowing your love of fine wine, we're sure your palate will enjoy this fine drop of red.'

David nodded his thanks, and revealed yet another character from his box of impersonation tricks, this time W.C. Fields. 'I cook with wine; sometimes I even add it to the food.'

There was a lot of goodwill in the room. Janice felt her pulse quicken as she prepared to give David what she believed were stunning gifts. She looked him in the eye and held up an envelope.

'And for that long-awaited overseas trip, please accept two double-passes for you and Judith to the Globe Theatre in London, and to the Royal Shakespeare Company in Stratford-upon-Avon.'

Janice was right. David was gobsmacked. He didn't expect such a gift. For once his response had nothing to do with cracking a gag.

'Wow!' was all he managed.

But Judith wasn't finished and produced another envelope.

'Of course, what else for the man who loves books, but a book voucher?' David smiled. 'And last but not least,' she said producing a boxed set of DVDs, 'a collection of every appearance by the Marx Brothers in movies and on TV.'

The onlookers laughed knowing David's passion for the vaudevillian brothers. Naturally he became Groucho for his response.

'Anybody who doesn't like this book is healthy.'

Janice paused. She waited for silence. It was the end of her speech and she wanted to make it perfect.

'I speak for everyone, David, the teaching staff, the office staff, the cleaners and caretakers, the canteen staff, the parents and your many adoring students, when I say thank you for just being you. Our loss is Judith's gain and we wish you both a long and very happy retirement.'

The applause was instant, generous and prolonged. David stood. He and Janice hugged and she kissed his cheek with love and sadness. It took some time for things to settle. Judith stood back and David had the floor.

No quips from the onlookers. This man was admired, respected and loved. They paid him the greatest compliment by remaining silent.

David struggled. His family unhappiness mingled with his sadness in leaving the job he loved. He had no religious faith but considered a silent prayer to help him get through his speech. It was something like, "Stick with me, Big Fella". He looked around the room.

'Crikey,' he said, being genuinely nervous.

What the hell do I say?

He turned and looked at Janice. Groucho came alive. 'Do you think I could buy back my introduction to you?'

The laughter was polite, reserved. David felt enormous pressure. He decided to be himself.

'Well, thank you Janice for your kind words. And thank you everyone for these superb gifts.' Those who knew him could tell he was under pressure. He threw in a gag—again. 'I can't remember what I said at my last retirement speech.' This drew some restrained laughter. 'I think it only fair to say I have some mixed emotions. Forty odd years is a bloody long time to stand in front of a bunch of kids and wonder if World War Three will ever be over.'

His colleagues were reluctant to laugh. He was emotional and it showed. He knew he must finish this speech.

'I've seen a few changes since I started teaching. Dress code for staff has gone from formal to informal to "I've just got out of bed". Older colleagues nodded. 'The boss has gone from headmaster to principal to Human Resource Controller, and finally to today's Media and Marketing Manager.'

Janice nodded. David became serious and that didn't happen often.

'Did you know there used to be a time when teachers were highly respected members of the community? It's true. Stationmasters and teachers were once pillars of society. Now the trains are stuffed and teachers are fulltime report writers.'

This serious stuff was spot on but didn't suit the occasion or David. When he switched back to his natural and cheeky nature, the atmosphere lifted in the packed room.

'Of course there are some things I'll never miss such as 9E on a wet Friday afternoon—any Friday afternoon. Yard duty. Gary on Mondays if St Kilda fluked a win.'

'Go Saints,' said Gary.

'Oh and professional development sessions where we're asked ...' David switched to a whining voice. 'Why did you become a teacher?'

Several colleagues understood this comment. They too had been to a training day where motherhood statements were the raison d'etre for the whole sodding event.

Finally David dropped any pretence to humour, and spoke from the heart.

'But there's one thing I will miss; big time—you. When Judith and I had that trouble with our son ...' David stopped speaking. When he resumed, he spoke softly. '... still have.'

He took a deep breath, looked around and told the gathering what he really thought.

'It was your fantastic support, your love which kept us going.' Again he paused. 'Thank you. I'll always remember that.'

He had more to say, more he wanted to say but couldn't. He became afraid.

If I keep talking, I'll break down and blubber. Shut up, Dave.

His colleagues saved the day. They began to applaud and kept on applauding. Janice moved in, and whispered in his ear.

'I'll see you before you go.' She squeezed his arm and left as David was swamped with well-wishers.

He shook hands, kissed and was kissed, had his back patted, and thanked enough people in a few minutes to qualify for a spot in the Guinness Book of Records.

When the crowd drifted away, he picked up his satchel, his bust of Shakespeare, his framed photo of the Marx Brothers, and his basket of presents, and headed for the door.

In the corridor stood a parent and her son, once one of David's students. The boy was unremarkable academically with a personality to match. The mother stepped forward.

'Mr Cadwallader, I'm Timothy's mother.'

'Hello,' said David unable to remember Timothy's surname, and unable to shake hands due to the presents and paraphernalia he carried.

The mother continued. 'I just wanted to say thank you for all the wonderful help you gave Timothy in your classes.'

'That's very kind but I was just doing my job.' He wanted to escape without being rude. The mother wasn't finished.

'For years, Timothy hated school. It was a real struggle just to get him up in the morning let alone go to school.'

David smiled at Timothy. The boy wanted to thank the teacher he admired but let Mummy do the talking.

'I want you to know, sir, that you have changed my son's life in a wonderful way. Thanks to you, Timothy now loves coming to school and any success he has enjoyed and will in the future is because of your brilliant teaching and kindness.'

She looked at her son who offered a small gift to David. 'For you, sir,' he said. The pause was embarrassing because David had no free hand. He raised the cane basket, and Timothy placed the gift therein.

David was touched. 'Thank you for your gift and for your lovely words.'

He wanted to leave. Mother wasn't finished.

'I hope you have a long and happy retirement. I'm sure your family will be glad to have you all to themselves.'

That was the killer sentence. *My family? What family?*

'You're too kind,' repeated the new retiree. 'But if you'll excuse me, I have to say goodbye to quite a few other people.'

Liar.

'Of course,' said the mother and took her son's arm. As they walked away, Timothy called. 'Good luck, sir. Have a happy retirement.'

David felt tears itching to escape. He headed down the corridor and paused outside the principal's office. Then he squibbed it. With head down, he walked straight to the car park, and loaded his possessions into the old MG.

A voice called from afar. 'See ya, sir.' He didn't recognise the student, but waved then drove out of the school, ending his long and distinguished career as a teacher. He started to cry and couldn't stop.

8

WHAT YOU DON'T KNOW can't hurt you—or so they say. As David drove home from his last day as a teacher, his son crouched in a lane a few suburbs away. Used syringes rested amongst the weeds which poked out between the bluestone pitchers. Matthew searched in vain for a vein. He'd scored from his dealer and now needed a hit.

His sister meanwhile searched for a basin. Rosie leaned out of bed and vomited. Her dreaded morning sickness erupted at any time of the day.

Back home, David knew it was crunch time with his marriage. He and Judith had ignored the elephant in the room for months. Love didn't keep them together. They stayed married because of their troubled kids.

Despite the shaky nature of his marriage, and its bleak future, David clung to his optimism. He'd always been a glass-half-full person, and now that his working life was over, he hoped his retirement might save his fractured marriage. Judith might look at things in a new light. They were both free to spend time helping their kids, and fixing their damaged relationship. As he got closer to home, his wife chatted on the phone.

'Yes, I know. I'll tell him.' The person listening grew impatient and forced Judith to comment. 'Tonight, I'll tell him tonight.'

David arrived in his much-loved MG with its distinctive engine roar.

'That's him now,' said Judith. 'I'll call you later.' Judith copped another reminder. 'Yes, all right, tonight.'

She wandered into the lounge knowing David would enter via the kitchen. Her heart beat faster. She had a number of things to get off her chest and none of them would be easy.

David plonked his gifts on the kitchen table and called. 'Judith, I'm home.' He looked through the mail and found nothing of interest. 'Judith?'

She entered, stood in the doorway, and spoke in a soft voice. 'I heard you the first time.'

David was excited. 'Look at these great presents. It was the best final day I've ever had.'

'Sit, please.'

He was still reminiscing about his farewell. 'Even Janice made a half-decent speech.'

Judith pulled out a chair and sat. She looked at David. He saw she was serious. 'I've got bad news.'

David instantly became serious. He too sat. 'It's Matthew, he's dead. Where is he?'

'I don't know.'

'You don't know where he is or you don't know if he's dead? Come on, tell me, please.'

'David, we've talked about this a hundred times. Matthew died the day he chose that lifestyle. I've got nothing new about him or Rosie.'

David exhaled. He was good at mood changes, and flicked the switch to *Excited*. He showed Judith his gifts.

'We got some fantastic presents—tickets to the Globe and the RSC.'

'I told you, I'm not going.'

Now he switched to *Despondent*. He spoke with a kind of whine.

'Oh but why?'

'You know why. It's over; we're over.'

He begged. 'Please don't say that!'

She went back to her soft voice. 'And you're not going either.'

He tried sounding reasonable and offered a practical concession. 'I know I said mediation was a waste of money but now I'll give it a try. I'll try anything, Judith. I want our marriage; I want us, to survive.'

Misery gripped his soul, and his brain took time to comprehend her last sentence. Confused, he asked for clarification.

'What do you mean, I'm not going either?'

'That's the bad news.'

He thought he knew what had happened. 'It's Mother.'

Judith felt awful telling David the details. 'It's Robert.'

'Robert? Is he okay?'

'He's been arrested.'

David's confusion started to build. His head filled with questions.

'Arrested? For what?'

Judith forced herself to speak. 'Fraud.'

David's face had pain and disbelief written all over it. 'Fraud?'

Judith leant towards her husband and touched his arm. 'I'm sorry,' she said, and meant it.

Shock can knock you sideways. David reeled in disbelief.

'No. How much?'

Judith didn't reply. She didn't want to. She didn't need to. David persisted. 'Not everything?'

Her silence spoke volumes, and the slightest of nods answered his question. He put his head in his hands and wanted to vomit. Then he clutched at a straw.

'Are you sure? There might be some mistake.'

'He rang from the police station.'

David embraced despair. 'Oh God; why me?'

'Robert took money from all his clients, and set up some Ponzi scheme.'

David sounded pathetic. 'But he's family; he's my brother-in-law.'

'I did warn you.'

'That's our entire super.'

'That's *your* entire super.'

David felt helpless, shattered. 'Jesus, Judith. What can we do?'

'Sorry, but what's this "we" business?'

'That was all the money I had. I switched my super on Robert's advice.'

'I told you he stole from my mother. Why do you think she finished up in that urine-scented nursing home? He ruined her life, and many others, and now he's ruined yours.'

David stared into space. 'Neither a borrower nor a lender be.'

Judith used sarcasm. 'I don't think Mr Shakespeare's listening.'

David wandered around the kitchen trying to make sense of the tragedy. 'I can't go back to teaching. I can't.'

'It's time for down-sizing, matey.'

David floundered in the ocean. Straws floated on the surface and he clutched at them. 'We could both go on the pension. You get more if you're a couple.'

Judith lost it. 'Will you stop this bloody acting? There's no more *we*. Our marriage ended years ago and certainly once our loving children dumped us. Get real, David. It's over. We're over.'

The anger in her voice and the bluntness of her message put him on the canvas. He looked pathetic, and Judith now regretted her outburst. She paused and then spoke in a soft and caring tone.

'I'm sorry about your money ... really ... I'm sorry.' He looked at her and nodded his appreciation. 'But we'll have to sell the house.'

Another punch to his breadbasket left him gasping for air.

'And go where?'

'That's your choice.' Judith hesitated. It was time for the sucker punch. 'I'll be living with someone else.'

A feather flattened the stunned David. 'What?'

'Oh come on, you must have known.'

David found some anger. 'Known what?'

Judith began to lose patience. Her temper started champing at the bit.

'Why are you doing this? Why pretend you're living in some parallel universe where everything and everyone is sweetness and light? We no longer share a bed. Our children have wiped us. We're a dysfunctional family, and our imperfect marriage is dead.'

Both fell silent. This conversation had been a long time coming, and once it arrived, neither knew how to proceed. Both dispensed with raised voices and anger. David was the first to speak and did so in a quiet, considerate way. He didn't look at his wife.

'What's his name?'

She paused. 'Don't go there.'

He paused. 'So, after thirty-eight years of connubial bliss I'm being replaced by Mister Anonymous. I mean, does he actually exist?'

'Let's talk money.'

David slipped into his Groucho voice. 'Man does not control his own fate. The women in his life do that for him.'

'You know I wouldn't mind the endless wisecracks if occasionally one, just one was even remotely funny.'

David switched from Groucho to Will. 'Our revels now are ended.'

'I suggest we sell the house unless you want to buy me out.'

David came alive and mocked his wife. 'Buy you out? And you call me the joker.' He stood and pulled notes and coins from his pocket, counting them as he spoke. 'Right. How does ... three, five, twenty ... twenty-seven dollars and forty cents sound?' Judith despaired at his childish behaviour. 'With a lawn-mowing round I could stretch to thirty.'

She snapped. 'I don't want to buy you out. I'm moving in with my partner.'

'Partner? Oh yes, Mister No Name. No, don't tell me, let me guess. He's a lawyer from Eltham called Sebastian. No?' He paused, thinking. 'Ah, how about a retired stockbroker with a holiday shack in Portsea?'

That was it for Judith. She stood. 'Let me know when you've grown up.' She started to leave causing David to become contrite.

'Don't go, Judith, please, I'm sorry. Please.' She stopped and looked at him. 'I'll stop the clowning.'

She considered his attitude, walked back to a chair, and lectured him.

'The best thing, the only thing we can do now is work through the situation.'

He nodded. 'Okay.'

'We need to list what needs to be done, get it done, and make the split as smooth as possible. Yes?

He was resigned to the inevitable. 'Yes.'

She sat. 'So, we sell the house?'

His answer was soft. 'Yes.'

'And if there's any money left, we split it fifty-fifty.'

His contrition changed to shock and anger. '*If* there's any money left?'

'We don't own the house.' She couldn't believe he'd forgotten such a major financial event. 'Oh come on, we did that deal with the bank so we could afford Matt's treatment. That rehab cost a fortune.' David looked confused. 'You've forgotten. God you're hopeless.'

Perhaps he forgot, or perhaps the whole drug scene was so painful, he just blocked it from his mind. He remembered he was now broke.

'Brother can you spare a dime?'

'We'll get a third of the sale price less what we owe.'

The reality check hit David between the eyes. 'A third?'

'From that we pay off the personal loan Rosie abandoned, the money we owe that lawyer we used to help Matt, and the money we owe my sister; remember?'

David shook his head. Talk about his world crashing down around him.

'What's left we split fifty-fifty. I won't quibble over the MG.'

'How kind.'

'I suggest you talk to a lawyer and make sure you're not being cheated.'

In a flash, David's unintentional anger joined the discussion. The only surprising thing was how long it had taken to vent his spleen.

'Well your brother's screwed me over so why not you?'

His anger triggered her anger.

'Now listen, matey, I told you time and again not to let Robert touch your money. You wouldn't listen, so don't hang that on me.'

He knew she spoke the truth. 'Sorry.'

She hammered him. 'Grow up, stop playing the martyr, and bloody well move on.' Judith did just that and left.

Alone, David's spirits were broken. The Bard may well have written the following speech just for David Cadwallader.

'When sorrows come, they come not single spies, but in battalions.'

Judith returned and stood in the doorway. 'There's an agent coming to see the house at five. I suggest you tidy your room.'

She left but returned when David called.

'No, Judith, wait, please.' He floundered. 'Where will I find a lawyer?'

'Look under lawyers.' She wanted to depart but he persisted. 'But wait, wait, please.' She sighed, her impatience on show. 'Can you recommend someone? Could your solicitor recommend someone?'

'Hardly; there might be some conflict there.'

'Conflict?'

Judith wandered back into the room. She had delayed her knockout punch, not wanting to hurt the man she once loved. She took a deep breath.

'My solicitor's my partner. We're moving in together.'

'Ah, it adds a precious seeing to the eye. So your mystery man is Stan the solicitor.

After a long pause, Judith spoke. 'It's not Stan, it's Sue the solicitor.'

David's love of a pun sprang into action. 'Sue the solicitor! Oh that's brilliant. Fire the arsonist, tap the plumber and sue the solicitor.' The clown collapsed. The penny dropped. He faced reality. 'Sue the solicitor?' Judith nodded. 'It's not a boy called Sue?'

Judith was glad her secret was a secret no more. 'She's a she.'

David was on the canvas, out for the count. 'I didn't see that coming.'

Judith showed some humanity. 'No need for salt in the wound.'

David wandered, thinking aloud. 'My wife left me for another woman.'

She anticipated his next question. 'And before you ask, I'm getting my divorce legal costs for free.'

'Oh. Is that ethical? I mean, can't you get struck off for sleeping with your clients?'

'We can do this the easy or the hard way.'

David couldn't remove his comic bone. He was programmed to deliver witticisms. 'I suppose a ménage a trois is out of the question?' Her expression was a perfect example of "if looks could kill". He shrugged. 'Worth a try,' he said.

64

This was new ground for both of them. This was the first time either had encountered a marriage split. Neither spoke as they reflected on their situation. David turned philosophical.

'I wonder what a woman feels like when hubby announces he's gay, and moves in with his first best friend? I mean are the wife's feelings the same a husband has when his wife shacks up with a bird?'

Judith ignored him. She had more news.

'There's one more bit of bad news.'

'Don't tell me,' said David. 'My doctor rang, and I've got two weeks to live.'

Judith stood. 'Your mother's had a fall.'

David couldn't resist. 'Well she can't be dead; you said it was bad news.'

'She's in hospital, and the number's by the phone.' Judith left and David sat in silence. After a long pause, he spoke in a soft voice.

'There is a tide in the affairs of men, which taken at the flood, leads on to fortune. Omitted, all the voyage of their life is bound in shallows and in miseries.'

Things got cracking between David and Judith. After a long and lingering illness, their marriage dropped dead overnight. They agreed on the business side of things. The house went on the market and was sold. Thanks to his crooked brother-in-law, David was broke and ashamed. He dreaded anyone asking him about his retirement, his overseas trips and his wife and children. Talk about a fall from grace. His was spectacular.

He needed somewhere to live, and the further from friends and family the better. After the house was sold and all debts paid, he and Judith split what remained. There was cash to splash for chocolates, socks and jocks but that was about it.

Judith was okay. She had her modest super, a reliable runabout, plus her friend, Sue the solicitor. She was doing okay with two properties, a swish automobile, and a thriving legal practice. David had zip—no job, no money, no friends, no friendly family, no spouse and soon, no wheels.

While everyone waited for settlement on the house sale, David put his beloved MG up for sale. It sat in the driveway with a *For Sale* sign resting against the front bumper.

He was polishing said vehicle when a bloke walked up the drive.

'G'day,' said David.

'I've come about the car,' said the bloke.

'Right place, right time,' said David smiling and receiving nothing in response. 'She's a beauty. Have a look.'

The would-be buyer and car salesman did a lap of the wheels.

Not too close, David. Don't invade his personal space.

They stopped beside the driver's door.

'Hop in. Make y'self at home,' said David, opening the door.

The bloke sat in the vehicle. David handed him the ignition key. The car started first time, and David sighed with relief. He began his pitch.

'She runs like a dream.' The bloke revved the engine. David spoke louder. 'I had a major service only last month; new tyres last year. Oh and it's waterproof, particularly when it rains.'

No response from the geezer in the motor who only laughed every Leap Year. David turned on the melodramatic music.

'Of course I'm gutted to sell but needs must. She's been a joy for ...'

The buyer killed the engine and made an offer. It was just below David's rock-bottom price.

'How much?' The price was repeated and David's misery plunged to a new low. 'But it's a classic. They're as rare as bantam's braces.'

The bloke looked at David for the first time then spoke.

'Take it or leave it, mate.'

I'm a lot of things, sir, but your mate ain't one of them.

The sale of his beloved MG was the final straw. A few tyre-kickers rang, promised to come and inspect, and were never seen or heard from again. At least this bloke turned up, but oh, what a disappointing price.

The family home was due to settle next week after which David would be off to greener pastures; literally because his present plan was to camp in a paddock. He swallowed his pride, looked at the bloke in the MG and nodded.

'Okay. I accept.'

With more cash in his pocket than he could ever remember, David wandered inside the now empty home; no furniture, no wife, no kids. David's books were in boxes; his sleeping bag in a corner. He opened one of the boxes and retrieved a book. It was Shakespeare's *Lear*. He flicked through the pages, stopped and read. He had emotion to burn.

'You heavens, give me that patience, patience I need
And let not women's weapons, water-drops,
Stain my man's cheeks! No, you unnatural hags,
No, I'll not weep.

I have full cause of weeping, but this heart
Shall break into a hundred thousand flaws,
Or ere I'll weep. O fool, I shall go mad!'

He closed the book and looked to where he thought heaven might be.
   'The wheel is come full circle, I am here.'

9

OH TO BE A FLY ON THE WALL. David arrived at his mother's South Yarra apartment to explain his massive lifestyle change. Her recent fall had produced bruised but not broken bones. He hoped she'd be her usual self and not listen. He hoped she'd be too self-centred to care. He was wrong.

'Why are you here? This is not your visiting day?'

'I thought you'd be pleased to see me, Mother.'

'Members of my family only visit because they feel guilty or want something. So I repeat, why are you here?'

David was there because he felt his mother should be told, face to face, the details of his fall from grace. He didn't want to upset her, and planned to use the drip-feed method where he would tell her a bit of bad news, then some more and so on, until when he reached the shocking news, his mater would be prepared.

But as his mother challenged him to state his business, he thought, bugger it, I'll tell her everything in one hit. And he did.

'I'm moving house, Mother. My marriage is over, my savings stolen, my children lost, and my life's a mess.'

She looked at him. Would she complain, curse or collapse? It was none of those.

'Is that all? Now I want you to fetch a prescription for me.'

'That could be tricky, Mother,' he said.

'Tricky? You drive to the chemist, collect the medicine, and return. What's tricky about that?'

'I've sold my car.'

'And why would you do that?'

'I'm moving house, Mother. My marriage is over, my savings stolen, my children lost, and my life's a mess.'

'Stop repeating yourself. I'm not senile. The script is on the kitchen table. If you start walking now, you'll be back before dark.

You certainly aren't senile.

'I'll catch the train,' he said.

'Public transport is for the working class. I've never used it.'

'Well the people of Footscray love the good old train, tram and bus.'

'Footscray?'

'It's in the western suburbs.'

'I know where it is. But what has Footscray got to do with anything?'

'I'm moving house, Mother. My marriage is over, ...'

'Yes, yes, all right, I get the message.'

David picked up the prescription and moved to the door. 'My weekly visits may become fortnightly, or even monthly, Mother.'

'Typical; any excuse to avoid your duty.'

He indicated the prescription. 'In the words of Captain Oates, "I'm just going outside and may be some time". Hooroo.' He forced a grin and left.

David chose to live in Footscray because it was cheaper, and on the other side of town thereby making him anonymous. In Footscray he was unlikely to bump into former students, colleagues or neighbours. He didn't want to explain his broken marriage, his new-found penury or the actions of his children—be they dead or alive.

Despite his life being a tragedy in technicolour, David remained a romantic. He enjoyed exploring his new locale. The shops, the smells, the station—he was now an enthusiastic trainspotter—all offered something to savour.

The Vietnamese enlivened Footscray, and their language, cuisine, fashion and appearance intrigued him. In his former Bentleigh locale, the overwhelming culture was European and familiar. Now, in Footscray, he was in foreign territory, and he no speaka da lingo.

The local market was an Aladdin's Cave. The noise, the produce—some of it alive and kicking—the bartering and aromas captivated the man whose life was steeped in the basics of Bentleigh and the classics of Ye Olde England.

Alas, without human contact and replete with woe, grog became his constant companion. It helped him forget, or try to forget, the disasters of his pending divorce, his stolen savings, and his off-the-rails kids. Have another drink, my son.

His modest flat, became his castle, bolthole and hideaway. His block enjoyed communal living with lavatories flushed in adjoining flats sounding in his.

The smells from Vietnamese cooking were nothing like his new cuisine of fish 'n ships, pizzas and burgers. A Gordon Blue chef he was not. His front door had a broken lock and after failing to fix it, he left it figuring he had nothing of value to steal. In truth, he didn't care.

He wandered home wearing a cap and scarf, and carrying his latest liquor supplies in a cheap plastic bag. The world of Footscray ignored him and he liked that. He anticipated nothing and remembered the oldest Brontë sister's words.

Life is so constructed, that the event does not, cannot, will not match the expectation.

A Vietnamese local, a chap about David's age walked towards him.

It's a fellow traveller.

David stopped, smiled and stuck out a hand. 'Good afternoon, friend.'

The local, believing the stranger to be a drug addict wanting money, avoided David with a new energy. He shrugged.

How does one say G'day in Vietnamese?

He crossed the road, and in his street approached two Vietnamese men, smoking and chatting.

'Hello,' said David. 'I do desire we may be better strangers.'

The men looked at one another then departed in different directions.

David spoke to himself. 'I'm a stranger in a foreign land.' He looked around his new suburb. 'I wonder if the RSC tour to Footscray.'

At his block of flats, a Vietnamese family with young children came into the street. David smiled and performed an expansive bow.

'Greetings,' he said. 'I wonder if …'

The mother pushed their children around David. The father spoke in Vietnamese, advising the former teacher to please leave his family alone.

'I'm sorry,' replied David. 'Do you speak English?'

The father followed his wife and children. David turned and called. 'English?'

The ex-teacher mused. He spoke in a dramatic and Shakespearean manner. 'Confusion now hath made his masterpiece.' He raised his voice and shouted to the Western suburbs. 'Where the bloody hell am I?'

David climbed the stairs and opened his unlocked front door. 'Paradise,' he said entering the flat. He removed his cap and scarf, and placed his shopping on the coffee table.

'I like this place and willingly could waste my time in it.' He studied his new home. 'Mind you I'm not so sure about the décor.' He indicated a wall. 'As darling Oscar once said, "Either that wallpaper goes or I do".'

He faced the fridge. 'Ah, vittles.' He opened the door to discover it housed a can of beer and some takeaway with mould. He slipped into his Groucho routine. 'Look at me. I've worked my way up from nothing to a state of extreme poverty.'

Fridge empty, he headed to the settee and his bag of shopping.

'Dear boy, one must have life's essentials.'

He placed a bottle of cheap wine on the coffee table. 'Ah, alcohol.' His French was excellent. 'Naturellement.' He put cheese next to the wine. 'Camembert,' he announced. It was cheap cheddar. His French pronunciation was parfait. 'Essentiel.'

He admired his food and drink, and then spotted a large book. 'And of course ...' he patted the book, '... the scribblings of one Will Shakespeare. The winning trifecta, I want for nothing, my life complete.'

His reverie was disturbed by the sound of door knocking.

David groaned and called. 'None today, thank you!'

The visitor knocked again.

'But hark, a voice,' said David, rising and heading to the door. 'And here I am fresh out of smoked salmon sandwiches.' He opened the door to discover a startled Vietnamese youth.

David greeted him. 'Ah, gentle adieus and greetings first visitor.'

The man spoke fluent Vietnamese. 'Danny có ở đây không?'

David shrugged. 'Pardon Monsieur?'

'Danny có ở đây không?'

David guessed. 'Danny?'

'Danny,' confirmed the youth.

'No longer here, old chap but ...' The youth fled. David called. 'Not a problem.' He adopted a Texas drawl. 'Now y'all have a nice day.'

He was about to close the door when he noticed the door of the flat opposite ajar, and a pair of eyes observing him. He smiled at the eyes. 'How do?' he said, causing the eyes to vanish and the door to close. He re-entered his own abode.

'That went well. I wonder if Danny kept a stash. And am I too young to become a drug baron?' He sat and twiddled his thumbs. 'Now what?'

He listened to his watch. It continued to tick. He sighed.

'How long till death?'

Depression and excessive alcohol consumption were landmines for David but far worse was boredom. He wandered towards the only window, examining the design of the room.

'What is this style of architecture? Lego?'

He tried and failed to open the window. 'One ... immoveable window.' He looked down on the world below and spoke with a plummy voice.

'This land of such dear souls, this dear, dear land, Dear for her reputation through the world, Is now leased out, I die pronouncing it ...' He flattened his vowels and sounded broken-hearted. 'Footscray.'

He studied the people below in the street. They couldn't hear him but he waved and addressed them.

'Greetings fair neighbours. Welcome to my humble abode.' He broke into song a la Noel Coward, singing about a room with a view. He stopped singing mid line as an idea exploded.

'Of course! I'll create the Noel Coward Appreciation Society, West Footscray Branch; even a choral society.' Again he sang a la the Master, this time about crazy canines, Hooray Henrys and tropical climes.

At least the boredom factor was kept at bay. He made a grand gesture. 'This is the life. Wine, cheese, and Shakespeare; what more could a ragged idiot want?'

He switched on his radio and gentle classical (or was it Baroque?) music filled the room. He was on fire.

'Culture. If music be the food of love, play on.' He picked up his phone and listened. More joy. 'And a dial tone. Bliss.'

He replaced the phone, turned off the radio, went to the coffee table, and poured a drink. He sat and proposed a toast. 'A man cannot make him laugh—but that's no marvel; he drinks no wine.' He sipped. He sipped again.

'Drink sir, is a great provoker of three things—nose painting, sleep and urine.'

He made himself comfortable. But was he happy? Of course not. His brave face and stoic language failed to mask his misery. He nibbled cheese. This was his evening meal—cheddar and a cab sav; several cab savs.

Dusk arrived then the night proper. In the darkness, David drank himself to sleep. Sofa replaced bed. This man could snore for his country.

At 2109 hours, David was clearly asleep. In his darkened room, his snoring told all. His shoes were off, his hair exhausted, the contents of his wine bottle reduced, and his cheese supply seriously depleted.

In the street below, not all of Footscray slumbered. Hoons on motorbikes chose to flaunt their macho image by racing and revving their machines. Rivals in a hotted-up Holden joined the party. It was loud. Throw in yelling, car horns and an approaching police siren, and it sounded like WW3 had kicked off outside David's flat. He woke.

'What? What's happening?' The petrol heads performed their finale. David sat up spilling the remains of a plastic cup, cheese crumbs and a newspaper.

'All right! I heard you the first time.' He tried to stand. 'Where am I?'

His phone came alive. He struggled to engage his brain and swore.

'Fustilarian!'

He started to move, kicking the settee. More swearing. 'Ow! God's teeth! Yes, all right, I'm coming!' He headed to the front door. 'Where's that bloody light switch?'

He found it and the darkened room was lit. The phone kept ringing. He approached the noisy contraption. 'Yea, think upon patience.' The phone stopped ringing and David's answering machine kicked in. He heard himself speak.

"This is David. I'm not here. Speak after the beep. Beep!"

Ever the comedian, David spoke the last word. "Beep," he said in a falsetto voice. The machine still had a beep of its own. He addressed the machine.

'Wait for the beep, Mother.' He hit the speaker phone button and fell onto the chair beside the phone. It sounded a beep. His mother sounded anxious.

'David, are you there? It's your mother.' David said nowt. 'David?'

Mr Comedy disguised his voice. He dropped the pitch and went all spooky. 'Footscray Funerals—how may we assist you?' He went to the wine bottle and poured himself a drink.

'Hello? David?'

He stopped the game and called back to the speaker phone. 'Yes, Mother, I'm here.'

'I didn't recognize your voice.'

Having endured so many phone calls from his ever-complaining mother, David knew exactly what she would say. He got in first.

Him: 'Are you having a terrible night?'

Her: 'I'm having a terrible night.'

Him: 'Do you think you're going to die?'

Her: 'I think I'm going to die.' He took a drink. 'David?'

He raised his glass. 'Your very good health, Mother.'

'And these new tablets are useless.' David drank again. 'David?'

She was not the only one who didn't listen. He called to her. 'How are the new tablets?'

She was confused. 'You sound far away. Where are you?'

He milked the situation. 'I've moved Mother, remember? Your impoverished firstborn now lives on the other side of the tracks.'

'But why are you living in *that* suburb?'

He tried to tidy his mess but failed. 'I'm like Fred Astaire, starring in *The Gay Divorcee.*'

'What did you say?'

'Just call me Wilkins Micawber.'

'I can't believe you've lost all your money.'

'I'm busy, Mother.'

He wandered into the bathroom to pee.

'And your suburb is full of foreigners.'

Being in another room, he needed to call even louder. 'Now don't be like that. Besides, there are advantages.'

'Birds of a feather, your father used to say.' For once she was listening, and queried his previous comment. 'Advantages?'

David appeared as he spoke in a stage whisper. 'You'll never visit.'

'I need you to take me to the heart specialist next week.'

David flopped on the settee. 'It'll have to be by taxi, Mother. I've come down in the world.'

'Your father would've taken me.'

David's stage whisper returned. 'You'd've made him.' He spoke in a normal voice. 'You could ask my darling brother.'

Now David had often made that suggestion about his brother, and his mother always gave the same answer. So much so that David joined his mother in her response. She started.

'Your brother has an enormously important job ...' David joined the chorus. '... and his children are going through a very difficult stage.'

He'd heard enough and moved to the phone to end the conversation. 'Must fly, Mother; I'm expecting some drug dealers.'

She was shocked. 'Did you say rug dealers?'

'They're huge fans of Noel Coward.'

More shock from Mother. 'Noel Coward?'

David's finger was poised above the OFF button. 'Bye Mother.'

Just as his finger began to touch the button, loud door knocking was heard. It was so loud, Mother heard it in South Yarra.

She cried. 'What was that?'

David groaned and headed to the door. 'It's another of Danny's friends.'

Mother was anxious and confused, and definitely a stickybeak.

'David? What's happening?'

The door knocking became louder. David was almost there and called.

'All right! All right! Keep y'shirt on!'

He opened the door and copped a shirtfront, that is, the visitor barged in forcing David to take evasive action. A young Vietnamese woman, wearing a silk tunic over trousers was frantic.

'Hey' he cried, alarmed.

The distressed woman faced him. 'Làm ơn giúp tôi. Ông tôi rất đau.'

David had no idea what she said and he stood close to her. Mother was several suburbs away so imagine her confusion.

'David! Who's that speaking?'

David tried to take control. He became annoyed. 'Whoa! I can't understand. Speak English.'

She couldn't. 'Anh ấy có thể chết. Xin vui lòng, thưa ông, gọi xe cứu thương.'

Mother became hooked. 'That sounds like a foreign person.'

David had no idea. 'Look, I don't speak Chinese.'

Mother was more confused. 'Chinese?'

David shouted at the phone. 'On Mother, shut up!'

Mother became outraged. 'Shut up?'

The Vietnamese woman began a mime routine. She clutched her throat and acted as if she were dying. 'Anh ấy đang rất đau. Ông tôi rất đau.'

David settled. Obviously the woman was distressed. He spoke slowly seeking answers.

'Okay, are you sick? Do you want ambulance?'

Her anxiety increased. 'Xin hãy nhanh lên. Tôi không biết số điện thoại khẩn cấp.'

Mother seized on David's question. 'Yes! I want an ambulance.'

The woman went to the phone and removed the handset. She spoke into it. 'Xin lỗi, madam, nhưng chúng tôi có một trường hợp khẩn cấp.'

Mother thought her world was about to end. A foreigner spoke to her and on *her* phone. Mother panicked. 'David!'

The visitor ended Mother's panic by hitting the END button. The phone was handed to a surprised and now annoyed David.

'Do you mind? That was my mother.'

'Làm ơn, ông tôi có thể chết.'

David sensed the woman needed help. He hit the emergency number but gave his visitor short shrift.

'And where's your phone? I see you young people yapping in your mobiles.' The phone was answered. 'Yes, ambulance please.'

David was about to explain his situation when the woman took off and ran from the flat. *What the hell?* David continued. 'I have an emergency with a woman who doesn't speak English.' The woman returned. David spoke to her. 'What are you? Chinese? Vietnamese?'

She became excited. 'Tiếng Việt. Tôi có thể nói tiếng Việt.'

David spoke into the phone. 'Do you have someone who speaks Vietnamese? I think a neighbour is ill but ...' He handed the phone to the woman. 'Here, you tell them.'

The woman sounded desperate. 'Xin chào. Xin vui lòng gửi một xe cứu thương. Ông tôi rất đau. Tôi nghĩ anh ấy bị đau tim.'

She gave the phone back to David.

'Hello? Yes, I think she lives next door.' He questioned the woman. 'Where do you live?' he spoke slowly. 'What's your number?'

The Vietnamese woman shrugged. 'Ông tôi rất đau.'

David shook his head. 'Your flat number?' She couldn't understand so David took control and spoke to the operator. 'Look my address is Flat 15, 21 Hudson Street, Footscray. ... Yes, I'll be here.' He hit END and replaced the phone in its socket. 'My social diary is currently free.'

The phone rang and kept ringing. The woman kept talking. 'Họ đến không? Xin vui lòng cho tôi biết?'

David tried to calm his anxious visitor. He spoke slowly, with emphasis, and used charade-like gestures.

'Right, ambulance is coming. You, go home. I will listen for am-bu-lance.' He made what he thought was the sound of a siren.

'Khi nào xe cứu thương sẽ đến đây?'

He looked like losing it. 'I no understand. You, go home. Ambulance com-ing.' He escorted her to the door. The answering machine message began.

"This is David. I'm not here. Speak after the beep. Beep!"

He returned in time to hear his mother.

'David! You cut me off! David?' He hit the speaker phone button. 'Hello!'

'I'm here, Mother. All's well that ends well.'

Not quite, as the Vietnamese woman burst in calling. 'Hãy chắc chắn rằng xe cấp cứu đi kèm bên cạnh!' She about turned and made a rapid exit.

Mother became incensed. 'Who is that person?'

David became annoyed. 'What person? I'm all alone.'

Mother smelt a rat. 'You've got a woman; a foreign woman!'

'Relax, Mother. I'm fresh out of concubines.'

'You've imported one of those mail-order brides.'

David snapped. 'Oh for God's sake, Mother. Some neighbour came in to use the phone. She needs a bloody ambulance.'

'I've warned you about foreigners.'

'And she sends her love to you too. Bye.'

David was fed up. He killed the call then removed the phone from its cradle preventing Mother from calling. He headed for the kitchenette.

'Coffee, my son; you need caffeine in your scotch.'

He pottered, making instant coffee. In keeping with this recent fondness for Noel Coward, he began to sing about bad times being nearby with all manner of dark clouds on view in the heavens.

His rendition was interrupted by an ambulance siren. It got louder. Surprised, he came out of the kitchen. 'That was quick. I must remember to have my heart attack on a Monday.'

He opened his door, saw the agitated Vietnamese woman, looked down the stairwell, and called to the ambulance officers.

'Up here; where the young lady is waving.' He nodded to the anxious woman then retired. He felt pleased, even happy. This was a new sensation. He took pride in his latest achievement.

'How far that little candle throws his beams! So shines a good deed in a naughty world.' Heading back to his coffee-making, he spotted the phone. He popped it back in its cradle and waited, expecting an immediate call from Mother.

'The line is free, Mother. Normal service has been resumed.' The phone remained silent. David felt a tinge of concern. 'That'd be right. Now she really does need an ambulance.'

He fetched his coffee and flopped on the settee. He felt hungry and craved takeaway. 'I fancy Chinese,' he said. It was not even 9.30pm but his new life involved drinking and retiring at that hour. He was contemplating bed when someone knocked on his door. It was a gentle, polite sound. Even so, he groaned.

'What now?'

He was about to stand when the door opened, his lock was useless. He turned to see the Vietnamese woman enter. She was quiet, respectful, and travelled in the slow lane.

'Xin chào? Ngài? Xin chào?'

David stood and greeted his visitor. 'Oh, it's you. Ah, is everything hunky-dory?'

'Tôi có thể nói chuyện với bạn được không?'

Had he understood Vietnamese, David would have discovered that the elderly gent next door had suffered an attack of very bad indigestion. No heart attack involved.

'Well your relaxed demeanour would suggest a silver lining. So are there bluebirds over the white cliffs of Dover? Was Dame Vera telling porkies?'

Neither understood a blind word the other spoke. The woman stepped closer. 'Tôi muốn thông báo với bạn rằng ông tôi không bị ốm nặng.'

David made a friendly face. 'That *sounds* like good news.'

The woman rubbed her stomach with one hand while holding a bamboo container with the other.

'Anh ấy chỉ bị chứng khó tiêu.'

David responded to her friendly behaviour. 'I'd offer you some refreshment only it's the maid's night off.' The woman looked around, unsure of how to behave. 'Ah, you admire my humble abode. Did you know that slumming is the new black?'

The woman held out the food container. 'Cái này dành cho bạn.'

David reacted. 'Is that for me?' He accepted the gift. 'Thanks, sir; all the rest is mute.' He sniffed the container. 'May one enquire as to the contents? It smells intriguing.'

'Đây là một món quà nhỏ để cảm ơn bạn vì tất cả lòng tốt của bạn.' She bowed. David responded in kind.

'But will it give me the runs?' She chose a blank expression. 'You know, the trots? Diarrhea? Delhi belly?' She shrugged and shook her head. He indicated the container. 'Shitty shitty bang bang?'

'Bạn có thích món ăn Việt Nam không? Đây là một món ăn rất đặc biệt. Tôi tự nấu nó.'

David guessed the gift was some form of Vietnamese food. He chatted. 'I've seen many Asian shops around here. I'm more familiar with Greek and Italian.' He spelt out his favourites. ' Souv-la-ki. Car-bo-nar-a.'

The conversation stalled. David placed the container on the table. She apologised. 'Tôi xin lỗi. Tôi không thể nói tiếng Anh ... English.'

David was stunned. He heard a familiar word, and seized upon it.

'English! Did you say, "English"?'

The woman smiled for the first time—a beautiful smile. She nodded. 'Eng-lish.'

'But that's wonderful! I know that word! I can even spell it.'

The woman's smile flourished. 'Eng-lish.'

'In fact, English literature and I—or should that be English Literature and me?—we've been having it off for years! We're pals, bosom-buddies, and "such is my love, to thee I so belong".'

The woman too was pleased but of course hadn't the foggiest about his comments.

'Vâng, tiếng Anh. Tôi không thể nói tiếng Anh; chỉ có người Việt Nam.'

David was on a roll. 'It's a glorious language, English—Chaucer, Dickens, Shakespeare.' He picked up the book of the Bard's work. 'Have you read even a part of their oeuvre?'

The woman stuck with what she knew. 'Eng-lish.'

David couldn't keep his wit under control. 'Or maybe Mills and Boon, Dan Brown or Barbara Cartland?' The woman smiled. Ignorance reigned. 'You should learn English; it's international. Even Americans speak a form of English. And with English as your language, you could order an ambulance yourself and not have to interrupt the boring old fart next door.'

Chaucer, American, and *boring old fart* were unfamiliar words to the woman, who decided to leave. She bowed.

'Cảm ơn ngài. Tôi phải trở về ông bà của tôi.'

David bowed, badly, in response. 'But you can't leave now. We have something in common. We both know the word *English*.'

'Tạm biệt,' said the woman and left.

David waved then followed her to his door and called.

'It was lovely to meet you.' Then as an afterthought, he yelled. 'And thank y'mother for the rabbits.'

He closed his door, returned to the settee and reflected on this most recent episode.

'That went well, Dave. First spot of social intercourse in the new locale, and your old chat-up charm is alive and well. Not.'

He investigated the food container.

'So what have we got here?' He dipped a finger in the food and tasted the contents. He liked it. 'Hmmm. Tis an ill cook that cannot lick his own fingers.' In fact he loved the taste of Vietnamese food, and got stuck into what was his first proper meal in ages. He spoke with his Sarf Londun accent.

'I tell you what, my son. You've done all right here.' He filled his mouth yet still managed to speak. 'Bloody good grub.'

10

NOT ONLY COULD THANH COOK, she could clean too. The morning after her grandfather's ambulance incident, Thanh scrubbed the oven in her grandparents' flat. It was a small oven, in a small kitchen, in a small flat. Thankfully, the elderly residents had the stature of a small jockey.

Grandmother came into the kitchen. 'Your grandfather sleeps. The medicine works.'

Thanh kept scrubbing. 'We were lucky the ambulance arrived so soon.' She stopped working and looked at her grandmother. 'We were lucky the man next door helped us.'

The old woman said nothing. Thanh returned to cleaning but spoke with her head in the oven.

'You know I gave the man next door some Vietnamese food.'

'There was no need to do that. Besides, you do not know him. He might be a criminal.'

Thanh finished and put away the cleaning materials.

'He is a good man. He telephoned the ambulance. If Grandfather had been having a heart attack, the man next door might have saved his life.'

'You do not understand. The man who used to live there was Danny. He sold drugs. Maybe this man does the same thing.'

'No, Grandmother, he has no drugs, except for alcohol. He has many books, some bad food, and a room full of loneliness.'

'Loneliness? How can you know that?'

She remembered her time in David's flat. 'You can see it in his eyes.'

Loneliness or not, the next morning David had a spring in his step. Drinking to excess at night invariably made him grumpy, if not bilious. But last night was unique, no, special, no, both. His penury, his divorce and dysfunctional family continued to haunt him but right now, those issues were pushed to one side.

81

David helped save a life, or so he thought. He became useful, helpful. He met someone new. He couldn't understand a word she said but hey, social intercourse is fantastic.

He knew depression would reach out and grab him later but for now, he was up and about and full of beans, well noodles. He showered, shaved and shot into the lounge saluting Will in the process.

'But, soft methinks I scent the morning air.'

He skipped to the phone, hit the answering machine, and an American voice spoke. 'You have no new messages.'

He headed for the settee and breakfast. 'Thanks for that, my lovely.'

Hair of the dog was a heart starter most mornings but not today. His Vietnamese neighbour had delivered some tasty tucker, and cold noodles never tasted so good.

Breakfast complete, he belched, and wiped his mouth with his inbuilt serviette, his sleeve. He was sans job, friends, family and interests, and so stated the bleeding obvious.

'Right then, what's on for the rest of my life? I could take up sitting in parks or pass wind professionally. I could join the self-pity society. The miserable have no other medicine, but only hope.'

He grimaced and wandered to his solitary, immoveable window. 'And what of the world beyond?' He looked out at his Footscray neighbours; ordinary folk going about their ordinary business.

'You're spot on about the natives, Mother. Not an abundance of Anglo-Saxons, not exactly a crowd of Celts.' He waved and called to the unsuspecting crowd. 'Good morning.' He pondered the scene below, and the words of the Bard came instantly to mind. He performed.

'All the world's a stage,
And all the men and women merely players;
They have their exits and their entrances;
And one man in his time plays many parts,
His acts being seven ages.'

He stopped. Thoughts of his disastrous life flooded back. 'But what can I do in this my seventh age? Race snails? Cultivate nasal hair? Worship wrinkles?'

Back on the settee, he poured a drink. 'I could deliver meals on wheels and pinch the puddings.' He drank then studied his glass. 'I could join Alcoholics Anonymous.'

Suddenly he slammed his hand on the coffee table, and exploded with excitement.

'Of course! Teach! Strong reasons make strong actions. It's a new take on an old job. I can teach the basics of English. Half the locals don't know their subject from their predicate.' He bubbled as new ideas kept coming.

'I can teach in here. Cash in hand. Now there's a purpose, a reason to exist. Simply the thing that I am shall make me live.' He raised his glass and toasted his new venture. 'To my English Language School.'

He almost skipped to the phone table, and grabbed a pencil and pad.

'Come on, come on; planning. Early to bed, early to rise, it's no jolly good if you don't advertise.' He wrote as he spoke. 'Learn English. Experienced teacher. Cheap ... No.' He crossed out Cheap. 'Reasonable rates. Contact ... blah, blah, blah ...'

Oh no, he suffered a massive mood change, threw the pencil on the table and swore.

'Pignut! They can't read an ad in English. It has to be in Vietnamese.' He pondered a solution. 'Don't panic, Dave. Find a translator. The library? No. I've gotta fly under the radar; stick to the black market.'

He moved to the window continuing to think aloud.

'Word of mouth advertising; start small, infiltrate the locals. What about Miss Ambulance from next door? She owes me.' He looked down at the street and became excited. 'And there she is!'

He tapped on the window, shouted, waved, and tried to get her attention. Had anyone looked up, they would have seen a sailor running through the Semaphore Code. He mouthed the words.

'Hey! Hey you! Oi! Hell-o.'

The young woman happened to look up and stopped when she saw the man next door auditioning for *A Chorus Line*. David saw her looking at him.

'You! Yes you!' He beckoned. 'Come here. Come here. I ... speak ... to ... you.' He saw her finally get the message and move towards the stairs. David bounced with joy. 'Yes! And hurry!'

He trotted to the front door. 'Go, Dave, action is eloquence.'

Then he worried. *What do I look like?* He headed to the bathroom. 'Appearances dear boy, appearances.'

He tried washing his face and combing his hair. For all the difference it made, he should have washed his hair and combed his face. As he abluted, he sang about bluebirds flapping their wings near the white, really grey cliffs of Dover.

Thanh returned to her grandparents' flat and told the elderly couple she needed to speak to the man who helped them last night. Grandmother was unhappy. They argued. Thanh escaped having promised to return soon.

David heard a door knock and went to answer it, quoting the Bard en route. 'It is not in the stars to hold our destiny but in ourselves.'

About to open the door, he saw a crooked picture. He adjusted it, then grabbed last night's food container and stuffed it under a cushion. Finally his mansion was open for inspection.

'And now for the Cadwallader charm.'

He opened the door, making a sweeping gesture. He oozed more charm than St Valentine at a speed-dating convention. 'A hundred thousand welcomes, dear maiden fair.'

The woman was nervous. She entered and bowed.

'Xin chào, thưa ông. Tôi nghĩ tôi đã nhìn thấy bạn vẫy.'

He closed the door, and followed her into the room. 'A general welcome from his grace salutes ye all.' He indicated the settee. 'Pray be seated.' She froze. He gestured again. 'Sit worthy friends.' Still she impersonated Lot's missus. He relaxed. 'Go on, take a pew.'

That worked. She gave a mini smile and sat on the edge of the only armchair.

Her thoughts were racing. *What is happening? Why am I here?*

He stood well back ensuring there was no invasion of personal space.

'Now, may I begin by expressing my sincere thanks for your splendid repast? It was delicious.'

'Ông tôi đang nghỉ ngơi. Cảm ơn bạn đã giúp tôi hôm qua.'

Both had no idea what the other said.

'But, dear lady, I have a problem arising from the following situation. I speak English; you speak Vietnamese.'

She felt better, recognising two words. 'Vietnamese,' she said.

He nodded and grinned. 'Now I plan to offer my services as a teacher. Here in my humble des res, I will impart the skill of a second language to anyone who is Vietnamese.'

She smiled and nodded again. 'Vietnamese.'

'Which is why I beg from you a favour, dear damsel, asking that you inform your family, friends and neighbours of this new and wonderful service teaching the basics of English.'

The woman smiled. This was another word she knew. 'Eng-lish,' she replied. Things were definitely on the improve.

'Oh I'm so sorry. I haven't introduced myself. My name is David. And you are?'

The woman failed to reply. He tried a new approach. At different times, he pointed to himself and then to her.

'Right. Me, David ... sir. You? ... You?'

She gave what she believed was the correct answer. 'Vietnamese.'

David smiled. 'Yes, I'm fine with geography; it's your moniker I seek. Right, let's see.' He looked around and spotted a photo of himself in a frame in the bookcase. He collected the photo and showed it to the woman.

'Look, this is me, David. There. Da-vid.'

She looked at the photo and had a stab at his name.

'Da-vid.'

Excellent. You're making splendid progress.' He kept pointing both to himself and then to her. 'So ... Me, David, you?'

She smiled, thinking she understood. 'Vietnamese.'

'No. Me, David.' He points at her. 'You?'

The penny dropped. The woman produced her biggest smile. 'Ah, Thanh.

David was thrilled. 'Thanh.' He offered his hand and they shook. 'Hello Thanh.'

She replied without hesitation. 'Hello Thanh.'

David was disappointed, realising his task was not so simple. 'No.' He repeated the previous routine by pointing to himself and then to her. 'Me David, you Thanh.'

Surely this will work.

It didn't. Thanh copied his words and deeds. Pointing at him, she said, 'Me David.' Pointing at herself, she said, 'You Thanh.'

He needed a new approach. He spoke his thoughts aloud. 'Hmmm, methinks reverse psychology, Dave.' He tried a trick and pointed to her. 'You David.' He pointed to himself. 'Me Thanh.'

It worked. The woman became a parrot. She pointed to him. 'You David.' She pointed to herself. 'Me Thanh.'

David triumphed and celebrated. 'Yes. Heaven sent thee good fortune. Now, speak.'

He tested her. He indicated himself. 'Da-vid,' she said. He indicated his visitor. 'Thanh,' she said. He repeated the routine. She gave the correct answers. Their happiness, nay excitement increased.

Then he tricked her. It was back and forth with him indicating—Thanh, David, Thanh, David. Suddenly he feigned pointing at her but quickly changed to indicate himself. As he pointed to himself, she said, 'Thanh.'

David kept pointing to himself and said, 'No.'

Thanh laughed, pointed at David, and said, 'Da-vid.'

He was delighted. 'O, well said, Lucius.'

He changed tack and jumped from Lesson 1 to Lesson 23. 'So, Thanh, I wish to teach English to local Vietnamese people, and I desire that you, please, should tell the locals. Vietnamese learn English. Understand?

This was far too much too soon. She indicated herself and said, 'Vietnamese.' She indicated him and said, 'English.'

He saw the potential and what potential. She was the key. If she told other Vietnamese non-English speaking people that he could teach them to speak English, his cottage industry would explode. Two benefits sprang to mind. It was something for him to do, and a bit of folding stuff in his skyrocket. The problem, however, was his inability to explain his plan in Vietnamese, with the obvious solution being, he had to teach Thanh to speak enough English to understand the project.

'Right,' he said. 'Let's try another tack. I will teach you some words of English.

She smiled. 'Eng-lish.'

'Then you can tell your friends I'm brilliant. What say ye, Thanh?'

Now they were on the same page. She indicated him. 'Da-vid.' She indicated herself, 'Thanh.'

David applauded. 'Bravo. Knowledge is the wing wherewith we fly to heaven.' He stopped and decided to come clean. 'Actually I should begin with a confession. My teaching experience is more with English Literature. Will that, do you think, be a problem?'

She paused and indicated herself. 'Thanh, Vietnamese.'

He ploughed ahead speaking fluently. He spoke his thoughts aloud to help himself understand his plan—the one he made up as he went along. She of course didn't have a clue.

'With English Lit I'm a seasoned professional but alas in the "how now brown cow" department, my experience and skills could best be described as, "not a sausage".'

Thanh wanted to learn. With difficulty, she spoke. 'Saus-age.'

David flew by the seat of his pants. He wandered and pondered. 'So, my kingdom for an idea.'

He raised his hands expressing frustration or was it ignorance? Flash! A moment of genius. He saw his hands. 'Ah!' He wiggled a hand and spoke. 'Hand.' He kept wiggling his hand. 'Hand.'

She twigged and mimicked him, wiggling her hand. 'Hand,' she said.

And thus began David Cadwallader's career as a teacher of the English language. From little things, big things grow.

'Very good. But there's no need to wave. Now,' he indicated his nose, 'nose.'

She copied him in word and deed. 'Nose.'

Muscles in his face were called into action. His laughter muscles hadn't been used for ages. His happiness glowed. 'Well done. Ah ...' He indicated his ear, 'ear.'

She copied him. 'Ear.'

He looked around then patted the settee. 'Settee.'

She leant forward and patted the settee. 'Sett-ee.'

He moved to the window and tapped the glass. 'Window.'

She assumed being tactile was the way to go, so stood preparing to move to and touch the window. She stopped when he spoke. 'No, stay there. Sit.' He sounded like a dog trainer. 'Sit.' She sat and again he touched the window. 'Window.'

From her seated position, she pointed to the window. 'Win-dow.'

He was on a roll. She was on a roll. He moved to the table on which the telephone rested. He touched the table. 'Table.'

She pointed. 'Ta-ble.'

He picked up the handset. 'Telephone.'

She struggled with three syllables but made it. 'Tel-e-phone.'

He indicated the single chair beside the phone table. 'Chair.'

Ah, a problem, the first pronunciation issue appeared. 'Care.'

'No, chair.' He made the *ch* sound. 'Ch, ch, chair.'

She copied like a parrot. 'No, care - c, c, care.' Her "c" sound was the *c* as in *car*.

'Almost,' he smiled, and made a show of sitting on the chair. 'I sit on the chair.'

She replied. 'I sit on the care.'

He spoke slowly sliding the sounds together. 'Ch ... air.'

She spoke very slowly and slid into the word. 'Ch ... air.'

'Bravo! Well done.'

There was a container with pencils by the phone. He picked up a pencil. 'Pencil.'

She was a fast learner. 'Pen-cil.'

David held up two pencils. 'Two pencils.'

'Two pen-cils.'

He added another pencil. 'Three pencils.'

More pronunciation problems surfaced. 'Tree pen-cils.'

'No three, three.'

'No tree, tree.'

David remembered a rhyme he learnt eons ago. 'When I say *three*, my tongue pops out.' He poked out his tongue then retracted it. 'This thing.' He again poked out his tongue then retracted it. 'That thing.'

Thanh needed time for this answer. It was tricky. 'When I say tree, my tongue pop out.' She poked out her tongue then retracted it. 'Dis ting.' Again her tongue popped out then disappeared. 'Dat ting.' She finished by poking her tongue out and leaving it there. It wasn't rude or disrespectful.

David reckoned he could match that. He put his thumbs against his temples, waggled his fingers and poked out his tongue. She copied him before they laughed together. It was a break-the-ice-moment, some chemistry between the two.

David immediately leapt back into teaching mode, and picked up the phone. 'I talk on the telephone.'

She put her hand to her ear, and mimed using the phone. 'I talk on the tel-e-phone.'

He replaced the phone and moved to the large bookcase near the door. 'Book-shelf.'

She just about got it right. 'Book-shell.'

He indicated the many books. 'I have books in my bookshelf.'

'I have books in my book-shell.'

He saw *The Complete Works of William Shakespeare* on the coffee table. He tapped it. 'This is a book.'

She leant forward and tapped the book. 'Dis is a book.'

He indicated the book. 'Written by William Shakespeare.'

She paused before tackling the tongue-twister. 'Witten by Will-iam ...'

David helped her. 'Shake-speare.'

She tried. 'Shak-es-peare.'

The teacher was chuffed—was he ever? He had no plan but what he did worked, or so he thought. His pleasure pleased his student. 'Brilliant, Thanh, we'll make a scholar of you yet. Boldness be my friend.'

He turned away from her thinking about his next move. He thought out loud. 'So, what next?' She assumed he wanted her to repeat his last line and did.

'Boldness be my friend.'

He turned and grinned then experienced another lightbulb moment. 'Of course, the Bard himself.' He made a dramatic hand gesture and spoke with feeling. 'To be or not to be.'

She copied his gesture, speech pattern and tone of voice. 'To be or not to be.' To an onlooker it was comical. To the participants, it was thrilling.

David's next speeches flowed. This was hometown territory for the lover of Shakespeare. Fifty years studying the Bard meant the following dripped off his tongue. 'I will wear my heart upon my sleeve.'

Thanh replied. 'I will wear my heart upon my scheve.'

'No,' said David and tugged his sleeve. 'It's sleeve, sleeve.'

She copied him, tugging her sleeve as she spoke. 'No, it's sleeve, sleeve.'

He spoke with feeling. 'Be not afraid of greatness.'

She had no fear and responded with gusto. 'Be not afraid of greatness.'

David loved this activity. He loved the teaching, the new relationship, and of course, the words. He began the next speeches softer, and built the crescendo with each new line.

'Speak low if you speak love.'

She kept getting better and mimicked him. 'Speak low if you speak love.'

He inched closer. 'Pleasure and action make the hours seem short.'

'Pleasure and action make the hours seem short.'

He extended a hand without being too close, and spoke with a lyrical quality. 'Shall I compare thee to a summer's day?'

Still she responded in kind without understanding a blind word. 'Shall I compare bee to a summer's day?'

He moved closer again, was almost within touching distance, and gazed into her stunning eyes as he spoke. 'Thou art more lovely and more temperate.'

She responded in kind. 'Thou art more lovely ...'

Stop! David instantly backed away. His "game" had taken a different turn. 'Right,' he said. 'Here endeth the lesson.' She was both surprised and confused. 'Fin-ish, Thanh.'

She thought this last sentence was part of the lesson. 'Fin-ish, Thanh.'

'No more. We stop. Con-clus-ion. Fi-ni-to. The end.' He gestured to her to stand. She did but still copied his words.

'The end.'

David indicated his watch. 'To-morr-ow.' He pointed to her. 'Thanh, you come here, to-morr-ow. Next day. Un-der-stand?'

She didn't understand. 'Un-der-stand?'

'You have done exceedingly well.' He indicated the door and ushered her towards it. 'See ... you ... la-ter.' He waved. 'Bye.'

She thought she understood, headed to the door, turned and spoke. 'See ... you ... la-ter.' She waved. 'Bye.'

Then David shouted and, in so doing, frightened Thanh. 'No wait,' he called. She froze. He made a sweeping bow. 'Parting is such sweet sorrow, fair maiden.'

She paused then copied him. Her bow was graceful. 'Parting is such sweet sorrow, fair maiden.' She nodded and left.

He followed and closed the door. His heart raced.

What have I done? Am I a complete fool?

He stood in the middle of his room, and felt fantastic for the first time in months, or was that years? He gave thanks to the Bard.

'Tis not enough to help the feeble up, but to support them after. They do not love that do not show their love.'

He clenched his fists in triumph as happiness flooded his breast. He couldn't remember the last time he felt this proud, nay excited. What a result. He raised his clenched fists and shouted. 'Yes!'

After her lesson with David, Thanh returned to her grandparents' flat. The journey took all of seven seconds. Her grandmother waited with questions aplenty.

'Why did you take so long? I was worried.'

'There is no need to worry, Grandmother.'

'That man is a stranger and may behave badly.'

'Please Grandmother; I have been treated with dignity and respect.'

The old woman remained stressed, and twisted her hands. Despite living in Australia for more than two decades, Thanh's grandparents had never assimilated into the Australian way of life. There was never pressure to learn English because their suburb, Footscray, had a thriving Vietnamese community. In some ways, they had moved to Little Saigon.

The inquisition continued.

'That man is not Vietnamese.'

'No, Grandmother, he is Australian, and his name is David.'

Shock struck the woman. 'You know his name?'

'Yes, and he knows mine.'

Grandmother went from being anxious to angry.

'This is not right. Can he speak Vietnamese?'

'Not a word. But I will teach him.'

The old woman sat down, stunned at Thanh's answer, and gasped. 'You will teach him?'

Thanh sat beside her grandmother, and squeezed the old woman's hands. Thanh spoke in a soft and reassuring way.

'Do not worry, Grandmother. David is a kind man—very kind.'

'But he is not Vietnamese.'

'Grandmother, where you come from does not determine your kindness. A kind person can come from Vietnam or from Australia or from any country.'

Grandma questioned Thanh. 'But what did he want?'

Thanh could see this matter needed time and tact. Her grandparents were old school, locked in their small Vietnamese world, and just old. Change was an enemy to their generation. They had waited decades to hear news of their family. Now it had arrived in the form of a precious granddaughter, and they felt responsible for her. Having her go alone into a strange non-Vietnamese man's home was possibly a terrible thing. He might seduce her. He might ruin her. He might rob or kill her. Thanh tried to put the issue of her new neighbour to one side.

'How is Grandfather?'

It was a good try but didn't work. The old woman became desperate.

'Answer me. Do you wish to bring shame on our family?'

Thanh felt sad. 'Of course not, Grandmother; I would never do that.'

'Have you no respect for your grandfather who is dying?'

'Please, Grandmother, I will always honour you and Grandfather. David was kind to me before, and just now, he was kind again.'

The old woman was sincere, albeit wrong, in her approach to David.

'He is tricking you. He cannot speak Vietnamese. You do not understand him.'

Thanh kept calm, and again her answer was gentle. 'No, but I will.'

'You will? How?'

Thanh smiled and felt happy just thinking about her recent visit.

'He will teach me to speak English.'

Only one word could describe her grandmother's face—shock.

11

NOW THAT DAVID HAD A NEW STUDENT, he spent far more time in the bathroom. To date, he hadn't asked Thanh for any tuition fees. He reckoned she was his entrée into the Vietnamese community, the key to launching his cottage industry teaching English to the locals. If he could teach her, she would do the word-of-mouth advertising.

Thanh gave him a reason for living, if you could call it living. Thanks to Thanh, David tried to improve his appearance—clean his teeth, comb his hair, shave, and change his underwear every three days instead of weekly.

But throughout this homemade makeover, Mother continued her nuisance calls and right now became a bloody nuisance. From the bathroom, where he continued to ablute, he called to his mother via the speaker phone.

'I'm busy, Mother.'

She maintained her consistent line of self-pity. 'I've telephoned the doctor. God knows when he'll arrive. I'm quite sure I'm dying.'

As usual, David wasn't listening to what she said. He'd heard it all before. 'Good,' he said, not meaning "good". It was the equivalent of a long-married husband saying to his wife, "Yes dear".

For once Mother was listening and queried him.

'What did you say?'

David popped his head into the lounge room. 'Now about next Tuesday, Mother. Any chance you could change to the afternoon?'

That set her right off. 'No, definitely not.'

'It's this public transport routine; a bit squeezy first thing in the morning.'

'Don't talk to me about public transport. Besides, you promised, and it's in my diary.'

He entered the room and started tidying. Not only was he cleaning himself, he cleaned his flat as well. Wonders will never cease.

'Don't panic. I'll be there.'

'You'd better.'

'Now Mother, would you believe I may have some good news?'

Mother scoffed. 'You never have good news. You take after me—permanently miserable.'

'I've gone back to teaching.'

'Oh, you stupid man, you're too old. You're on the pension.'

'I agree; the idea is a tad radical.'

'Radical? It's preposterous.'

'I'm teaching Shakespeare to people who can't speak English.'

He stopped tidying and waited for her response.

'Your father was insane.'

David grinned having heard what he expected then resumed spring cleaning. 'I'm sure some university offers a degree in the subject.'

'Will you ever grow up?'

'Never. What's to come is still unsure.'

'And are you rid of that foreign woman?'

There was a brisk and "friendly" knock on David's door. Excited, he moved to kill the phone call.

'Must dash, Mother; opportunity knocks.'

She didn't quite hear. 'Who?

'Bye,' called David and ended the call. He moved to the door calling, 'Enter'. He heard more knocking. He called again. 'Come in.'

The door opened, and Thanh entered wearing a different stunning Vietnamese outfit. David gasped. She held another bamboo food container. He came alive greeting her with a flourish.

'Mistress, what cheer?'

She was nervous. She remembered the concerns expressed by her grandmother. *Is this man kind? Will he do me harm?*

She bowed then indicated him. 'Da-vid,' she said. She pointed to herself. 'Thanh.'

He was not impressed, quite disappointed in fact. 'No, no, no. You say, "Good morrow, sweet Lord!" and then you curtsey, like this.' He curtsied, making a darn good job of it. She was confused.

He took control. 'Look, I'll show you. Come here.'

He escorted her into the room, stood to one side, and performed.

'Good morrow, sweet Lord, and then you curtsey.' He again curtsied and remained in that position, as he turned his head to the spellbound Thanh and asked, 'Got that?'

He invited her to repeat the routine. Just as she was about to begin, he interrupted. 'Wait, wait!' He led her back towards the door then moved aside giving her plenty of room. He called. 'Enter!'

She paused then, stepped forward, spoke and curtsied as she had been taught. 'Good morrow, sweet Lord, and then you curtsey.' Frozen in her curtsy position, she turned her head to David. 'Got that?'

He wanted to laugh but settled for a smile. 'Yes, all right.' He beckoned her to move. 'Come dear lady, be thou seated.' She remained confused. He pointed at the armchair, and repeated his dog-training routine. 'There, Thanh, sit!'

She sat while he stood in the middle of the room and resumed his role of teacher.

'Now, conversation should be pleasant without scurrility.' She stood interrupting his flow. 'Hang on, I haven't finished.'

She bowed and offered the latest container of food.

'Xin lỗi, thưa ông. Đây là món ăn truyền thống của Việt Nam.'

He accepted the gift. 'More food? How kind.' He placed it on the kitchenette table, speaking as he did so. 'I must say I found your previous offering delicious. And pray, what is this comestible called?'

He faced Thanh seeking an answer. He knew she couldn't understand but had no interest in mocking or belittling her. David believed the best way to help Thanh was simply to speak as he would normally, thus helping her become familiar with the flow and content of the language.

She'd been working on her answer in her flat. She pointed to the container, and spoke with confidence.

'Shitty shitty bang bang.'

He laughed and why wouldn't he? With barely a miniscule knowledge of the English language, Thanh delivered a witty retort—a clever pun. She gave her delicious concoction an incorrect 1 star review with a side serve of scorn. She smiled at his laughter. He pushed ahead.

'Jokes already,' he said. 'I'm impressed. Now, once more unto the breach, dear Thanh.' He pointed to her chair. 'Sit.' She did.

He well knew the importance of revision and launched into it.

'Right, my name is ...' He pointed to himself.

She was super keen and set off like a parrot. 'My name is ...'

'No, no, no,' replied David shaking his head. 'My name is ...' Again he pointed to himself.

This time she understood. 'Da-vid.'

'Yes,' said the teacher, who then pointed at her. 'And?'

She remembered. 'Thanh,' she answered with speed and accuracy.

'Well done, so my name is David and ...'

She was on the ball. 'My name is Thanh.'

David applauded and complimented her. 'Excellent. And again. 'My name is David and ...'

'My name is Thanh,' she fired back.

'Brilliant. Now, moving on.' He held his hand aloft and wiggled it. 'What is this?'

She did not hesitate. 'Hand.'

He pointed to his nose. 'And?'

She pointed to her nose. 'Nose.'

He pointed to his ear but did not speak. She did.

'Ear,' she said, batting a thousand.

Ah, but perfection can be hard to maintain. He moved towards the window indicating same. She was quick off the mark.

'Sett-ee,' she exclaimed then immediately realised her mistake. 'Window,' she added.

David nodded. 'Self-correction already; well done.' He pointed to the telephone table.

'Tab-le.' She performed well. He pointed to the telephone.

'Tel-e-phone,' she replied.

'Correct,' said David, sitting on the chair. 'Now, I sit on the ...'

She took a deep breath. Pronunciation was tricky. She worked her way through the problem and slid into her answer. 'I sit on the ... ch-air.'

'Yes,' exclaimed David. 'Superb. Well done you.'

His praise excited her. She wanted success, more success.

He moved to the bookshelf and pointed. 'Book-shell,' she said.

'Bookshelf,' he corrected.

She took her time. 'Book ... shelf.' Another hurdle crossed.

He spied the Shakespearean tome on the coffee table. He moved in and tapped it.

'Book,' she said.

David felt his pulse get busier. 'Yes, perfection. Thanh, you have done extremely well. I am delighted with ...'

She interrupted him and tapped the book. 'Will-iam Shak-es-peare.'

That line became the icing on the cake. Her ability to remember words after a single lesson had both of them genuinely excited. And what words to remember—the name of the greatest poet and playwright in the English language—in any language.

'Indeed,' said David. 'We know what we are, but know not what we may be.'

He turned away from her and walked to the phone table to collect a pencil and pad. But Thanh hadn't finished. She decided to volunteer the rest of her knowledge. Her words were slow at first but gradually built in tempo and volume. She made mistakes but continued. Once she began, he turned to face her and froze. Was he impressed, stunned or delighted? Perhaps all three. She started.

'To be or not to be. I will wear my heart upon my sleeve. Be not afraid of greatness.' This was difficult. She concentrated like crazy, even closed her eyes and trawled the depths of her memory. Last night, as she tried to sleep, she went over and over the words spoken by the man next door.

'Speak love if you speak low. No. Speak low if you speak love.' Things got even harder. David was transfixed. 'Pleasure and action make the summer. Shall I compare bee to a temperate day? Dow art more lovely.'

She smiled, which in itself was a thing of beauty. David shook his head in amazement, and for once was speechless. He applauded.

'Puking lout! Your first English sentences are straight from the Bard.'

She caught his enthusiasm and repeated his words. 'The Bard.'

David's excitement bubbled. 'The swan of Avon; the greatest playwright ever; William Shakespeare!'

Again she tapped the book. 'Will-iam Shak-es-peare.'

David rejoiced in her success. 'William Bloody Shakespeare.'

She soared to catch his happiness. 'William Bloody Shak-es-peare.'

He laughed. He had to. 'And you're a parrot.'

On cue, she proved his claim. 'And you're a parrot.'

Phew. The action slowed. He found it hard to believe a person with no English could remember and repeat so many new words—words until yesterday she had never even heard, let alone understood. He spoke from the heart.

'You know I've introduced Shakespeare to thousands, well I tried to, but never have I seen such enthusiasm for the good old Tudor talkfest.'

Thanh smiled. 'Talk-fest,' she beamed.

Then the momentous lightbulb moment arrived. The penny dropped. David gave birth to an idea. Was it crazy? Many would call it ridiculous.

'Of course, of course,' he shouted, 'Elizabethan English; Saigon and Windsor. I know the lingo, and now have the perfect guinea-pig to teach.' He moved closer to Thanh, and asked a direct question. 'Tell me, Thanh, do you fancy a bit of the Bard? Will-iam Shak-es-peare?'

She had no understanding of the question or what David intended. But her new-found happiness, and his new-found enthusiasm and sincerity meant she had no choice.

'Will-iam Shak-es-peare,' she proclaimed.

He was off in a world of imagination. He turned away from her thinking aloud. 'My seventh age, my new life starring an ageing guru creating a multicultural miracle.' He indicated a banner headline. 'Boat people fluent in Shakespeare.' Buzzing with excitement, he turned back to her.

'Thanh, we'll be the talk of the nation and Foot-is-cray.'

She knew that word and mimicked his mispronunciation. 'Foot-is-cray.'

David's delight overflowed. 'People will stop you in the street. Do you not know that I am a woman? When I think, I must speak.'

She became a first-class mimic. 'I must speak.'

'Elizabethan English declaimed by a woman from Vietnam.'

Now she excelled. The idea which so excited her teacher, included the name of her beloved homeland.

'Vietnam,' she repeated with a sparkle.

His imagination caught fire. 'We'll hear *forsooth, verily* and *skimble-skamble.*'

The latter in Shakespeare's time meant rambling and nonsensical, and she spoke it with flair. 'Skim-ble skam-ble,' she announced.

Again he turned to face her and posed a direct question. It was time to put up or shut up. 'So what say ye, O Mistress mine?'

Thanh sensed he sought an answer, and spoke with pride.

'Tôi rất vui khi học tiếng Anh với một giáo viên tuyệt vời như bạn, thưa ông.'

Naturally David had no idea that she said, 'I am very happy to study English with such a great teacher as you, sir,' but he was delighted with her answer.

He questioned her. 'Really Thanh?'

Her intelligence shone because, when replying, she used the same intonation as David. 'Really David?'

He paused and smiled. She paused and smiled. Their adventure was about to begin. All aboard. He stared into her eyes and spoke.

'When words are scarce they are seldom spent in vain.' He moved around the room. He had a plan. When he first tried teaching her a few words of English, he flew by the seat of his crumpled and in-need-of-a-clean pants. Now he was shaved, shampooed, and shipshape. He knew what to do. Using the Bard as his guide, his confidence soared. He would teach Thanh to speak Elizabethan English. He started.

'Right, mistress, say after me.' He pointed to his shoes. 'Shoon.'

She now knew the routine and pointed to her shoes. 'Shoon,' she replied.

He pinched and tugged his trousers. 'Trossers.'

She tugged at her gorgeous silk trousers. 'Trossers.'

He raised a leg and patted it, flexing from the knee. 'Forks.'

She understood and remained seated while tapping her knee. 'Forks.'

He placed his hand against his throat. 'Ruffs,' he said.

She mimicked him in action and word. 'Ruffs.'

Then he used one hand and ran it around his wrist. 'Cuffs.'

She copied exactly. 'Cuffs.'

Using both hands, he indicated where a belt or similar would be placed around a waist. 'Hoops,' he said.

She did as he did. 'Hoops,' she replied.

Things changed though when he left his hands alone and motioned with his lips. He puckered and said, 'Sweet friends.'

She showed no sign of embarrassment or of being uncomfortable. She pursed her lips and then spoke, 'Sweet friends.'

He patted his belly and even thrust it forward. 'Fulsome.'

She copied his belly patting. 'Fulsome.'

Without hesitation he indicated his crotch. 'Cod-piece,' he said.

She showed no emotion or reaction although her indicating was more genteel. 'Cod-piece,' she said.

Things changed. Until now, the stationary Thanh sat and repeated Elizabethan vocabulary. Now David wanted action. He moved towards her and offered his hand. She sensed his request and stood, taking his hand. Not for a moment was she worried. He drew her into the centre of the room.

'Come again, good Kate. We will have rings and things and fine array.' He led her across the room and she finished standing on the other side.

She caught his excitement. 'Will-iam Shak-es-peare,' she cried.

He took control. 'I am thy Lord and thou art my mistress.' He pointed to himself as he did when first he conducted introductions. 'My Lord.'

She knew the routine and pointed at him. 'My Lord.'

He pointed at her and said, 'Mistress.'

This was easy as she pointed to herself and replied, 'Mistress.'

He played a game which excited her. The words she spoke were strange, unknown, but the spirit of the game was all. He spoke at her.

'Women speak two languages—one of which is verbal.'

She loved the challenge. 'Women speak two languages—one of which is herbal.

'Verbal,' he corrected.

She tried but failed. 'Fur-ball,' she said.

This was a first-draft. He didn't worry about basic errors. It was the thrill of teaching, of contact with a fellow human, and the glorious richness of the language which drove him forward.

'Kindness in women shall win my love.'

'Kindness in women shall win my dove.'

Again he spent a moment to guide her back to the path.

'Love,' he said in a loving voice.

'Love,' she replied in kind.

His enthusiasm increased. His passion for the language inspired him to greater heights.

'She is a woman, therefore to be won.'

His eyes gleamed. Her eyes matched his as she spoke.

'She is a woman, therefore to be won.'

'The sight of lovers feedeth those in love.'

'The sight of lovers feedeth those in dove.'

Soft but firm described his correction.

'Love,' he said

'Love,' she replied in kind.

He moved away then turned back to face her.

'I bear a charmed life.'

She moved as he did in the opposite direction then turned. 'I bear a charmed life.'

He pointed at her and spoke with a serious tone. 'You have witchcraft in your lips.'

She returned the favour, and gave as good as she got. 'You have witchcraft in your lips.'

In his finale, he spoke with force. 'And all the world's a stage.' He stamped his foot while extending his arms in triumph.

She copied him to the sound and letter. 'And all the world's a stage.'

They froze in their histrionic poses. He dropped out of character and roared with laughter, and she smiled the biggest of smiles.

Later that night Thanh huddled over her sewing machine. Her father would have been proud. She had become a piece worker soon after arriving in Australia, making garments for a song. Clothing sat on the floor, finished items in one pile, and to-be-finished in another. Her grandmother entered the room.

'You have not finished your work,' she said, stating the obvious.

Thanh kept working. 'I will work late to get it finished.'

'We need the money. Your grandfather needs new medicine.'

Thanh stopped sewing and looked at the old woman. 'I know that, Grandmother. I will work late to get it finished.'

'You waste your time doing other things.'

Thanh was exasperated. She loved and respected her family but had found a new friend who taught her wonderful things in a wonderful way.

'Please, Grandmother. I said I will finish.'

The old lady was unhappy. She believed her granddaughter showed disrespect to her family by spending time with a strange man, an old man and one who was not even Vietnamese.

'Why do you waste your time with that man? Does he pay you? Does he take advantage of you?'

Thanh fought to remain calm and polite. 'I have told you, Grandmother. He is a good man, a kind man, and he teaches me to speak like William Shakespeare.'

'Who is this William Shakespeare? Does he speak Vietnamese? And can this William Shakespeare get you a job?'

The old woman left the room. Thanh felt sad, lowered her head and resumed her sewing. She pondered her situation.

I think William Shakespeare is like David, a good man.

12

IT WAS EARLY NEXT MORNING, and David was rarely up early. But an early start was not the only change since he began teaching Thanh. Now he cleaned his teeth regularly. And it was not just his appearance which changed, as his spiritual health fared better too. His self-esteem grew in stature, and really, the bloke just felt happy for the first time in a long time.

He remembered a song his grandfather sang when he took wee David sailing. It involved the Sun wearing a hat. The tune was catchy but the concept fantastic; the brightest of stars wore a titfer. It was 60 years since David first heard that song and right now he sang it and gargled at the same time. Now that's tricky.

Above the sound of running water, teeth brushing, gargling, and spitting, his melodious warbling still did not cover the sound of his door receiving a knock.

He purred with happiness. His student had arrived for her next lesson. This idea of teaching Thanh to speak Elizabethan English was still in its infancy, but he thought it had great potential. David was back teaching, and doing so with a subject he adored. The fact the student was a beautiful young woman who was as enthusiastic as any student he had ever taught, made the anticipation of their next lesson, excitement plus. He couldn't wait to begin.

He dried his face and hands, poked his head out of the bathroom and called, 'Enter.'

He combed his hair and attempted to make himself presentable. The door remained shut. Again, David stuck his head around the bathroom door and in a stage voice demanded, 'Enter.'

The door didn't move. Curious, he positioned himself in the lounge room and waited for his favourite student. He pondered pleasant thoughts.

Perhaps she has both hands full holding even more delicious Vietnamese grub. Perhaps a more detailed request may work.

He called. 'Come, oh mistress mine.'

The door stood still and silent. Then it moved. Just as it started its inward trajectory, David noticed the floor beneath the kitchen table had not been swept. 'Oh Gawd,' said the now houseproud tenant, who picked up a brush and pan and dusted. He had his back to the front door which opened as he pottered.

With his posterior pointing to the visitor, he uttered a polite question.

'How now, good woman; how dost thou?'

The reply made him freeze, leaving his bum staring at the ceiling.

'Dust?' said his visitor. 'I never dust.'

David's next words were laced with disappointment. 'I know that voice,' he said, then softer, 'do I ever?'

Judith, his estranged wife, stared at his backside, and couldn't resist her reply. 'I know those cheeks,' she quipped.

David placed the brush and pan beneath the table, stood and turned.

'Judith,' he said without feeling.

'You've remembered,' she replied also without feeling.

David forced a grimace. 'Long time no argue.'

She indicated the front door. 'Front door unlocked I see.' She paused then pointed a finger at him. 'Gotcha.' She used that finger to tap her nose. 'Handy for the mistress mine.'

David panicked. *Why is she here? It must be serious. He thought the worst.*

'What's happened? Is it Matt? Rosie? What?'

Judith entered, and sat on the settee, speaking as she moved. 'Don't panic; I've no news of our dysfunctional family. This is business.' She opened her satchel and withdrew papers. 'These are divorce papers you need to sign.'

He slipped into his Groucho persona. 'Whatever it is, I'm against it.'

She ignored his gag. 'If I post this material, you'll procrastinate. So I'm here, in person, to get the legal stuff moving. Once it's complete, I'll be gone, leaving you to get serious with your mistress mine.' She looked around the room. 'So, where's she hiding?'

He ignored her. They were good at ignoring one another. He moved closer and held out a hand.

'The papers, if you please.'

She handed him the documents. He glanced at them then felt in his pockets for a pen. He had no luck so Judith offered hers. He gave a forced smile, took the pen and walked to the phone table.

She issued orders. 'Put your mark by the X—three times.'

He studied the paperwork in detail. 'Beautifully prepared documents; no doubt the work of Sue the solicitor.' He gave another forced smile.

She didn't bite. 'Get on with it.'

David saw the perfect way to express his feelings about what was in front of him, and used his mate, Groucho to make his point.

'A child of five could understand this.' He called to an imaginary person. 'Send someone to fetch a child of five.'

Judith was unimpressed. She needed his signature now. 'Just sign.'

He turned the pages, found the blank lines marked with an X, and signed. He wanted her gone more than she wanted to leave. Having signed where required, he handed the papers to Judith then turned away but stopped when she spoke.

She held out a hand. 'And the pen.'

Another forced smile from David who returned her pen. She placed the documents and pen in her satchel while he pretended to be human.

'So, Tea? Coffee? Rat poison?'

She looked around then ran a finger along the top of the coffee table. She was sincere. 'I'm pleasantly surprised at your housekeeping.'

Thank God she didn't come last month.

David was not sincere. 'You're too kind.'

'And I'm doubly impressed you've found a woman to do for you.'

'I would normally say "find your own woman" but am reliably informed that's already in hand—or hands.'

'Touché.'

Judith prepared to leave. She went all coy and gossipy. 'The curiosity's killing me. What's she look like?' Judith brushed past him en route to the door, and spoke without looking. 'Send me a photo.' She stopped when someone knocked on the door. David groaned.

Not now, Thanh. Wait till the harridan's gone.

Judith turned back to David, delighted. Ah, the mysterious maiden appears. I get to take a peek.' She pretended to be shocked. 'Oh no! Don't tell me—she's a mail-order bride!' Now she taunted him with a "who's been a naughty boy" type grin. 'Why don't I open the door?'

She was dying to do just that. He preferred root canal surgery, and turned away, fearing Judith's ridicule. Then he thought otherwise.

Why am I upset? Thanh's not a mail order bride or even my girlfriend. I don't need to apologise or explain.

Judith reached the door, dying to meet who she believed was David's mistress. He cringed. He feared humiliation but turned around when Judith spoke.

'Bloody hell!'

Thanh was not the door knocker. David's two visitors were surprised to see Judith. They entered and moved to a smiling David.

His former principal, Janice, arrived carrying a basket of goodies. 'David,' she said, as they embraced.

'Good dawning to thee, friend,' said mine host. Janice stepped aside to reveal her follow visitor, Juliet, one of David's erstwhile Year 12 students. She threw her arms wide, chewed gum, and grinned. 'Hello sir, it's me.'

They too embraced and David again used the Bard to greet his guest.

'How do you, pretty lady?'

David indicated the settee and both new arrivals sat. Judith closed the door and, being an incurable stickybeak, joined the party.

'Curiouser and curiouser, cried Alice,' she said nudging herself back into the conversation.

Janice explained her arrival. 'We're sorry to barge in uninvited, David, but Juliet came to school to ask about her favourite teacher and, well, here we are.'

Judith sat and David addressed her. 'I thought you were leaving.'

The stickybeak simply had to stay. 'I've changed my mind. I will have that rat poison.'

Janice was confused. *Why is David's estranged wife in his faraway bedsit? Are they back together? Janice offered David a chance to ask them to leave.*

'Is this a bad time, David? We can come back later.'

He wanted none of that. 'Nay, nay, be truly welcome hither.'

There was a lull in the conversation. This was the first time David had seen, let alone spoken to anyone from his previous life since his major fall from grace. Bad news travels fast, and Janice and the staff all knew of David's travails. Juliet broke the ice. She was pleased to see him.

'It's great to see again you, sir. An' I'm doin' real well at uni.'

David was delighted. 'So wise, so young.'

Janice tried to explain how she found him. It made things worse.

'David, I had trouble tracking you down so I rang your mother and she told me ...'

David felt embarrassed and thought it best to be open about his failure. He need not have done so but second guessed Janice's answer.

'About my spectacular fall from grace.'

There was an awkward pause. Janice was too polite to ever raise David's condition. She tried to rescue the situation, and used a soft voice.

'About your new address.'

Oops. There was another awkward pause. Judith now wished she had left. Juliet again broke the silence. She knew how to lighten a mood.

'Hey sir,' she said, slipping into a Groucho Marx impression. 'While money can't buy happiness ...'

David seized her cue and became Mr Marx himself, '... it certainly lets you choose your own form of misery.'

David and Juliet enjoyed the repartee but the atmosphere soon swung back to sadness. Janice reached for her bag of goodies.

'Now, David, you left in such a hurry, you must have forgotten these few things. The staff wanted you to have them.'

Janice lied. It was one of those delicate moments. Was this charity? Yes. Would this gesture embarrass or insult the impoverished recipient? Probably. But before any judgement could be made, Juliet slapped her gift on the coffee table.

'And sir, I've remembered your favourite choccies.'

David was overcome. He was thrilled people remembered him, went out of their way to find him, and to visit bringing simple gifts. He felt a lump in his throat. He got control of his emotions and spoke.

'You, and your lady, take from my heart all thankfulness!'

Judith finally worked her way into the conversation. 'Well, with friends like these, who needs a char?'

'Indeed,' said David rubbing his hands together. 'Right, manners David. That's two teas and a rat poison.' He began to move to the kitchenette but stopped and gave a gentle command to his visitors. 'Ladies, please, just talk among yourselves.'

He pottered fearing a social disaster. He had nothing to offer. Instant coffee, stale milk and a used teabag being the sum total of his larder.

Thanh, I need you. Some Vietnamese finger food, if you please.

Back in the lounge room, the three women were bereft of ideas. The only thing they had in common was their host, and his situation was hardly the stuff of polite conversation. He was broke, and his spouse was shacked up with another woman. Not ideal topics for a chat. The silence lingered. Again, the youngest visitor cracked the impasse.

'I think he looks terrific,' said Juliet.

At least it was a start, however, it didn't get the conversation flowing.

After another heavy pause, Janice addressed the ex. 'So Judith, are you well?

She failed to take the bait but instead raised a new topic—a doozy. 'I've just discovered he's got a woman.'

Okay, how does one respond to that? Janice didn't touch it. Juliet thought it was great news. 'Cool,' she purred, and meant it.

Before the strained situation worsened, David returned to apologise.

'I'm so sorry, ladies, but I'm fresh out of cucumber sandwiches.'

Everyone knew this was code for "I haven't got anything even half decent to offer you so could you all please bugger off?"

Janice twigged and stood. 'Thanks David but we really must be going.'

David tried to sound sincere. 'Nay, I pray you tarry.'

Janice gave a subtle gesture to Juliet who had been warned about a possible early departure. She stood beside her former principal. 'Oh yeah, I f'got, sir. I've got a tutorial on how to pronounce cer-e-moan-ey.'

Judith too got the message and stood, looking at her watch. 'Good heavens, is that the time?'

David feigned shock and disappointment. 'All of you? And just when the party was starting.'

The best way to remove the obvious embarrassment was to leave. The visitors knew this and began to depart. They hadn't taken two steps when a door knock was heard. The women froze. David died. He didn't believe in miracles. He knew there was a slight possibility this could be a Tibetan herdsman looking for directions to the South Pole, but somehow his brain refused to accept that the person outside was anyone other than Thanh. He cringed. Having his estranged wife meet Thanh was bad enough. Having the entire world do so made his miserable life more miserable.

But why am I ashamed or afraid? I've done nothing wrong.

Nobody moved. David seemed incapable of action. He thought if he did nothing, the person would go away and the visitors would depart. Juliet yet again broke the silence.

'Someone's at y'door, sir.'

Thanks Juliet.

Okay, so now the truth was out in the open. Now David's private life was private no more. But as yet the identity of the door-knocking person remained a mystery. Not to David, but certainly to his guests. That situation changed when a loud voice was heard.

'My Lord,' called Thanh.

Oh dear.

That sounded like a female and her greeting didn't fit the everyday female greeting. A woman addressed David as her Lord. The scene could, with accuracy, be described as *interesting*.

Judith showed her true colours. If her former hubby had been playing away, she wanted the facts out in the open. She fancied getting her own back.

He gave me stick about my girlfriend. Now it's payback time.

She spoke, enjoying the humiliation of her ex.

'Methinks a woman's at your door—my Lord.'

Thanh remained outside the flat. She heard no reply to both her knocking and calling. She tried again, moving up a notch in volume.

'Tis thy Mistress, my Lord.'

Okay, so that was the sucker punch. David now had no hope of avoiding his secret love becoming a secret no more. He was a cross between annoyed and embarrassed. Thanh would set tongues wagging. Janice sensed his discomfort and tried to help.

'I don't suppose there's a fire escape?'

David ignored her question, made a decision, and took control.

'Tis my Mistress indeed.' He faced the door, and called, 'Enter.'

Was there ever a better time for a drumroll? The three women stood staring at David. They desperately wanted to stare at his visitor. They got their chance.

Thanh entered. She wore another striking traditional Vietnamese outfit and looked breathtaking. She couldn't see the women on the other side of the bookcase. Carrying yet another food container, Thanh walked past the bookshelf and straight to David. Her appearance gave David's heart a jolt, and fascinated the three women, especially Judith.

Thanh stood before David, bowed and then offered her latest dish. He accepted it, and they both held the container. David bowed and smiled his appreciation.

She spoke with pride, describing her latest concoction. 'Shitty shitty bang bang,' she proclaimed. David beamed.

Judith gaped. 'It *is* a mail-order bride.'

Janice's mouth had been open for some time. Finally she whispered. 'Well, bugger me.'

Juliet sported a massive grin, being seriously impressed. 'Cool!'

When Sue the solicitor came home that night, Judith had two glasses of fine wine ready and waiting. Judith said nothing but handed her lover a glass. Sue was curious.

'So?' How did it go? How was your ex? I bet he was surprised.'

'Cheers,' said Judith raising her glass.

Sue was hooked and nervous. 'Don't tell me he didn't sign the papers?'

'All done,' said Judith.

'Well what then? What's with the mystery?'

'He's got a woman.'

Sue shrugged. 'Big deal. So have you.'

'Have a guess, describe her.'

Sue considered the facts. 'Well if he's living in a public housing shoebox in Footscray I think it's a fair bet that she's not an entrant in the current Miss World.'

Judith shrugged. Sue gasped.

'Could be,' said Judith. Sue's mouth fell open.

'No?'

'She's young, gorgeous, a brilliant cook and feeding him.'

'Feeding or feeling?'

Judith shrugged. 'Possibly both.'

Sue gasped again. 'You are kidding?'

'She's from Vietnam. My boring-old-fart ex has got himself a stunning mail order child bride.'

Sue dropped her glass.

13

THANH'S GRANDMOTHER WAS A STICKYBEAK. Thanh slept on the living room settee—a practice she shared with her neighbour—and packed up her bed linen every morning before her grandparents awoke. When Thanh went shopping, Grandmother got nosy and rifled through Thanh's belongings. The old woman purloined an exercise book and confronted Thanh when her granddaughter returned.

'What is this book?'

Thanh was shocked to see her elderly relative holding something private, and to discover her Grandmother was a sneak.

'That is my lesson book which I use for my lessons in Elizabethan English. David gave it to me.'

'David, David, David,' snapped the old woman. 'He is not from our country, and far worse, he is probably strange.'

Thank took a deep breath trying to remain calm. 'No, Grandmother, I have told you. He is kind and gentle.'

'If he loves this William Shakespeare then he must be strange. Grown men do not love other men.'

Thanh shook her head. Coming to Australia, and living in a new culture was not always easy.

Thanh and David got serious. Each day, after breakfast, she would knock on David's door, enter, and resume her lessons in Elizabethan English. They both adored these sessions. It was new to him and a challenge. It was new to her and she thrived.

David began each lesson with revision then launched into new studies. Learning Elizabethan English by simply hearing the words was a quick and easy way to start. But being able to read was vital. David wanted Thanh to see the words she spoke so gave her an old exercise book from his teaching days. This is what Grandmother discovered.

Over his long career, David taught thousands of students, and knew Thanh would have been in the top group in any class. She was quick, clever and enthusiastic. She wanted to learn. And as the days and lessons rolled by, her grasp of Elizabethan English grew ever stronger.

At first, the teaching technique involved rote learning where Thanh copied David, parrot fashion. Her understanding of the words didn't exist. But over time, that began to change.

She entered David's flat where his enthusiasm for the task continued to bubble. He directed her to sit while he stood in the centre of the room.

'Come, fair maiden, let us commence thy next lesson and begin with revision; repeat after me.' He pointed to his shoes, trousers and legs, and said, 'Shoon, trossers, forks.'

She knew the routine and, more importantly, the answers. She copied her teacher in action and word.

'Shoon, trossers, forks,' she said.

David used his hands to indicate his throat, his wrist and his waist. 'Ruffs, cuffs, hoops,' he said.

Again she copied him to perfection. 'Ruffs, cuffs, hoops,' she replied.

David picked up a book he'd researched the night before. It had illustrations of Elizabethan clothing. He placed the opened book on the coffee table and beckoned Thanh to come closer. He pointed to items of clothing, speaking the names. Thanh's face was a picture. She loved the illustrations, and her understanding took root. He paused then gave her a test.

'What is this?' He pointed to some shoes.

'Shoon,' she replied.

'Excellent.' Then he pointed to other items, and each time Thanh identified the clothing or accessory. David rejoiced.

This is the life; teaching what I love to someone who loves to learn.

David left the book and resumed his visual revision. He indicated his lips, his belly and his crotch. 'Sweet friends, fulsome, codpiece,' he said.

Without being prompted, Thanh repeated his routine. 'Sweet friends, fulsome, codpiece.'

One of the many benefits David received, having started to teach Thanh, involved his food intake. Her gifts of Vietnamese food meant his diet improved overnight. Their relationship inspired him to do something about his lifestyle. He bought fruit and vegetables; an amazing occurrence because if you'd seen his diet BT, (Before Thanh), you would understand how colossal a change this was. But back to the lessons.

He moved around the room introducing new words. He held up his favourite jacket, the one with leather arm patches. 'Gabardine,' he said.

She remained patient before answering. 'Gab-ar-dine.'

He held up two carrots and a stick of celery. 'Vegetives,' he pronounced.

Again she tackled a new word, 'Veg-e-tives.'

He held up a cup. 'Cannikin,' he said.

She was not in a hurry. 'Cann-i-kin.'

He indicated all three and spoke with a constant tempo. 'Gabardine, vegetives, cannikin.' She copied his rhythm and diction.

Then he pointed to each in turn and she replied with the correct answer. 'Gabardine, vegetives, and cannikin.'

'*And* cannikin,' said David. 'Thou hast added a conjunction sans prompting.'

She smiled having no idea what he meant.

'Well, now that you have chosen to show off your superior intellect, Mistress, let us tackle some words created or used by the Bard.'

'The Bard of Avon,' she replied.

'Indeed. Right then, try these on for size—*scallywag, sanctimonious* and *swagger.*'

She straightened in her chair and took a deep breath. '*Scallywag, sanc* ...' It wouldn't come.

'Sanctimonious,' he said.

She started again. 'Scally-wag, sanc-ti-mon-i-ous, and swagger.'

The last word she spoke with confidence, with body language that suggested a swagger. Surely not? Her teacher was delighted. He knew these words were far too advanced for her knowledge of basic English skills, but David believed in pushing his students, and in setting tasks which forced them to stretch their intellect and imagination. Sure, he teased her but it was obvious Thanh was intelligent. The fact that she added an *and* to her collection of three words showed how she had begun to pick up the flow of the language.

Their lessons became mutually rewarding. David loved teaching, loved the language of Shakespeare, and his passion for helping someone, for passing on his knowledge and enthusiasm, gave his self-esteem and spirits a serious boost.

Thanh too received many benefits. She obtained knowledge, which gave her confidence. She found happiness in pleasing the man she admired, and ever so gradually, she gained an insight into the human condition, thanks to the words of the Bard.

'Excellent,' said David. 'Thy progress is commendable. But now, resolve me with all modest haste. Brevity is the soul of wit.'

Thanh loved these quote sessions. Again her understanding of the words was zero, but she loved the challenge of speaking with accuracy.

'Brevity is the soul of wit.'

David was in his element. 'No legacy is so rich as honesty.'

Off she went. 'No legacy is so rich as honesty.'

'Be not afraid of greatness.'

'Be not afraid of greatness.'

David added variety to his lessons when using quotes. He added a crescendo, placed an emphasis on certain words, and always added emotion throughout his speeches. 'I must be cruel, only to be kind.'

Thanh improved her pronunciation and became expert at mimicking David's interpretation and presentation.

'I must be cruel, only to be kind,' she repeated.

It was as if David used Shakespeare to instruct Thanh in how she might choose to live her life. 'Listen to many, speak to a few.'

'Listen to many, speak to a few.'

Now he smiled as he spoke. 'With mirth and laughter let old wrinkles come.'

She tried the grin and copy method but slipped up on the pronunciation. 'With mirth and laughter let old winkles come.'

This caused David to laugh out loud. 'Wrinkles,' he cried, rolling the *r*.

Thanh, as she had always done, tried to copy him exactly. She laughed but made a mess of her *r* rolling. 'Wrink-les!'

This lesson, this game was fun writ large. Learning was a side issue, a secondary benefit. The real winner was the renaissance of David Cadwallader and the discovery of a new culture for Thanh Nguyen.

As the days went by and new lessons were held, Thanh's grasp of the language improved. Her memory was terrific. She was good. But even more important was the development of their relationship. Genuine friendship blossomed between the couple. David addressed her as Mistress Thanh. She addressed David as My Lord or Master David or Sir. She delighted in her title and loved their banter. She soon realised that he often teased her in their conversations. This thrilled her no end. And to top it off, her understanding and knowledge continued to grow.

She entered his flat for her latest lesson. They bowed and he spoke.

'Mistress Thanh!'

'Master David!'

'Tis a new day, Mistress, and a new lesson.'

'Aye, sir.'

He questioned her. 'Dost thou wish to speaketh well?'

Her understanding meant their conversation flowed. She knew what he meant and more so, knew what she meant in reply.

She spoke with strength. 'Aye, sir.'

He spoke with sincerity and pride. 'Thou art so fine a student.'

She spoke with sincerity and gratitude. 'Thou art so fine a teacher.'

During each lesson, he would stop and explain a particular word. One such word was *addressed*. In Elizabethan English it meant *prepared*.

He questioned Thanh. 'Mistress, art thou addressed?'

She had completed her homework, and indicated her exercise book. 'Aye sir.'

He moved to the centre of the room. 'Then what pray tell are these?' He pointed to his shoes.

She loved being tested. 'Shoon.

He tugged at his trousers.

'Trossers,' she said.

He raised a leg and tapped it. 'Forks,' she said.

He didn't speak but simply pointed to his lips.

'Sweet friends.'

He patted his stomach even pushing out his gut.

'Fulsome,' was the immediate answer.

But there was more. David had explained that a distended belly on a woman who was with child had a special word. He patted his stomach and spoke.

'And with woman?'

She replied immediately without emotion. 'Childing.'

Next he indicated his throat, his wrist and his crotch. Each movement was simple and brief.

She copied his movements and spoke. Ruff, cuff, codpiece.'

'Bravo,' said David, 'now for emotions.'

This was new. At first they only dealt with physical things. Thanh could see and touch a chair, shoes, a pencil and the window. But what about invisible things like happiness, anger or confusion? These took time to explain, and David's teaching expertise won the day—eventually. Over several lessons he introduced various states of mind. He played charades and acted an emotion. She had to guess.

He took a threatening and angry stance, and added vocals. 'Ahhhh,' he cried, imitating anger.

Thanh took her time. She no longer looked at a physical object.

'Mistempered,' she said, and David smiled. She felt warm inside.

David became a simpleton, someone who struggled with a disability.

'Errr,' he uttered.

Thanh pondered then remembered. 'Motley-minded,' she said.

She was good. David switched to being bossy. He showed contempt, pointed towards the door, and shouted, 'Out!'

Thanh instantly remembered this contemptuous behaviour and answered without hesitation.

'Tilly-Vally,' she answered and was spot on, again.

Now David pretended to be confused. He scratched his head, looked puzzled and whined, 'Ahhh.'

Thanh remembered this state of confusion. 'Diffused,' she said.

Then David mimed being a vocalist. His mouth framed silent words and his arms and hands added meaning to the lyrics. Thanh thought she knew the answer.

'Reduce,' she offered. To Shakespeare, reduce meant to bring back. David shook his head and kept miming.

'Recure,' said Thanh more in hope than anything. Wrong again as in Elizabethan English, recure meant to recover.

Thanh worried. Two attempts without the correct answer. David's histrionics continued.

Thanh tried again. 'Record,' she called with confidence. It meant to sing and David stopped his singing and applauded.

Excited, he pointed at her and cried, 'Aye.' She shared his excitement.

But David wanted her good work to become consistent. 'Now, constancy,' he demanded. He had taught her many quotes which she could repeat. Now he added variety. He would begin a quote and she had to complete it. He started what was to both of them a game.

'What's mine is yours ....' he said.

To which she replied, '... and what is yours is mine.'

The game was on in earnest.

'Better a witty fool ...'

'... than a foolish wit.'

'Better three hours too soon ...'

'... than a minute too late.'

He challenged her. Yes, her understanding was limited but that would come with time. He reckoned education was as much about attitude and ambition as it was about application.

He looked at her. 'Ambition should be made ...'

She looked at him. '... of sterner stuff.'

'Boldness ...'

'... be my friend.'

He moved to one side of the room speaking as he walked. He looked out through an imaginary window. 'But, soft! What light through yonder window breaks?' He stared towards the imaginary Sun.

Thanh rose and copied his movement, heading to the opposite side of the room, speaking as she walked. 'It is the east, and Juliet is the one.'

David continued staring and spoke with a calm yet correcting voice. 'Sun.'

Thanh hated making a mistake, and spoke through gritted teeth. 'Sun.'

He continued without looking at her. 'Poor and content is rich ...'

Thanh replied without looking at David. '... and rich enough.'

Now their game became serious. David metaphorically lunged at Thanh with Shakespearean quotes as his sword. She returned fire with fire, and gave as good as she got. Through language he spat at her.

'Asses are made to bear, and so are you.'

She challenged him. 'How poor are they that have not patience!'

'Was ever woman in this humour woo'd?'

'Done to death by slanderous tongue.'

He built the ferocity with volume and venom. 'Frailty, thy name is woman.'

She called his bluff. 'Nothing can come of nothing.'

He reached his tipping point and wanted her gone. He pointed and shouted. 'Get thee to a nunnery.'

She too was fed up and finished their session by pointing and commanding. 'Off with thy head!'

In this humble public housing flat in working-class Footscray, studying Elizabethan English, the language of Shakespeare, became little short of marvellous.

In Julia's sumptuous South Yarra apartment, the elderly matriarch, impeccably dressed as always, led her GP into the sitting room. The doctor was more than 50 years younger than his patient, and had only treated Mrs Cadwallader for two months. His father had been Julia's GP for decades.

She sat in her favourite and expensive arm chair. Everything about Julie was expensive. 'You must be the only GP who still does house calls.'

He opened his bag and removed a blood pressure monitor. 'You must be the only patient who demands them.'

'Requests, if you don't mind.' The GP placed the device on Julia's arm. 'Now I want you to know I feel terrible, and insist you find something terrible.'

The GP measured her blood pressure. 'Well let's just see, shall we, Julia.'

'I told you to call me Mrs Cadwallader.'

'It's a relaxation of the old rules,' he smiled.

'Well that's the last time you'll ever relax in my home. Understood?'

He humoured her. 'Certainly, Madame Lafarge.'

'The Bard only, if you please.' He grinned and checked the result. 'Your father was an excellent doctor because he only did what I allowed him to do.'

'Yes, he did mention your particular request.'

Julia called a spade a spade. 'Nothing downstairs,' she said.

The GP listened to her heart and lungs.

'That's not quite the way things are done these days,' he said.

'More's the pity,' said Julia.

'Perhaps you'd prefer a female doctor.'

Julia scoffed. 'A female doctor! What a ridiculous suggestion.'

'You do realise, madam, it may be the case that you are actually in rude health.'

'Impossible,' she snorted. 'There must be something wrong with me! How can I be miserable if I have nothing about which to be miserable?'

'Mrs Cadwallader, there are many women, some much younger than your good self, who would gladly swap their health condition for yours.'

'I'm not interested in other women. Now what conditions have you found, and the more exotic the better? I don't want anything common.'

The GP began to put away his equipment.

'Well, madam, I believe you do have a certain condition.'

'Excellent,' said Julia.

'The bad news, I'm afraid, is that there is no cure.'

That stopped Julia in her tracks. "You mean it's going to kill me?"

'Perhaps not because to my knowledge, no-one has ever died of your condition.'

He closed his bag and smiled. 'I'll see myself out.'

'Wait a minute,' cried the grande dame. 'What is this exotic condition which won't kill me?'

At the door, he turned and told all. 'It's called self-pity. Good day, Mrs Cadwallader.' He left and she boiled.

'Self-pity,' she hissed then roared. 'That's not a disease.'

Twelve weeks had passed since Thanh began learning Elizabethan English. Her enthusiasm and intelligence never ceased to amaze her teacher. Their latest lesson finished and David was tired, creeping towards exhausted. Because she had mastered so much Elizabethan English, he now needed to plan their lessons in detail. The planning and teaching took its toll. Old man Cadwallader felt the pinch. Not so Thanh who at the end of their lessons, wanted to continue. He couldn't. He collapsed on the settee.

'O Mistress, thy lesson endeth.'

'Nay, sir.'

'Thou art apprehensive beyond measure but I am stuff-ed.'

Thanh saw he was genuinely tired. Amazingly, she knew how to question his wellbeing using the words of the Bard.

'O, my good Lord, why are you thus alone?'

He wasn't impressed, thought her wisecrack inappropriate, and he too replied using Will's words.

'Prithee, cease thy quillets.'

She would have none of it and asked a genuine question. 'For what offence have I this fortnight been a banished woman from my Harry's bed?'

Now he took notice. Now he lost his tiredness. This wasn't a quillet, a wisecrack, this was a damn speech. He sat up. His student asked a specific question relevant to his current condition, and doing so quoting exactly Shakespeare's Henry IV Part 1. They had studied that scene a week or two past. She had taken the play home and "done her homework".

Remembering the text was remarkable in itself but more so was her interpretation. She wasn't just quoting, but acting. She knew enough of the meaning of the text to make her point. He was impressed but annoyed because her words hit home. She spoke the truth about him and it hurt.

Out of nowhere, their relationship ran into conflict.

David forgot his tiredness.

'Hang on! I hath not taught thee thus.'

She piled on the pressure. 'Tell me, sweet Lord, what is't that takes from thee thy stomach, pleasure, and thy golden sleep?'

'Whoa, back off, lady.' He became defensive. 'Let's not get personal.'

She spoke plainly. 'Why dost thou bend thine eyes upon the earth, and start so often when thou sit'st alone?'

This was too much. He switched to anger. 'Hey! Stop this!'

She didn't stop this but grew more insistent. Did she tease him? Did she try to prove her mastery of Elizabethan English? Did she show off? Whatever, she kept at him.

'Why hast thou lost the fresh blood in thy cheeks ...'

He pointed at her and shouted. 'Thanh!'

'And given my treasure and my rights of thee to thick-eyed musing and cursed melancholy?'

Now that was over the top. His anger flashed. 'Enough, woman! Hold thy tongue!'

Her next speech summed up David's current predicament.

'Thy spirit within thee hath been so at war and thus hath so bestirred thee in thy sleep, that beads of sweat hath stood upon thy brow.'

There *were* beads of sweat upon his brow. He fumed and fired back.

'O most pernicious woman!'

Would nothing stop or silence her? No, nothing. She attacked.

'And in thy face strange motions have appeared. Oh, what portents are these?'

David threatened her and meant it. 'I'll give thee bloody portents!'

She went for the killer punch. 'Some heavy business hath my Lord in hand, and I must know it, else he loves me not.'

He bellowed. 'Enough!' Then David fell back on the settee. He was close to exhaustion before this fracas began and definetly so once it ended. He genuinely didn't know what to say. Thanh was brilliant in her choice of words, her ability to remember them exactly, and in her delivery. He wondered at her brilliance.

Is this down to me? Have I just pointed her in the right direction and her intelligence has taken over? Or wait! Has my student discovered my real nature? Has she done a Will and held a mirror up to my life?

Thanh tingled. She had studied this part of the play for more than a week. To find the perfect opportunity to display her learning was a fluke, unexpected. She didn't plan it. It just happened.

She soon realised his response was not what she expected or wanted. He was upset, seriously so. She thought he would be pleased. Instead he slipped into silence and depression.

'Depart, Mistress,' he said without looking at her.

'My Lord ...'

'Depart,' he shouted. She hesitated. 'Get thee hence!' cried David.

Thanh felt pain in her heart. She wanted to please him with her learning. Instead she angered the man she admired. Nothing could be worse. With sadness aplenty, she returned to her grandparents, enduring scary thoughts.

Have I offended my Lord and Master? Will he ever want to teach me again?

14

IT WASN'T A NIGHT TO REMEMBER. Earlier that day, Thanh gave David a serve, unintentionally of course. Ever since she left his flat, he'd patted the black dog. Did he have depression? He was certainly miserable and, like his mother, overloaded with self-pity. But for nigh on three months his life had found a new purpose. Teaching Thanh had given him a reason to get out of bed, to eat good food, to take care of his health, and to get stuck into useful activities. But tonight, the old woes came back to haunt him. No money, no marriage, no family, and no hope. And when Thanh used Shakespeare to give David the rounds of the kitchen, the old demons roared back into his life.

In the dark he sat on the floor leaning against the settee. He drank from a bottle of cheap wine with not a glass in sight.

His phone rang. It had to be, could only be his mater. He didn't even try to get up and answer it.

After several rings, David's dulcet tones sounded from within the answering machine. Julia was worried and still angry as a result of her GP's comments about her self-pity.

'David! Why haven't you been to visit me? David! Hello?'

He replied but because he hadn't hit the button on the machine, she couldn't hear. He answered from the floor.

'Pray woman, baffle me no more.'

Hearing nothing made Julia even more anxious.

'Why won't you speak to me? Do you want me to die?' She paused feeling sure he would react to her last question. Nothing. 'David?'

He called to the phone. 'I'll race you to the grave, Mother. Last one there's a sissy!' He raised the wine bottle and took a swig.

More than half a century ago, Julia had introduced her two young sons to Shakespeare. She took them as wee boys to see plays and films. She often read to them. Her efforts bore fruit with one of her sons, and David became a huge fan. Right now, she fell back on the words of the Bard.

'O wonderful son, that can so stonish a mother!' That stopped David drinking. 'But is there no sequel at the heels of this mother's admiration?'

David sat in the darkness and shook his head. 'Alas, no!'

The answering machine sounded a beep and Mother was no more.

David shared a drink with his mate, Misery.

David was tired. Alcohol without food made for a dangerous mix, and to someone who was depressed, the consequences could be disastrous. He crawled to the front of the settee, put the wine bottle on the coffee table, and hauled himself onto his now all-too-familiar bed. He wanted to puke. He wanted to die. He belched and tasted bile. It was vile.

He groaned in both physical and mental anguish. Eventually he fell into a fitful sleep. He should have stayed awake. In a fitful sleep, David wandered into his own nightmare.

In his dream, David was trapped in his tiny flat. He sat in the dark and heard a strange sound. It was a cackle, several cackles, laughter from weird women, sisters, the three witches from the Scottish play.

David had no time for superstition and failed to understand what the sisters from Macbeth were doing in his lounge room.

The witches were people he knew—very well. Headgear hid their faces, and flowing robes disguised their bodies but their voices told all. The room was dark but David well knew his visitors. Cruelty was their game.

The first sister to speak was Judith. She mocked her former husband. 'Oh David, guess who's just become a granddaddy again?'

David was stunned. It was good news. He spluttered a reply. 'Me? A grandfather—again? Is it a girl or a boy?'

Judith tormented him snatching away his hope of any happiness.

'They won't say,' she snarled. 'Your kids have cut you off—forever!' She launched into a cackling laugh, oozing hatred and worse.

Then a second witch cackled, continued the torture, speaking close to his ear. It was Janice, his former principal.

'Oh David, guess who's just retired, and is off to see the world?'

Shock gripped David. How could my kind friend now become nasty? He failed to understand her statement. He stuttered.

'Retired? See the world? But, but, but, but how can you afford it?'

Janice, the kind and understanding former colleague oozed malice. She spat her answer.

'Because I've still got *all* my super.' Her evil laugh rubbed salt into David's wound of poverty. He despaired.

How can I escape this nightmare?

He tried but failed as the third sister leered at him. It was his favourite former student, Juliet. They once shared a joyous relationship. But no longer as Juliet the witch became Juliet the bitch. Her taunting remarks cut David to the bone.

'Oh sir,' she called, and became Groucho Marx. 'You may look like an idiot, and talk like an idiot, but don't let that fool you.'

He knew the response and had to speak as his hero. 'I really am an idiot.' His woe compoundeth.

The women closed in around their victim and mocked him using the words of Groucho Marx.

Witch Judith started. 'Next time I see you, remind me not to speak to you.'

Witch Janice sprang from another angle. 'Either you're dead or my watch has stopped.'

Witch Juliet piled on the evil. 'Go, and never darken my towels again.'

David spoke in his nightmare. He had to speak. He fell back on Will.

'I had rather have a fool to make me merry, than experience to make me sad.'

The witches joined forces and bubbled away behind their target.

'Double, double toil and trouble;

Fire burn, and caldron bubble.'

The Cadwallader witches repeated their famous lines, chanting softly as David exclaimed to the world.

'A merry heart goes all the way, a sad one tires in an hour. The meaning of life is to find your gift. The purpose of life is to give it away.'

The evil witches, having cast their spells, cackled their glee then walked out of David's nightmare, issuing instructions as they left.

'Therein the patient must minister to himself.'

David fought back and shouted to the world.

'Throw physic to the dogs, I'll none of it.'

The heinous laughter of the witches took forever to fade. David's nightmare ended. He woke, discovered he was shaking and perspiring. He automatically reached for alcohol. He drank unaware his next nightmare was just around the corner.

After Mother's phone call and his dream about witches, David sat on the floor, in the dark, resting against the settee. Misery was his mate; the pal who refused to leave. All the good times with Thanh, all the progress she had made thanks to David's passion and planning, were swamped by negative thoughts. David was depressed, mightily so. Not afraid to mix his drinks, he drank from a can of vodka and orange. Strictly speaking, he was not an alcoholic although training hard to become one.

Across the hall, Thanh slaved away at her sewing machine. Her grandparents had retired but Thanh, like David, faced her own demons. Had she insulted her beloved teacher? Had she ruined their beautiful friendship?

She knew he suffered although why he looked and sounded sad, to her remained a mystery. Thanh knew little of David's personal life. She knew he was despondent, but could she help? Perhaps teaching her something new might help. She remembered topics he promised but had yet to start.

Perhaps if I remind him of these new topics, he will concentrate on his teaching, and that will lift him out of his misery.

Even though it was night time, and she only ever went to her lessons in the day, she decided she would not let the sun go down on their disagreement. She simply had to apologise, and do whatever she could to help her friend and mentor.

She crept out of her flat and tip-toed to David's door. She listened. Could she hear snoring? She knocked. Nothing. She knocked louder.

David knew that knock. He too felt bad about the things he said, and how they'd parted. Then his pride arose. He snatched the mantle from his mother, and wallowed in self-pity. He called.

'Go, go, begone, to save your ship from wrack.'

She heard him and became even more determined to help. She called trying not to disturb the neighbours.

'My Lord, art thou within?'

He wanted to see and speak to her but pride dictated his moves.

'Avaunt,' he cried.

She knew this meant "go away" but ignored the order and knocked again. Silence. He decided to ignore her, hoping she would leave.

She paused, opened the door, crept inside, and squinted in the dark.

She whispered. 'My Lord?'

David whispered with feeling. 'Avaunt, and quit my sight!'

Thanh followed the sound. She squinted in the darkened room. When she looked down she made out the dissolute wreck of a man. She was shocked, and knelt to help him.

'My Lord, thou art ill.'

Now he was angry. 'Begone woman. And I am not thy Lord.'

Thanh was frightened and told him. 'I am gasted, sire, to see thee so.'

'Harken Mistress, taketh thy bleeding heart to someone who doth give a damn.'

Thanh added confusion and shock to her fear. 'My Lord?'

'I am a miserable old man and wish to wallow in self-pity without help from any do-gooder including and especially thy good self.'

Thanh was convinced her behaviour had caused David to become like this. She begged for help.

'Oh sire, what canst I do to earn thy forgiveness?'

He tried to rise. She helped as he leant on the settee.

'Hark! Taketh thy Pho noodles, thy forsooth, verily and palabras, and bugger off!'

Thanh was distressed. This was a David she had never seen. Her shock forced her to speak Vietnamese telling him she was afraid.

'Xin thưa ông, tôi sợ.'

He snapped. 'And you can stop that bloody gibberish!'

He collapsed on the settee, a broken man. Thanh's heart went out to him. She looked at his loneliness and determined to rescue her hero.

'I wilt not forsake thee, my Lord.'

He turned to look at her, to tell her to get lost. He raised a hand and pointed at her. He wanted to curse and banish her from his life. He stared at her grieving face. He paused then surrendered. His hand collapsed. Here sat the former teacher who became a destitute, broken man. His head slumped on his chest. Thanh paused then spoke.

'If it pleaseth thee, sire, I canst proffer thee money.'

Wow, did that ignite the blue touchpaper. David was incensed, and revived in an instant. He sat up, and bellowed.

'What?'

'I know I must neither a lender nor a borrower be, but for all my learning, surely a small repayment I couldst make.'

Now he was angry. 'I want not thy money, housewife. Canst thou not see? There's no fool like an old fool. Now prithee begone.'

She ain't moving. 'Nay, my Lord.

His anger became fury. 'Nay?'

Thanh resorted to what might be termed friendly blackmail. 'Thou promised a lesson with shopkeepers and I must keep thee to thy word.'

Did she want the lesson? Yes, but her real desire was to have him snap out of his trough of despair.

He stared at her. He remembered his promise, and pride tickled his conscience. He'd given his word. Would he go back on that? No. He glowered at her and hissed.

'Witch.'

She gave no ground. Their staring match continued until he became the first to crack. He waved, ordering her to move.

'Well, get thee yonder. Thou art not yet in my shop.'

She rejoiced. It was a double burst of happiness. David had stepped out of his misery, and she was back in the business of learning.

Knowing how to shop in a non-Vietnamese shop was important to Thanh. She could easily shop using her native tongue but other shops, where only English was spoken, were beyond her reach. She skipped to the light switch and the room was lit.

He managed to stand and stagger to the kitchenette. He turned a chair around making it the counter in his shop. He looked for a tea-towel. She dashed home and collected a cane basket. She returned and bounced towards him, smiles aplenty.

'My basket,' she beamed.

He mocked her, sending up her behaviour. 'Ooooo, my basket.'

He stood behind the back of the chair and indicated the space in front and beside him, and then himself. 'Behold thy green-grocer.'

She stepped forward, excited and enthusiastic. 'Good morrow, sir. Tis a fine new ...'

David held up his hand. 'Wrong,' he declared.

This took the wind from her sails. How was she incorrect?

'Wrong, my Lord?'

David placed the tea towel on his head, and tied the ends beneath his chin. 'Thy shopkeeper art a woman, woman!'

Thanh understood, smiled and stifled a giggle. She bobbed in a small curtsy and cleared her throat. This was fun.

'Good morrow, Mistress. Tis a fine new day methinks.'

David spoke with a Greek-Australian accent. 'Ti thellis?'

More shock for the shopper. Thanh looked confused so the impatient shopkeeper repeated the question.

'Ti thellis?'

Thanh wasn't expecting to deal with a man pretending to be a woman speaking Greek.

'My Lord?'

David switched back to being himself. 'Ha! Gotcha! This country's a melting-pot of nationalities and language. Be prepared.'

She recovered and it was his turn to be surprised when she spoke.

'Intelligence hath seldom failed, my Lord, but for mine own part, it was Gleek to me.'

Just how smart is this woman?

David was impressed. 'Touché.' He remembered a quote by Byron and told her so, 'With just enough of learning to misquote.' She smiled in appreciation without understanding. 'Now, pray continue.'

Examining the imaginary fruit and vegetables, Thanh rehearsed her shopping spiel. 'Prithee Mistress, I desire thy finest vegetives and fruit.' This was a good start.

David switched back to the Greek woman, the part-owner of the greengrocery.

'Okay lady, what-a you want?'

Thanh looked and pointed. 'There, Leather-coats.'

David looked puzzled. 'Leather-coats? Them is apples. How many you want?'

'Prithee, three leather-coats.'

David mimed selecting three apples, and Thanh passed her basket towards him. He mimed placing the apples in her basket.

'One, two ... three. Now, something else, lady?'

She planned to make an Elizabethan salad. 'And violet buds for my sallet.'

David pretended he'd never heard of these things even though it was he who taught Thanh her vocabulary.

'Violet buds? Sallet?' He mimed handing over the goods.

Thanh was firing and produced her list. 'Then love-apples.' She pointed and said, 'Prithee, two firm and ripe.'

David continued pretending to be confused. 'Love apples?' He mimed placing two love apples in her basket. 'Two tomatoes.'

She pointed to different imaginary items, naming each in turn. 'And whortleberries, brambles and apricocks.'

The Greek woman lost patience. 'What are you talking about?' "She" pointed to the imaginary items and named them. 'This here is a blue-a-berries.'

'Nay, whortleberries.'

'And here,' "she" contradicted her, 'this is a black-a-berries.'

Thanh knew her vegetives and fruit. 'Nay brambles are there, and here, apricocks.'

David shook his head. He was dealing with a mad woman, and muttered under his breath. 'Bloody idiot.'

Then "she" walked to the imaginary back of the shop and called to "her" husband, the greengrocer formerly of Athens.

'Hey Con. We got any apricocks?' Con answered saying he didn't understand the question. His Greek wife repeated the request, speaking with emphasis. 'A-pri-cocks?'

Con called back his answer. David re-entered the shop, walked behind the counter, and told the customer the news.

'He say they same as apricots.'

Thanh understood. For her, this exercise was a raging success.

'Prithee of each one handful,' she said.

She offered the basket and the Greek woman mimed placing the fruit therein. Now "she" wanted payment.

'That's-a ten a-dollar.'

Thanh made no attempt to pay but looked at the produce. 'Dost thou have vegetives from Sir Walter Raleigh?'

The Greek woman pretended she had no knowledge of English history, and made a mess of pronouncing the sailor's name.

'Wall-ter Rill-ee?'

Thanh became excited. She spotted her quarry. 'There,' she said, pointing.

The greengrocer looked at the items indicated by the loopy customer, and the shopkeeper's exasperation exploded.

'Them is potatoes!'

Thanh remained calm and placed her order. 'Prithee, five Walter Raleighs.' She remembered how David had explained that the explorer, Sir Walter, supposedly introduced spuds to the Emerald Isle—a tall tale to be sure, to be sure.

The miming of the transfer of spuds took place. David wanted this activity to end.

'That everything, lady?'

'Nay, Mistress,' said Thanh. 'I pray thee, peppercorns.'

She looked but couldn't see them. The Greek woman turned sarcastic and pointed.

'There. Next to the apricocks! Help-a-yourself.'

Thanh did so and bubbled with happiness. She shared her news. 'I maketh for my Lord and Master, poached partridge and peppercorns.'

'That's-a fifteen-a dollar,' said Con's missus, holding out a hand.

Thanh mimed payment of the purchases. 'Five ... ten ... fifteen.'

David mimed accepting the money but stayed in character. 'And you be careful with the part-a-ridge. It can give you the runs.'

Thanh was confused. 'Mistress?'

The Greek shopkeeper grabbed "her" stomach and groaned. 'The runs. Ohhhh.'

Thanh twigged and smiled. 'Ah,' she said, 'shitty, shitty bang bang.' She bowed. 'Good morrow, Mistress.'

What a triumph for Thanh. She'd rehearsed her shopping routine for days. Her grandparents observed rehearsals and, as neither spoke English, Elizabethan English to them was double Dutch with fries.

Thanh waited for her teacher to assess the performance. He went from Mrs Greengrocer to Mr Grumpy. He returned to the settee and collapsed. She craved a response but not the one he provided.

'Depart woman, we will proceed no further in this business,'

Thanh was up on her toes, as bright as a button. 'Doest I well, sir?'

How can I get rid of this woman?

David nodded. 'Aye, yea; now prithee begone.'

Thanh changed in a trice. 'Nay, sir.'

David's anger flared. 'Aye, sir. I am sickly ...' He pointed at her, '... and of thee.'

She had an answer for everything, and stood her ground. 'But, sire, thou promised me the post office.'

He groaned, (a) because he wanted to be miserable, (b) because she spoke the truth and (c) because a teacher's work is never done.

He whined. 'The Post Office?'

She pointed to the former shop. 'Fruit, vegetives, and then the Post Office.' He didn't respond and so copped a reminder. 'Keepeth thou thy word, my Lord.'

He lay back on the settee hoping, wishing this wasn't happening. She folded her arms and tapped her foot. He surrendered.

'Oh, yea.' He pointed at her. 'But thou must Mistress Quickly be.'

'Aye, my Lord. Now I canst sendeth thee my letter.'

He attempted to stand and she helped him. They walked together back to the greengrocer's shop which was transformed. By reversing a chair and using imagination, they created a pop-up post office.

She moved away from the "counter" and took out a real envelope. He positioned the chair and felt his age. He swore.

'Pluto and hell!' She looked at him with concern. He wanted it finished and urged her to begin. 'Well, henceforth do what thou wilt.'

She hesitated, not wanting to repeat the gender mistake.

'Your pardon, my Lord, but art thou now Mistress or Master?'

He snapped. 'Master; an ageing, ailing, piss-ed-offeth bloke. Now prithee begin.' Thanh entered the post office only to freeze. 'Not there' he snapped, pointing and becoming Mr Rude. 'There. Can't you read?' He pointed to the imaginary sign, 'Queue here!'

Thanh moved to the right place and, holding her basket, waited to be called. He mimed fiddling with imaginary objects on his imaginary counter. Time dragged. He kept her waiting. She became impatient, and cleared her throat. Hint, hint. Finally he called. 'Next!'

Thanh approached the counter and stated her order.

'Prithee, sir, one stamp for mine letter.

David is offhand. 'Anything else?'

She is confused. 'Sir?'

He indicated his imaginary counter laden with imaginary items.

'Look, I've got all this junk to sell. Wotcha want?'

'Junk, sir?'

'Yes, look—coins, pens, books; the lot.'

Thanh had only rehearsed purchasing a stamp. 'Nay, sir. Prithee one stamp.'

The man behind the counter grumbled. 'You can't just buy one lousy stamp.' He tried the hard sell. 'How about a toothbrush in your football team's colours?' Thanh had no interest. 'A CD of the world's most unheard of vocalist? A calligraphy set for the illiterate?'

Thanh was definite. 'Nay, sir. Prithee one stamp.'

He scoffed. 'One stamp?'

'Aye, sir.'

He ramped up the selling pressure. Perhaps he was on a commission. 'But look here. A map of South America which doubles as a poncho; or a cardboard corkscrew for teetotallers.'

She shook her head. 'Nay, sir.'

'Today's post office is a two-dollar shop on speed.' He indicated each imaginary item as he tried to make a sale. 'Mobile phone charger for left-handed, unmarried Norwegians. Rain gauge for lapsed Catholics. Winnie the Pooh books with real fake honey.'

She'd had enough. 'I pray thee, sir, one stamp for thy letter.'

She said *thy* when she meant *my*. David seized on her mistake.

'*My* letter? Surely tis *thine*?'

For the first time, Thanh was angry at herself. 'Forgive me, sir. Tis mine indeed.'

Having finally tripped her up, he grinned. 'So, how can I help?' She had already stated her order, and held out a hand for her purchase. He got the message. 'One stamp it is.'

He mimed handing over a stamp, and she mimed the payment. She became annoyed, turned to leave but stopped when he called.

'Hey, just a minute!' She looked back at him as he held out a hand. 'Your change.'

She was embarrassed, humiliated in front of other imaginary customers in the post office. She returned to the counter and collected her change. He grinned and walked past her en route to his spot on the settee. He spoke with a Texan accent.

'Now y'all have a nice day!'

She fumed, believing he didn't play fair. In truth he did because David reckoned that Thanh should be prepared for any eventuality.

He lay back on the settee trying to relax. She stood behind him with folded arms and overheated temper. She looked at him, and spoke with a soft but menacing tone.

'Sir, thou art a cretinous, clapper-clawed codpiece!'

He leant back, relaxed and savoured her grasp of Elizabethan insults.

'Oh well-said, mistress. I love thy wit.'

She moved closer, still behind him, and added more volume and venom to her next insult. 'A measley, onion-eyed lewdster!'

He loved it. He loved the way Shakespeare gave his characters delicious words to attack their enemies.

'I like it! More! Insult me again!'

She did with a rich bitterness. 'Thou flap-mouthed, bat-fowling, fen-sucked bum-bailey!'

David rejoiced. 'Yes!' he cried not looking at her. She departed but stopped at the door. He wanted more and didn't know she'd moved.

'Go on, another insult, I beg thee. More.'

She came back and stood behind him. Her anger died. She didn't mean those curses. This is the man who changed her life. He grinned, waiting for another insult. She paused, being humble and grateful.

She whispered. 'I cannot, my Lord.'

He remembered the curses, how he taught her to use that language, and that gave him satisfaction. He urged her to speak again.

'I love it when thou speakest dirty.'

She stood behind him, quite close. Her strong feelings of love and gratitude to this man were overpowering. She paused knowing she had to speak. Finally she did with softness and sincerity.

'I knowest I love thee.'

The words hung in the air. She turned and left. He laughed until the penny dropped.

That's not a curse. What was that?

He stopped laughing, smiling even, and became serious.

'What?' he asked. He turned to confront her. She was gone. 'Hey!' he got up and hurried to the door, calling. 'Woman! Hey come back. Mistress!' Too late.

He wandered back into his flat and pondered her words. He repeated them. 'I knowest I love thee. What the hell was that all about?'

He scratched his head. He was genuinely confused. 'One minute she's calling me every name under the Sun, the next she says she loves me—and with confidence. I *knowest* I love thee.'

His confusion was disturbed by his ringing phone. He ignored it and spoke aloud.

'Steady, Dave. She's young enough to be your child bride.' But he kept thinking about what she said. 'I knowest I love thee.'

In a sort of trance, he moved to the phone and hit the speaker button. He ran on autopilot, consumed by Thanh's remark.

'Hello Mother,' he said.

She sounded terrible. 'David, I'm dying. I can feel it in my bones.' He said nothing, lost in dreamland. 'Did you hear what I said?'

He replied thinking only of Thanh. He had no idea what his mother had said. 'That's nice.'

She never listened to other people. 'I hope you've arranged the speakers for my funeral service. I know my time is up.'

David fantasised. 'Can one desire too much of a good thing?'

Mother continued her selfish monologue. 'There comes a time when a person knows ...' She stopped. Remarkably she heard what her son said, and was surprised. 'What did you say?'

David did the same thing. He too stopped, and concentrated on what she said. 'I'm sorry. What did you say?'

Now they were on the same wavelength.

Julia became suspicious. 'Have you been drinking?'

'I fear, mistress, I may be drunk on love.'

She became angry. 'Oh you wretched man. You've still got that mail-order bride.'

David drifted back to his fantasy world, in a daze. 'I knowest I love thee.'

She regarded him as a fool. 'You gorbellied, folly-fallen maggot-pie!'

Delight swamped David. 'But that's what *she* said!'

'She's a gold-digger. She only wants your money.'

'Ah, but there's no gold here, Mother.'

'Then it must be sex. And you're obviously popping those ... Niagara pills.'

'Not guilty, m'lud. The young lady's best friends and mine remain steadfastly distant.'

Mother despaired at her son's stupidity. 'How can you be so gullible?'

David had a spring in his step, and a girl in his sights. 'Well you know what the great man told us, Mother. Love looks not with the eyes but with the mind.' He leaned in close to the speaker phone. 'Good night! Good night! Parting is such sweet sorrow.'

He hit the OFF button and Mother was no more. But he was much more than no more. He'd had a revelation. His mind fairly buzzed.

What's happening? Do I have romantic feelings for my student? More to the point, does she have romantic feelings for me?

Then doubts appeared and he gave voice to his thinking.

'You're wrong, Davy; hopelessly so. You're clutching at Cupid's straws. Jove knows I love: But who?' Was David confused? Was he heck? 'Yet I heard her speak.'

He couldn't forget that crucial sentence. 'I knowest I love thee.'

He wandered the room debating his situation. 'Nah, it's my hearing. What she said was, "I goest to make tea". Oh, help me, Will. Crabbed age and youth cannot live together.'

He looked for a drink, found the can, and raised it but stopped before taking a swig. His need for a drink faded. What mattered now was love.

'But what if she *does* fancy me?' He touched his hair and his face. 'Though I look old, yet I am strong and lusty. And older men make better lovers.'

He panicked. A terrible thought flooded his mind.

'Oh God, what if I have to prove it?' He looked down at his "codpiece". 'Is there a lock on the tool shed? Can I still ride a two-wheeler? Do I need Viagras for my Niagras?'

Confusion, even fear, dominated his thinking. He moved to a mirror and examined his countenance. It wasn't pretty.

'What I need is a shave, and a transplant.' He patted his stomach. 'And a bloody corset. Oh, you're right, Oscar. Youth is wasted on the young.'

He fled to the bathroom being chased by despair.

'Aaaaah!'

15

ON THE MORNING AFTER LAST NIGHT'S conflict, Footscray was open for business and Thanh went shopping. She cared not for apricocks but instead for a bag of fruit, rhyming slang for a suit. Forget postage stamps, she wanted cloth. Her plan involved doing something special for the man she loved, her dedicated and brilliant teacher, David Cadwallader Esquire. Outside a shop selling dress material, Thanh window shopped. She liked what she saw and entered.

The sales attendant was the owner, a middle-aged woman who, in the main, sold dress material to women. A dry cleaning business, with hanging garments wrapped in plastic, stood in one corner where the woman's husband operated equipment. The couple were dinky-di Aussies.

The woman approached Thanh. 'Can I help you, love?'

'Good morrow, Mistress. I maketh for my master, new trossers.'

'Trossers?'

'Aye, Mistress.'

'The only tosser here is my old man, and you can have him, for free.'

The husband called. 'I heard that.'

Thanh continued. 'And prithee, Mistress, a gabardine.'

'A what? Look, can you speak English?'

'Verily, Mistress; the finest Elizabethan English.'

The woman was clueless. 'Who's Elizabeth English?'

'Prithee cloth, Mistress, for gaskins and a doublet.'

'Look, are you taking the piss?'

Now it was Thanh's turn to be confused. 'Mistress?'

'And stop calling me Mistress.'

The husband called from the dry cleaning area. 'I wish someone'd call me a mistress. Me number's in the window.'

The woman took control. 'Look, we only sell cloth here, love. Try one of them Vietnamese shops.'

'Thou hast thy finest frippery, Mistress and I hast chinks aplenty.'

The woman started to lose it. 'For Gawd's sake, woman, what the hell are you talking about?'

Thanh pointed at rolls of material. 'Yonder, Mistress, thy finest cloth.'

'That's dress material. D'you wanna make a dress?'

Thanh pointed to the dry cleaning. 'Yonder, Mistress, gabardine and trossers.'

The woman fumed. 'I don't understand. Look, are you on drugs?'

Hubby saved the day. He called. 'She wants material for a gent's suit.'

His wife scoffed. 'And what would you know?'

The husband came in holding a suit. He lifted the plastic and indicated the jacket and the trousers. 'Gabardine and trossers,' he smiled.'

Thanh came alive. 'Aye, verily, a doublet and gaskins.'

The woman added confusion to her anger, and shouted at her husband. 'Well why didn't she say so?'

The husband's light had been well hidden under a bushel for a life time. 'All difficulties are easy when they are known.'

His wife stood gobsmacked. Thanh beamed and replied.

'Knowledge is the wing wherewith we fly to heaven.'

Hubby winked at Thanh and returned to his dry cleaning. Thanh's smile lit up the shop. Thunder face Wife lived up to her name.

'Hang on, just a minute. What's going on here?'

Thanh moved towards some rolls of cloth and pointed. 'Here, Mistress, thy finest cloth.'

'All right, you wanna make a suit. What size is the gent?'

Thanh didn't understand. 'Mistress?'

Mr Dry Cleaning called. 'How art thy Master?'

Thanh understood. 'Oh, quite fulsome, beyond thine codpiece.'

The woman added suspicion to her basket. 'Codpiece? Hang on, this is a respectable shop.'

Hubby called again. 'He's about my size with a verandah over the tool shed. Seven will be plenty, and make sure you give her a good price.'

The woman finally understood. 'Speaking of which, love, let's have a squiz at your spondulicks.'

Now Thanh understood Elizabethan English but a serve of English and Aussie slang had her bamboozled. 'Mistress?'

The woman wanted her own back. 'What's the matter, love, you no speaka da Elizabeth English?'

'Thy chinks, madam,' yelled the dry cleaner.

'Whose cheeks,' fired back his wife?

'Not cheeks, chinks,' he replied. 'It means cash in Shakespearean speech.'

'Shakespeare? Wot's he got to do with the price of fish?'

Thanh saw the situation spinning out of control. 'Prithee Mistress, I desire not much ado about anything.'

The gloves were removed. 'Listen sweetheart, don't you come the raw prawn with me.'

Thanh backpedalled. 'Forgive me, Mistress, I would willingly bite thee by the ear.'

'What!' The woman screamed and prepared to defend her honour if not her ear. Hubby raced out of his dry cleaning area and faced his seething spouse.

'Hold it, hold it, hold it.' His wife simmered, with Thanh afraid.

'The wife pointed at Thanh. 'She just threatened to bite me.'

'No she didn't. She used a term of endearment. She was being friendly.'

'Friendly? Well what the hell does she do when she hates me?'

Hubby explained. 'In Elizabethan English, to nibble on someone's ear was an expression of love and friendship.'

The contretemps was interrupted when a customer came into the shop. The owner called to the new customer. 'Be with you in a tick, love.'

'See,' said hubby. '*In a tick* is Aussie slang. All this young lady did was use slang from the days of good Queen Lizzie the first.'

The wife suffered. She wasn't making a sale and now, for the first time in 37 years discovered her husband had a working knowledge of Elizabethan English—whatever that was.

'I want a word with you,' she said, pointing at him. 'You lied to me. You said you were as thick as pig shit and now you reckon you're the ants pants, and as flash as a rat with a gold tooth.'

Hubby translated for Thanh. 'My Mistress speaketh skimble-skamble.'

Thanh smiled without being confident of her situation.

Wifey attacked Hubby. 'I know you, mate. You are a deadset bogan and a boofhead.'

Hubby bowed to Thanh. 'Behold, thy clodpole.'

Thanh enjoyed the jousting.

Hubby was threatened by his missus. 'You, shut your gob.

'Dun's the mouse,' he spoke to Thanh whose smile grew bigger.

The other customer, unhappy about the lack of service, not to mention the lunatic behaviour, decided to leave. The wife took off after her.

'Hey, Mistress,' she called then swore silently. 'Shit.' Louder, she tried again. 'Madam,' she cried, catching the customer and persuading her to return.

While they chatted, hubby showed Thanh some different rolls of material, helping her choose an expensive cloth for which he undercharged her.

With cloth in basket, Thanh departed, smiling at the still busy owner. 'Rest you merry, Mistress,' said Thanh and left.

The wife looked at her dry cleaning husband. He waved and translated. 'All the best, Madam.'

The Cadwallader family was a perfect example of the term *dysfunctional*. The parents didn't speak to one another or to their children. The children didn't speak to one another or to their parents. Each lived in his or her little world and most made a mess of their life without help from anyone.

David had no savings, a modest government pension, a drinking problem and no future. His relationship with his mother was strained to the point of breaking.

Judith had a partner who was wealthy but difficult. Judith returned to work as a matron in a small nursing home. Her divorce from David came through and she and partner Sue spent their weekends at Sue's holiday house in Sorrento. From time to time Judith thought about her daughter Rosie, her son, Matthew, and her former husband and his mail-order bride. But that's all she did—think.

Matthew had a serious drug problem. He obtained drugs by dealing drugs. His parents once spent serious money on rehabilitation for their boy. It didn't work. Counsellors helped but the power of the drug dragged Matthew back into his world of pain. At times he thought about his parents and sister but never enough to try and make contact. His life expectancy grew ever shorter.

Rosie fell in love with a man and his evangelical religion. She married Aaron and supported him in his ministry. Her parents-in-law were heavy hitters in the same church, and Rosie did her best to be a good wife. Getting pregnant proved easy, and Rosie delivered a son and 15 months later, a daughter. Rosie too thought about her parents, and even more so when Aaron became abusive. She couldn't speak to his parents because they supported their son. She couldn't speak to her parents or her brother because she'd broken all ties.

With their children suffering serious harm, the best news for David and Judith came in the adage—what you don't know can't hurt you. Had the parents known their son lived a destructive lifestyle, their hearts would have been broken. Had the parents known their daughter suffered abuse being threatened in a so-called Christian marriage, their broken hearts would have been buried forever.

As previously mentioned, the appropriate word is *dysfunctional*.

David was up and about with a new reason for living. His student, his beautiful and talented female student, had, the night before, confessed to being in love with—wait for it—him.

He was overweight, unkempt, had a drinking problem and homeless teeth but somehow, miraculously, was found to be attractive by a young and gorgeous single female.

He thought about *Pygmalion* and how Henry Higgins enjoyed a relationship with a much younger woman. Were Higgins and Eliza lovers? And what about that professor falling for a schoolgirl in *Lolita?*

Am I Footscray's answer to Humbert Humbert?

In his bathroom, David got serious. He now believed he had a duty to improve his appearance. No woman wants a slob as a lover. Lover? The word terrified him. He'd been dormant in the intimacy department since he couldn't remember when. He chose not to think about his former wife's possible sleeping arrangements.

He scrubbed his teeth, gargled, spat and gargled again. His last haircut was self-inflicted. Being broke forced his hand, and having used blunt scissors meant wearing a cap became essential.

He tried combing what didn't want to be combed. His hair went on strike and nothing would cajole it back to work.

As to his behaviour with Thanh, David had behaved impeccably, maintaining a professional working relationship throughout. Oh he teased and tricked her with wordplay on a constant basis, but never had he done anything of which he might be ashamed.

If she had taken a shine to him—I knowest I love thee—it was she who made the running. He smiled.

Who would have thunk it, hey? David Casanova Cadwallader.

He considered his wardrobe. The Bard said that apparel oft proclaims the man. David's brain pinged. 'Of course,' he said, remembering a cringe worthy item he rarely wore, and went hunting for it.

Looking radically different, and never having been so clean since his wedding night, David fine-tuned his eyebrows, and jumped when he heard a friendly knock. His heart grabbed excitement. His blood gushed.

She's here. Oh God.

Many times the anticipation of an event becomes more exciting than the event itself. Will knew that. Would that happen now?

Oft expectation fails.

He called from the bathroom. 'Pray enter.'

Thanh did so carrying a large cloth suitcase. She too was excited.

'Good morrow my Lord.' She lifted the case onto the settee, unzipped same and fossicked. She had her back to the bathroom.

He was not quite shaking, but certainly nervous. He delayed his entrance and called again.

'I am without attending to my ablutions. Prithee be seated.'

She refused. 'I cannot my Lord. I bring thee great news.'

Shit! David's nerves went from taut to highly strung.

What is her great news?

He continued hiding, and called again. 'Oh? Pray tell.'

Thanh fussed with the contents of her case. She called back. 'Nay my Lord, I must gaze upon thy countenance.'

Bloody hell. She can't keep her eyes off me. What about her hands?

'Really?'

'Prithee make haste, sire. My heart it beats apace.'

If her heart was beating apace, his was sprinting. He decided. It was time to bite the music and face the bullet. He girded his loins, worrying what might happen if his loins might need to be ungirded, then stepped into the room.

The fact that someone, anyone, had said they loved him, turned David the penniless pensioner, into David the penniless lovesick teen. He lost all sense of reason. Love made him dolally. He leant against the door frame and made a pathetic attempt at being a male model. He would have had more success as a female model. His hair was impossibly slicked, his eyebrows confused, and he wore a fake silk dressing gown with a hint of Asia. A hunk he was not.

Thanh did not notice his entrance. To announce his arrival, he fell back on his hero, the Bard.

'Sweet lady, ho, ho.' She turned, lost control of her jaw with gobsmacked being an accurate description. David explained his makeover.

'I feel much younger today.'

Sadly for him, she was shocked not stunned.

'Why, how dost thou, man? What is the matter with thee?'

The awful truth dawned, and David died. He looked a fool, was a fool, and did his best to rewind with loins ungirded.

'Right. Why stand we prating here?' He changed the subject and pointed to her case. 'I see thou hast to market been.'

Now recovered from the shock of her teacher's "casual clothes day" outfit, Thanh buzzed with euphoria.

'Oh yea, sire, tis truth indeed. I hath bought goods yet speaking only our beloved Elizabethan English.'

'So wise so young. And that is thy good news?' He wanted to leave.

She wanted him to stay. 'It was a test of what thou hast taught me.'

'I see.' He definitely wanted to leave.

She tingled with excitement. 'The stall-holder sold me the finest love apples and the filthiest Walter Raleighs.'

'Really?'

'But he chargeth me too much, my Lord, and thus I told him so. I cursed him as thou hath taught me.'

David forgot his embarrassment. 'Thou cursed him?'

Thanh left her case and moved to David. She touched his arm. It tingled. She looked into his eyes making him weak in the knee department. She spoke with energy.

'Thou wouldst have been so proud, my Lord. Behold.'

She stepped back and re-enacted her time in the Footscray market. Over the months of her tuition, he explained how people might swear and curse one another. Thanh took everything David said as gospel.

He didn't dwell on the topic but she did. Her grandparents would have died had they understood her homework dealt with curses and spells.

Now she had the opportunity to prove her worth. Now all her homework and rehearsing had been put into practice in public. Thanh wanted to thrill David, to show exactly what his teaching had done. She not only got the words correct, her acting verged on the brilliant. Her fury exploded as she repeated what she said to a market stallholder.

'A pox upon thy house, sir, and upon thy children and thy children's children.'

She froze waiting for his response, desperate for his praise. He was in shock. He recovered.

'An excellent curse, and spoken well. He smiled and she was pleased. He still clung to the hope she loved him. 'And that is thy news?'

Surely she must elaborate on "I knoweth I love thee".

Thanh smiled. 'Nay, sir. I hath saved the best till last.'

David almost wet himself. His mind went into overdrive. He was confused, excited and afraid.

The best he could muster was, 'Oh?'

Thanh spoke. 'As I left the market, I declared the sting of my wrath.' David deflated. Thanh repeated another of her Footscray Market free concerts. 'May thou forever kiss the coarseness of thy mother-in-law's foul-smelling arse!'

David's dream was dashed. He hoped for romance and got zip. Never had that great philosopher, Groucho Marx, been more relevant. *If you find it hard to laugh at yourself, I would be happy to do it for you.*

Thanh remained frozen in her curse-giving posture. She hoped her performance was first class. She prayed her Lord and Master would agree. His reply contained surprise and praise.

'Blessed fig's end! Thou hast spoken with the voice of angels.'

Thanh rejoiced. She bowed. 'I thank thee, my Lord. Thou art a most excellent teacher.'

But her delight contrasted with his despair. To him, life was worthless. He'd made a giant miscalculation. He thought this divine young woman fancied him, and he could not have been more wrong. The word *Idiot* was tattooed upon his forehead. He prepared to leave.

'Prithee excuse me. I have my fantasies to ablute.'

Thanh became distressed. He cannot leave now. 'But stay, my Lord.' He paused. 'I have yet to speak of my great news.'

Talk about an emotional rollercoaster. The good news was yet to come.

I was right all along. She does have love in her heart for me, this boring old fart.

He enquired with hope. 'That was not thy great news?'

She beamed with happiness. 'Nay my Lord. I speak roundly of something most wondrous. Tis news to make heaven even the happier.'

David started shaking. 'Goodness. That sounds ... wondrous.'

She loved the fact he used a word she chose in her previous speech. She paused. This was it. This was the full and frank expression of her true feelings for David. She looked into his eyes in a new and wonderful way.

'My Lord,' she said, milking the moment, 'I am in love.'

David feared having a panic attack.

It's true. It is true. I knew all along it was true.

Finally he spoke. 'How now, what is in you?'

'I hath my heart betrothed and can no longer keep from telling thee.'

He replied, managing only a sotto voce, 'Bloody hell!'

She was desperate to explain. 'This matter hath troubled me greatly, sire, but now I feel my heart new opened and love I fain would pledge.'

He steeled himself for momentous news. 'Then pledge, pray pledge.'

Thanh had never been more serious. She paused then knelt and clasped his hands. They sweated and shook.

'It is thee, my Lord, who hath released my heart's desire. It is thee, gracious sire, who hath given me courage and skill to love. I pray thee, grant me thy blessing and tell me thy heart soars as does mine.'

She looked at him, her eyes beseeching his approval.

'It does.' He nodded, fighting back tears and celebrating the momentous news. 'It soars. It soars.'

Thanh stood with heart afire. She lifted his hands and kissed them with a tenderness he found exhilarating. She spoke from the heart.

'Because of thee I hath confessed my feelings to the man I love.'

David was halfway to paradise before she finished her sentence, and could only respond with a groan of pleasure and joy.

'Ohhhh.'

However, his response was neither poetic nor romantic. This was because halfway through his groan or moan, his brain managed to decode her words, and confusion now hath made his masterpiece. He asked a simple question.

'*Because* of me?'

Thanh could not stop smiling. 'Aye, my Lord.'

If the penny had not yet dropped, it was well on its way. 'To the man thou dost love?'

Thanh bubbled. 'He speaketh not Elizabethan English, yet when I spoke what thou hath taught me, he knew my love for him was true.'

David struggled. 'Verily?'

'Aye, verily. And this is what I spoke.' She moved closer and placed a hand on his cheek, paused then repeated what she said to her boyfriend. 'When I saw you I fell in love, and you smiled because you knew.'

David had confirmation. He was out, replaced by Mr X. David strolled down Memory lane. 'I was adored once too.'

'I thank thee, most gracious Lord.'

He snapped back to reality. 'Oh and doth thy Romeo have a name?'

'Aye, he is called Huu.'

David was unsure. 'Who?'

Thanh was pleased. 'Aye, Huu.'

He thought he misheard and made one final enquiry. 'Who?'

She couldn't understand his confusion. 'Yea, Huu.'

Always the joker, David remembered contemporaries of Groucho, namely Abbott and Costello. 'I don't suppose Who's on first?'

Thanh had much more to share. 'And I hath told him of thy great kindness, and he fain would make thy acquaintance.'

A fine offer but David wanted none of it. 'Alas I am busy this day.' That statement could be nominated for Lie of the Year.

'His family will be honoured to welcome thee, sire.'

Shock grabbed David. He lost control of his destiny. 'His family?'

'They wish to herald the great man who helped their son find love.'

David snapped. 'Nonsense.' He saw this offended Thanh, and tried to repair the damage. 'I mean, I goeth not to social events.'

That didn't pacify Thanh. She loved her teacher, and wanted him to meet her true love and his family. David grasped at straws.

'Besides, I hath nothing to wear. Methinks I am a punk.'

She offered a cheeky smile. 'I knoweth that, my Lord.'

Now it was his turn to be upset. 'Thou knoweth?'

Thanh dived into her case speaking as she delved. 'And therefore hath made provision.' She displayed the cloth she had recently purchased. 'Here is cloth to maketh thee trossers and a gabardine.'

He wanted none of that. 'Nay Mistress, you'll do no such thing.'

'But I have begun already, my Lord.'

He snapped. 'Begun already?'

She dropped the cloth on the settee, produced a tape measure, and approached the shop dummy.

What a transformation, a switch in the balance of power. Months ago, David was the boss. He gave the orders and Thanh followed. He set the agenda and she did as told. Now the roles were reversed. Thanh became the boss and David lost control.

'I need thy final measure, my Lord.'

She walked behind him and placed her arms and the tape measure around his waist. It all happened so fast. She was business-like, he upset.

'Hey! What doest thou, Mistress?'

She went to the settee, picked up a pad and pencil and made notes. She returned to measure his arm but first patted his stomach.

'Quite fulsome, my Lord. Eight wild-boars roasted whole at a breakfast.'

'Stop this nonsense,' he protested.

She had a job to do and did it. She lifted one of arms and measured its length. He kept complaining.

'Enough! I protest! How dare thee!'

She made another note and then knelt beside him. 'If thou please, my Lord?' She held aloft one end of the measuring tape but he had no idea what he was supposed to do.

'What?'

She spoke without emotion. 'Wilt thou place the measure at thy codpiece?'

He took a few seconds to understand. She would never shove anything in the vicinity of his crotch. He fumed but took the tape and held it against the top of his inside leg. Tailor Thanh placed the tape at his ankle and checked David's inside leg measurement. He dreaded that she might ask if he dressed on the right or the left.

In the last 12 hours, he admitted he allowed certain lascivious thoughts to linger in his mind but none of them involved being fully dressed and measured.

As he held the tape, he voiced his dissatisfaction.

'This is an outrage!' Once she had the measurement, he tossed away his end of the tape. She stood and made a note.

'I wilt not allow thy business to unfold,' he said.

Thanh refused to take him seriously and delighted in her response. 'Methinks the gentleman protesteth too much.'

David knew he had lost control. He couldn't bully her out of her plan, so he tried a different approach. He went all gentle.

'Forbear this talk. I've done nothing to deserve thy fussing.'

Thanh knew that was nonsense. 'On the contrary, my Lord, thou hast done everything.'

He argued in vain. 'I'm a recluse with no need of garments new.'

'Thou wilt be resplendent, sire.'

His anger reappeared. 'Bugger resplendent; I desire to be alone.'

She shook her head. 'Thou canst not mean that, my Lord.'

He did mean that. His fantasy of romantic love was just that—a fantasy. Now Thanh portrayed him as some hero when all he wanted to do was drink and die. He lost it—big time.

'Damn thee mistress. I wish to be as happy as a bastard on fathers' day, so pray sticketh thy inside-leg measurement up thy fundament and closeth the door behind thee.' He pointed to the door and roared. 'Out damned spot! Out I say!'

The following silence was loud. His anger was rude, crude and hurtful. She was stunned and afraid. Then his anger became shame.

Thanh was speechless. She loved her teacher, adored him. She knew she could never repay his kindness. But at last, she had an opportunity to do something practical to express her gratitude.

She would make him a beautiful suit which he could wear to meet her lover and his family. She would be so proud. Now, her offer had turned to mud. She began to put away the things she brought.

'Prithee forgive me, my Lord.'

Inside, he died. His reaction was way, way over the top and hurtful. He drowned in shame. She risked a quick look at him then started to leave.

David tried desperately to repair the damage.

'No, wait. Don't go.' She kept going. 'Thanh! Prithee, stop!'

She stopped and turned. He moved to her. His face told all.

'It is I who must beg forgiveness,' he said.

She shook her head. 'Nay sir.'

He disagreed with her. 'Yea sir.'

He knelt and took her hands. He looked up, and tears appeared.

She looked at him and remembered the hundreds of words he had lovingly introduced her to since first they met. She remembered his patience, his enthusiasm, his sacrifices and love. She well knew he had no need to apologise to her.

She placed a hand on his cheek and spoke some words of Shakespeare in a calm and kindly way.

'Pray you now, forget and forgive.'

'I must explain,' he said.

He kissed her hands and she helped him to stand. She took control becoming bright and happy again.

'Well then, come, my Lord.' She indicated the settee and mimicked his behaviour to her all that time ago when first they met. She pointed.

'David, sit!'

16

MANY PEOPLE ARE PRIVATE and don't discuss their secrets. Some who experience failure in relationships, employment, finance and elsewhere tend to keep such information under their hat. I mean, why discuss loss? It's possible to get to know someone, even become close friends, and yet never know what may have happened in their past.

David was a good example. He said nothing to Thanh about his marriage failure, his "lost" children, his parlous financial status, or his Moaning Minnie mother. He was a private person.

The more time she spent with David, Thanh discovered that David's life was far from happy although the details remained a mystery.

The same could be said about David's knowledge of Thanh. In their early meetings, it was "Hello Thanh" and "Thanh, sit", and once their teacher/student relationship began, the lessons dominated with little time for small talk. David prepared so diligently and Thanh studied so diligently, that Elizabethan English consumed their time together. But that was about to change.

It was unusual to see David lead the way to the settee. He stood waiting for Thanh to sit then sat next to her. Both were nervous. He turned to her and fell into Shakespeare.

'I am not bound to please thee with my answer.'

She knew he suffered and used the Bard to comment.

'When words are scarce they are seldom spent in vain.'

He nodded, not sure where to start. He wanted to explain why he behaved the way he did. There were reasons for his unacceptable outburst. He kept it simple.

'I am sad. I am old.'

She placed a hand on his arm. 'Methinks young at heart, my Lord.'

He put a finger to his sweet friends. He wished to speak and required her to listen. She understood and he began.

'We each suffer the slings and arrows of outrageous fortune but my pain is worse because of my years. I have lost my family and my fortune. I have lost my will to live.'

There was resignation in his voice. She understood his suffering as his pain became her pain. She tried to help.

'Thou art mistaken, my Lord.'

He reflected on events he had pushed to the back of his mind. He spoke without looking at Thanh, and found it hard going. He stood and moved and spoke with his back to her.

'My life before Footscray was beautiful until it fell on stony ground. The man before you is sad. I am estranged from my family. Once I had dreams of writing, of travel with my wife, and of watching my children grow and be happy. Now my dreams have flown. My darling boy is involved with drugs and may well be dead. My daughter's cruel faith demands no contact with non-believers so my grandchildren hath never even heard of me. My wife despises me and lives with a woman. And my mother berates and belittles me without end.'

He stopped, felt shame, and dredged up memories of things he hated. He despised himself and wept in silence which dominated the room.

Thanh spoke in a soft and loving voice. 'I wilt not forsake thee, sire.'

He didn't hear her, being lost in his painful memories.

'And all this now, at the end of my life, when passion is spent and hope is gone. Why not the beginning or middle of my life? Now, tis too late—too late.'

She objected. 'Nay sir. True hope is swift and flies with swallow's wings.'

He ignored her, not from rudeness but despair. Had he money or courage, he might have sought professional help but he was too proud, too stubborn, too stupid. He bottled up his demons, and now they leapt out to mock and taunt him. He spoke of his lost dreams.

'I was to stroll the streets of Dickensian London; explore Top Withens and Hardy country; and by the Avon, I would worship with Will. He looked to the heavens and called to his hero. Oh Will, wherefore art thou, Will?'

Thanh felt helpless. How could she help the man she loved? How could she rescue him from this quicksand of despair? She found help from her friend, Mr Shakespeare.

'It is held that valor is the chiefest virtue, and most dignifies the haver.

David set off down memory lane, lost in his own world of dreams. 'Then, within me, a book; a sparkling, inspiring text of how to fall in love with the most beautiful language. But alas, my dream is no more and I am undone.'

She understood his despair and reached out to help. 'Nay, sir, nay.'

He slipped further into self-pity. 'Oft expectation fails, and most oft where most it promises; and oft it hits where hope is coldest; and despair most sits.'

He could not halt his tears. Having been locked away for weeks, even months, they burst forth without restraint. He cared not. He wanted to cry, to bare his soul, to reveal his inner man.

She let him weep. Just being with him was enough. She waited. After he settled and wiped his face—with his sleeve, of course—she spoke with a gentle sound imbued with love.

'It is not in the stars to hold our destiny but in ourselves.'

He forced a closed-lips grin, and turned his tear-stained face to her. He performed the most difficult task; looking at his confessor and friend. He gave advice.

'If ever thou suffer misfortune, do so when young.' He indicated himself. 'Behold this pathetic figure. I wear the grotesque robe of self-pity.' He slipped back into misery. 'I am dressed to die but worse, I am too old to care.' He slumped and she moved to him without hesitation.

'Prithee, my Lord, lift up thy heart.'

He recovered somewhat. 'Look at thee; healthy, young, the world at thy feet, with time and scope to dream. Age, with his stealing steps, hath clawed me in his clutch.'

She was desperate. 'I beg thee, sire, desist from thy sadness.'

He rammed home his point. 'And thou hast family, grandparents to love and care for, thy young man and his family. Mine hath absconded and I am undone. Pray forget me. Flee. Live thy life, thou who hath everything and youth.'

He surrendered, stopped caring. He wanted her out of his life. He wanted out of his own life. His past was horrendous. Misreading her love for romantic love, made him a fool, and then he insulted the one person who loved him, and who had done so much to help him repair his life. Now life had no purpose. It was time to wallow in self-pity, and drink himself to death.

She disagreed, and refused to quit. Her heart and mind were super busy. She paused only because to speak would cause her pain, serious pain.

'With my life, twas not always so, my Lord.'

Again he became blind to her presence. He was the centre of his world, and called on the Bard to express his grief, and explain his self-loathing.

'Last scene of all, that ends this strange eventful history ... mere oblivion, sans teeth, sans eyes, sans taste, sans everything.'

It was hardly a game of tennis but in a delicate manner, she returned serve. 'Oh, I have suffered with those that I saw suffer!'

Another pause lingered. Her words finally registered but his sadness dominated. He turned and looked at her.

'Hell is murky!'

She removed some photos from her clothing. 'My Lord, I hath keepsakes.'

He re-entered reality. It wasn't instant, but gradual. His mind needed a major reboot. He looked at her possessions and sought an explanation.

'What?'

She held out her possessions. 'Here is my family, sire.'

He moved back to the settee, sat beside her and took the photos. What he saw reinforced his case.

'Family?' He indicated the people. 'See, healthy, strong and young; young!

She pointed to someone. 'There is my father, my Lord.'

David had a point to prove. 'See, a young man, healthy, professional— and with a future.'

'Alas, not so, my Lord.'

Vietnam 1977

Quang and Hoa Nguyen were reunited on the fishing boat. The couple embraced and wept for joy. Their three older children were delirious with happiness now their dear father was with them. Little Thanh, not yet 2, looked on in amazement. The family had fled from Saigon, suffered enormous hardship and near death experiences, and, yes, they made it. They were safe and on their way.

But after their wild reunion celebrations, the parents settled and took stock. Their situation offered a challenge. The boat was about 14 metres long and could possibly squeeze 60, maybe 70 people on the deck and in the hold. Try double that as 140 were crammed aboard the vessel. Its captain wanted as much money as possible and so health and safety regulations—what regulations?—didn't apply.

This was a coastal fishing boat, a typical Vietnamese vessel, and the Vietnamese were not a seafaring race. Sailing the seven seas in search of new lands was not a Vietnamese trait—poetry yes, exploration no. Their relationship with the sea focused on food, on fish. Now, hundreds of small craft, just like the one carrying the Nguyen family, were sailing out into the South China Sea in the hope of making land in a new and safe country. Good luck with that.

Only minutes into their journey, terrible sounds were heard. People stood and looked. They were still in the mouth of the river but nearby a boat, just like their vessel, was in trouble. People screamed, fell or jumped in the water. The boat was overcrowded, old, not meant for ocean travel.

Quang and Hoa hugged their children, shielding their view as dozens of refugees, just like them, floundered in the sea and drowned. Lifeboats didn't exist and life jackets were plastic bottles or bits of wood—useless.

Hoa looked at her husband and whispered. 'If that boat cannot survive in the river, what hope have we got in the ocean?'

He indicated the children. Scaring the little ones was the last thing they wanted.

On board their small boat, conditions were appalling and, as the journey stretched into day 2, it was obvious people would suffer major hardship. Passengers were so crowded that movement around the deck proved impossible. Seasickness gripped many, and those suffering, vomited where they sat. Toilet facilities were basic for the regular crew of 5 or 6 fishermen. Toilet facilities for 140 didn't exist. People did what had to be done there and then. Complaints were vocal at first but soon faded. Everyone, literally, was in the same boat.

Children grew hungry so grizzled and wailed. Parents despaired. Those in the hold below deck found it hard to breathe. Those on deck were soaked as waves, whipped up by storms, crashed onto the deck. The sea became the shower and lavatory-flush combined.

Quang and Hoa looked out to sea and saw nothing. The horizon disappeared. They could not tell where the sea ended and the sky began.

To think they had left their business and extended family, cheated the re-education camp system, and made a miraculous escape to end up in this situation.

They were shot at by the Communists, nearly attacked by a madman, chased by government soldiers, almost drowned, and made it, only to end up on this old, unseaworthy boat in the wild and heartless ocean.

We should have stayed in Vietnam.

The third night was the worst. They had little food, the babies and elderly struggled to survive, and people stopped complaining because it did no good, when out of nowhere, in the pitch black night, someone saw a glow on the horizon. What choice did they have? The captain headed towards the light. What was it; help or hell?

They got closer and whatever it was scared the already terrified sailors. It seemed to be a giant creature poised on the surface of the sea. They were only about 200 metres away when the boat's engine died. The captain cursed and shouted orders.

People below deck were forced to move. And go where? Those on deck had to make way for the new arrivals. The sardines squeezed ever closer.

The boat drifted towards the glowing object. Now they could see it was an oil rig with lights on different levels reaching up into the black sky. Could anyone on board the fishing vessel speak English?

One man with the basics was appointed spokesman.

People on the oil rig spotted the boat. A dialogue began.

In broken English it meant, "Our engine has failed and the people on board have little food or water. Could we come aboard the rig and be rescued when your supply ship next calls?"

'Not a chance.'

'What about the two pregnant women, the babies and the elderly?'

'Nobody comes aboard the oil rig.'

An engineer used a small boat to cross to the refugee vessel and repair the engine. A modest amount of supplies was ferried to the desperate passengers.

The engineer from the oil rig pointed in the direction of the nearest landfall and wished them luck. The refugees sailed away.

So far so good, and hopes rose. Quang and Hoa finally had a reason to believe they might survive. If the storms stayed away, and the engine kept going, and the directions were correct, their flight from Vietnam might yet have a happy ending; the key word here being *might*.

The next day, someone saw something on the horizon. It came closer. It was a boat. Not big but bigger than their small fishing craft. Someone said the word *pirates* and fear gripped the hearts of all on board.

Quang and Hoa feared death but worse, they feared what might happen to their children if the little ones became orphans.

Who will care for our kids?

Footscray 1999

Thanh pointed to the photo of her father. 'He was murdered, my Lord.'

David remained self-absorbed and despondent, and ignored Thanh's statement. He handed her the photo. 'We will proceed no further.'

Thanh offered another photo. 'And my mother, my Lord; she was raped.'

Now David reacted. He stopped thinking about himself, and processed the meaning of what Thanh had just said but had difficulty accepting the gravity of the situation. He stared at her in disbelief. He took back the photos and gasped. 'Raped? Murdered?'

She handed him another photo. 'And my brothers and sister.' She paused finding it difficult to speak. 'Like my parents, they too, my Lord, are all dead.'

David was now out of his self-pity zone, concentrating on every word Thanh spoke. 'All of your family are dead? All of them?'

Thanh nodded, produced a much folded piece of paper, and offered it to David. He held it with care as she explained.

'The tale of my family, here 'tis translated into the modern English.'

He opened the letter and stared at it. He looked at Thanh.

'I may read this?'

'Aye, my Lord, and prithee aloud.'

He looked at her, took a deep breath and spoke. He felt pressure to be sensitive. He worried, fearing what he might find as he read aloud.

'The Americans left Vietnam, and my parents were afraid. The government sent my father to a re-education camp. My mother fed four children on bo-bo grains.' David was unsure and turned to her. 'Bo-bo grains?'

'Tis grain for horses, my Lord. It swells inside and fills the belly.'

He pondered the explanation then resumed reading.

'Many people disappeared and were never seen again. The authorities were cruel and dangerous.' He looked at his student. 'Who wrote this?'

'My older sister, in Vietnamese, before she died.'

So much death in Thanh's family made David shake his head in disbelief. He returned to the document.

'My mother bribed officials to have my father released. But the authorities stole our home. Many people tried to escape and my parents joined them.' Again he queried what he read. 'Escape?'

'At least one million Vietnamese, sire, and nearly all by sea. We became the boat people.'

'With gold hidden in our clothes, we took food and water and were smuggled out of Saigon. Then we walked for days. We could have been arrested or killed. My mother told us to be as quiet as a mouse but my baby sister, Thanh, would often cry.'

David looked at her. She tried to smile but failed.

'They said I was a noisy baby, my Lord.'

He looked at her solemn face then continued. 'We sank up to our necks in mud, and nearly drowned. My parents were separated but managed to save us. When we reached the harbour, hundreds waited for boats. Our boat was old and small and we were about 140 people.'

'Very crowded, my Lord.'

David resumed reading. 'We left Vietnam and prayed we would be safe. While still in the river we heard screams. An old boat sank and many people drowned. Our journey was hard. We had little food or water. The ship's engine stopped and we drifted. We managed to get going again and hoped we would be saved. Then we saw another boat. We prayed for help but instead met unimaginable horror. The other boat had pirates who did unspeakable things.'

Thanh reached for the letter. She did not want to hear again what had made her cry herself to sleep for years.

'We cannot proceed with this plan.'

She had her hand on the letter but he held firm. Their eyes meet. His voice was calm and filled with respect.

'I would like to continue ... if it is not too hard for thee.'

She paused, released her grip and sat back. Her voice was soft but firm. 'Nay, sir, it is hard but prithee continue.'

David had no idea of the turmoil inside Thanh's mind and body. She felt physically sick and her mental demons screamed as they tried to torment her. David began to read again.

'With clubs and knives, the pirates attacked my father and all the men. They were thrown overboard. Some swam and clung to the end of the boat but the pirates clubbed their hands forcing my father and the others to let go, and drown. The boys too were grabbed and made blood-curdling sounds as they were tossed overboard. Some mothers had dressed their sons as girls to trick the pirates. It didn't work. In the sea, the fathers tried in vain to save their sons. They had no hope. The screams were chilling. No males survived.'

He turned to Thanh and offered her the letter.

'I cannot continue.'

She pushed the letter back.' Yea, my Lord, thou must.'

'I cannot. It is beyond belief.'

'They say, my Lord, that the largest cemetery in Vietnam is the South China Sea.'

He blew air and shook his head. He looked again at Thanh and she nodded. He continued.

'One old man had gold fillings, and the pirates pulled out his teeth with pliers. The girls and women were taken to the pirate ship. Some women smeared engine oil and stinking fish on their faces and hair to deter the pirates from raping them. Nothing stopped the madmen.'

'Nothing stopped the evil and terror. Some young girls bled to death. Some were attacked even after they died. I sat on my baby sister, Thanh, to hide her. I heard my mother cry out as she was raped. Some women begged to be thrown overboard.'

David was in a mess. Thanh wept in silence. Confused, he looked at Thanh. 'Why would the women want to be thrown overboard?'

Thanh whispered. 'Drowning endeth the rapes, my Lord.'

David now suffered a double blow. The appalling details made him ill. Thanh's misery was horrendous but before discovering her life story, he had complained while she said nothing. Her misery was light years worse than his, yet he made a song and dance about his hardship. Thankfully he was near the end of the tale.

'The pirates stole our money and left the women to bleed to death. Our boat drifted and we lived on rain water. We fell asleep listening to our mother sobbing. She prayed for death.'

David became speechless. He looked at the woman, who, as a child, endured this outrage.

'I was lucky to be so young.'

David neared the end of the letter. 'We drifted towards land but the people sent a fishing boat which towed us back out to sea. We drifted until a cargo ship saved our lives. The day we were rescued, my mother died.'

Thanh explained what was not recorded in the letter. 'We were placed in a camp. My sister told her story to the refugee official before she died. As a two-year-old without a family, I was sent back to Vietnam. My mother's unmarried sister had moved to the country and she adopted me. After many years she died, and with the help of agencies, I hath discovered my only living grandparents and so am here, in my new country.' She smiled although it had none of the brilliance or mischief she so often displayed.

David returned the letter. He was in shock. 'Forgive me, I had no idea.'

'Some nights,' said Thanh, 'I canst hear my mother wailing. Today I hate going near the sea and fear any journey by boat.'

He shook his head in disbelief yet wanted to know more. 'So you grew up in Vietnam?'

'In a rural village, sire, like William Shakespeare.'

He found it difficult to speak. 'Thou art amazing.'

'My grandparents sponsored me and now I sew clothes and learn to speak the most beautiful language from the most wonderful teacher.' She touched his arm.

He felt chest pain, which mixed with his shame. The fact that he'd never bothered to explore her life made his self-loathing worse.

'I do not know what to say.'

'Much good fortune is mine, my Lord.'

His misery grew stronger. 'Thou hast brought me great shame.'

This upset her and she protested. 'Nay sir, and thrice times nay.'

He slipped back into that trough of despair. 'I hath bemoaned my fate when beside thine 'tis nothing–nothing!'

'We both hath lost our family, sire.'

He spoke with conviction. 'But thou hath lost family and thy innocence, and now sew clothes for a pittance being told by some, "Go home Asian".'

She spoke with passion. 'But my *good* fortune, sir; freedom, work, new friends ... and thee.'

He stood and wandered away, not being able to look her in the eye. 'My suffering pales beside thine, and I am ashamed.'

She feared for his mental state. 'My Lord.'

Without turning, he pleaded with her. 'Leave me, I beg thee.'

She struggled to speak. 'Nay sir, I wilt never leave thee.'

His voice cracked, and his snot and tears combined; meet David Cadwallader, the blubbering wreck. 'Forgive me then leave me.'

Tension crammed into the room. She wanted to stay but feared if she pushed too hard, he might again lose control and do something terrible. She believed the best response was to do as he asked. Don't argue, just leave. She stopped beside the bookcase, and spoke to David's back.

'A friend is one that knows you as you are, understands where you have been, accepts what you have become, and still, gently allows you to grow.'

She paused, letting the words of the man she once called Will-i-am Shak-es-peare hang in the room. Then she left, leaving silence behind her.

Alone, David believed he'd plumbed a new depth. Never had he been so wretched. Never had he felt such soul-destroying failure. And worse, far worse, nothing could save him. Nothing was worth saving. If ever going to sleep and not waking in the morning was a good ending, now was the perfect time. He told the world what he truly thought.

'Life's but a walking shadow, a poor player, that struts and frets his hour upon the stage, and then is heard no more; it is a tale told by an idiot, full of sound and fury, signifying nothing.'

He made a mournful sound, a word from the language of Death.

'Ahhhh!'

17

JULIA COULD NOT MOVE. After breakfast, she tripped in her sitting room, fell and stayed there. She was in serious trouble. Calling for help was a waste of time. The walls of her apartment could quell the decibels of a riotous party, and her carpets and drapes absorbed sound. Her cleaner came on Wednesdays and today was Friday. Death by starvation or dehydration is indeed terrible but does the mind go before the body?

She could think of only one solution. She must crawl, drag herself or do whatever was necessary, and get to her phone.

She started. Her wasted muscles failed to respond. They were next to useless. Julia never believed in the "use it or lose it" mantra. She cried, and cried out. Ten minutes after she started her journey, she'd only just left the starting blocks. Her phone was nearby but it may as well have been a mile away. She couldn't travel in a straight line, and had to go via the furniture. She needed something to grab hold of in her inch-by-inch trek. A rest became essential and the rests became longer with every pit stop.

Her nonagenarian bones were brittle. Had she broken a hip? Many people her age received a hip replacement but that was due to wear and tear. Did she have a fracture? Whatever muscular or skeletal problem she had, her pain was bracing tending to agony.

As she struggled in South Yarra, across town in Footscray, her older son matched her misery. Two nights ago, he endured grief and humiliation. Once Thanh left, he drank, and kept on drinking over the next two days. On the third day he was as sick as a dog with his mental health even worse. He discovered his student, his companion and friend, had lost her entire family in mind-numbing circumstances. For months, he'd grumbled about his lot in life and never once enquired about Thanh's background. The only reason she finally spoke up was to try and show him that life goes on, and people can rise above tragedy.

William Shakespeare suffered his own tragedy when his young and only son died. But the great man kept writing plays and poems, which still delight, inspire and educate millions of people. Will and Thanh got on with life—what about David?

He slept badly on his second bed, the settee. His thoughts were in turmoil and he saw no reason to carry on living. His student loved her young man; they would marry, and David would lose her. She was the reason he attacked each new day in his impoverished world. She would leave and, right now, he could touch his sadness.

Then the phone rang and his woes increased. He sat up, dislodged an empty can and swore. 'Rabbit-sucker!'

He forced himself to the phone and hit the speaker button.

'Yes, Mother, I'm here.'

He found it hard to hear her. 'David, I'm dying,' she croaked in a raspy voice.

'Have you taken your tablets?' She didn't answer. 'Mother? Have you taken your tablets?'

'I'm dying.' This time she spoke louder. Her message was the same but her delivery had changed. David noticed this and worried.

'Mother, are you all right? Are you ill?'

'Fall,' was all she said.

'Have you had a fall?'

'Yes. I'm on the floor.'

'Right, I'll ring an ambulance and have Mrs Perry open your door.'

'Hurry.'

'I'm going to hang up, Mother, so I can ring for an ambulance.'

'My hip hurts.'

'I understand, Mother. Stay where you are.'

Stay where you are? What a brilliant comment. Do you think she's going to start tap-dancing and follow that with the splits? Moron.

For once, he didn't enjoy ending a phone call with his mother. He stopped bemoaning his lot in life, and worried about her. He didn't want her to die, and certainly not alone, collapsed on the floor. He requested an ambulance, then rang Mrs Perry, a resident in his mother's building. She had a key to Julia's apartment for an emergency just like now.

David rang his mother's phone. It rang out. 'Oh Jesus, no,' he cried. 'Not now, not like this.' David despaired.

What do I do? Ring my brother?

He tried his mother's number one more time. As it started to ring, someone knocked on his door. Life had two certainties for David. If his phone rang, it was his mother. If someone knocked on his door, it was Thanh. He didn't want to end the call so yelled to the door. 'Come in.'

Thanh entered carrying her cloth case. It was three days since she was last in David's flat. At that time each discovered the tragedies in their respective lives. A time apart seemed wise and gave Thanh time to sew. She wasn't her father's daughter for nothing, and he would have been so proud.

David spoke. 'I'm on the phone. My mother's had a fall.'

Immediately Thanh became serious, dropped her case and hurried to David's side.

'What canst I do, my Lord?'

The phone was answered.

'Hello,' said a voice.

'Mother?'

'Mr Cadwallader, it's Veronica Perry.'

'Oh Mrs Perry, thank goodness. How is my mother?'

'I think the term is "resting". I helped her into her favourite chair and the ambulance people have just arrived. Would you like to speak to her?'

'Yes please.'

'Hello,' said a croaky voice.

'Hello Mother. How are you?'

'Terrible.'

'That's good. Now Mrs Perry will let me know what happens, and I'll come and see you as soon as I can.'

'Which we both know means next year, if I'm lucky. The ambulance people are here now. Ow!' Mother winced then snapped. 'I said, "Nothing downstairs"!'

That's a good sign. It's when she goes silent I have to worry.

Mrs Perry took the phone and told David she would call again as soon as Mrs Cadwallader had been assessed.'

'Thank you, Mrs Perry. You're a wonder. Goodbye.'

He replaced the phone and looked at Thanh. She smiled, and that alone made him feel better. The last time he looked at her they were both in tears.

'Dost thou have good news, sire?'

'Possibly, and the ambulance people have arrived. We can but hope that all's well that ends well.'

'Hope is a lover's staff, my Lord. Walk hence with that and manage it against despairing thoughts.'

He looked at her in wonder. In a few months this woman had gone from no English to fluent Elizabethan English, being able to grasp the intricacies of the Bard's words.

'Aye, tis verily so.'

'Then rejoice, sire, because I have even more good news.'

He was stunned. A few days ago she revealed the horrific tale of her murdered family. Those memories tore at her heart—and his. Now she was beaming, bouncing on her toes, and dispensing joy with gay abandon.

He suffered and worried. 'Pray tell.'

'Sire! I bringeth sweet offerings.'

Normally her presence would make him feel great. Not so this morn. Now the excessive alcohol and depression left him wretched. Bugger the good news. He felt shithouse, headed to the settee and collapsed. His mother, his despair, and the demon drink combined to make him faint.

Immediately she went to him, concerned for his health. 'My Lord, thou art ill.'

'Not ill, mistress.' He burped. 'Hung-over.'

She copped a blast of his foul breath. 'And methinks a friend of thy wine.'

He slipped back into his old miserable self. 'Begone woman so I may gorge myself on misery.'

'Gladly my Lord, but first thy fitting.'

She tried to help him stand. Being manhandled, he said what he felt. 'Ah! Stop those bloody drums.'

He was upright—just. She collected something from her bag.

'Here sire, thy new gabardine.' His jaw dropped. 'Tis for thy meeting this day.'

He remembered. Thanh had arranged for him to meet her young man and his family. He wanted none of it. 'Nay,' he protested.

Thanh held the coat as would a shop assistant for a customer. 'Come my Lord, thou wilt be resplendent.'

He upped the protest. 'Nay! Begone!'

She took one of his hands and guided his arm into a sleeve. 'Come sire, be thou trimmed.'

He was being trimmed, er, dressed and was not happy. 'Cease thy labour! I do not desire this.'

Although complaining, he put his other arm in the other sleeve while she collected his trossers. She had them over her arm, and approached as he grumbled and stumbled.

'Now sire, away with thy old trossers.'

Without thinking, she took hold of his belt buckle, and attempted to remove his ancient strides. He exploded.

'Hey! Desist woman! Desist I say!'

She stopped, realising she had overstepped the mark, and turned her back to him.

'Prithee forgive me, sire.' She even raised a hand to shield her eyes. 'I wilt mine eyes avert.'

He glared at her. He did not want this generosity. But after what he had learnt about her family, and after all the joy she had brought him since he arrived in Footscray, he could not deny her this small pleasure.

He muttered. 'Thou art evil, mistress; evil!'

He continued to mutter but followed orders. He undid his belt and removed his old trousers revealing even older underpants. He once used them to wash his beloved MG, but since Wilkins Micawber became his financial adviser, it was a case of waste not, want not.

He performed this drop-your-daks routine in the standing position which, for a man in his condition, was not wise. In removing the second leg, he lost his balance and fell forward. Thanh panicked thinking he was about to replicate his mother, so grabbed his arm.

'My Lord!' she exclaimed.

He shrugged off her helping hand, and steadied the ship. 'Begone woman, I am still able.'

They stood facing one another, he with the bare and ragged legs. She offered him the new duds, and he offered her the old. They exchanged trossers. She placed the old in her bag and he placed his legs inside the new. She stepped forward to steady him, and again he rebuffed her.

'Yea, enough! I may be old and with ale but I am still manly ...' He zipped up the new strides, speaking as the zip struck 12. '... just.'

She was much impressed, thrilled with her handiwork, and so pleased to see the man she loved and admired finally looking resplendent. She circled him giving a wee tug of his jacket here and there.

'Oh my Lord, verily thou art a picture. Shall I compare thee to a summer's day? Thou art more lovely and ....'

'Enough Mistress! I do not want this. I have lived long enough.'

She hated his unhappiness. 'Come sir, what nonsense is this?'

161

He explained. 'Thy family's suffering makes my suffering seem as none. And now you bestow great kindness I do not deserve.'

She spoke the truth. 'Hither I wilt repay thy kindness.'

'Kindness? I hath burdened thee with my self-pity.'

'Nay, sire, thou hast showered me with love unbounded; with that precious gift of language, thou hast made my tongue sing words of truth and beauty.

'Piffle!'

She got serious. 'We both hath suffered the slings and arrows of outrageous fortune, my Lord, but that is time past. Now, this day, we hath love, hope and life to share and enjoy.'

He shook his head. It was his defence. He wanted to thank her and rejoice but pride and self-pity crushed his ability to be honest.

'What tomfoolery is this thou speaketh?'

She had two items on her agenda. The first, the suit, was complete. She began the second, and spoke with a soft and gentle voice.

'One request I wouldst make, my Lord.'

'Request?'

'At my betrothal, sire ...'

He snapped, his anger on show. 'I told thee, I goeth not!'

She didn't argue. She let his anger and rudeness fade. She paused, having considered this moment for weeks and having long rehearsed her line.

'Wilt thou be my father?'

That shocked him. He was speechless. He needed more details. He needed an excuse. The volume of his voice dropped a decibel or three.

'What?'

'I am to be given away, and if I could choose one person in the entire universe, sire, it would be thee.' She moved closer and eye contact ruled the day. 'Say thou wilt, my Lord. I know love dwells in thy heart. Share thy love and I wilt be proud beyond measure.'

He suffered, felt ashamed. Her kindness was overpowering. He wanted to weep and stuttered a reply.

'I cannot. Nay.'

She took his hand, looked at him with more love than he could imagine, and delivered the knockout punch.

'I knowest I love thee.'

His resistance vanished. He nodded then whispered. 'Yea, yea I shall.'

Thanh was overjoyed. She bounced on the spot. She kissed his hands.

'Thank thee, sire, thank thee.' She ran to her bag and removed a new shirt and tie which she placed on the settee. Then she produced his only half decent pair of shoes which she'd pinched then cleaned and polished till they shone. She bought him a new handkerchief. She ran back to him.

'Shoon, my Lord and thy napkin.'

He was bowled over by her enthusiasm and love.

'Mistress! What doest thou?'

She placed the shoes at his feet and tucked the handkerchief in his breast pocket. It would match the shirt and tie on the settee. She collected her bag and started to exit.

'Hasten my Lord; all the world's a stage and we are both surely players. Now, I must Mistress Quickly be.'

She blew him a kiss and departed in a hurry.

He shook his head in wonder at all that had transpired since he and Thanh had their heart to heart only two days ago. He removed his jacket and dreadful shirt before putting on the new one. He put on his new tie then sat on the settee and put on his shoon. He talked to himself.

'What fools these mortals be. What a deformed thief this fashion is.' With shoes, shirt and jacket on, he stood. 'Then up he rose, and donn'd his clothes.'

He wandered to a mirror and admired the new David. He adjusted his napkin and smiled. But his happiness vanished as the phone rang.

'Just when life offers a glimmer of hope.' He crossed to the table and hit the speaker button. 'Mrs Perry, what news?'

'Mrs Who?'

'Mother? Why are you answering the phone?'

'Because I can.'

'But your fall? What did the ambulance crew say?'

'Apparently I tripped over my self-pity.'

'Are you sure you're all right?'

'I won't be unless my son deigns to assist his dying mother.'

'You sound normal, Mother.'

'I've run out of my heart tablets. I need you to go to the chemist, immediately.'

'I'm sorry, Mother, but I'm rather busy.

'Busy? You're never busy.'

'I've been invited to a soiree in Footscray.'

'That's sounds like an oxymoron.'

'I'm going to meet Thanh's fiancée's family.'

'Oh you're not still living with that money-grubbing foreign bride?'

'Not quite. And there's more news, Mother. My new teaching career has taken flight.'

'What new teaching career? You've never mentioned that.'

'Au contraire, Madame. It must have been one of those rare conversations when you failed to listen to a word I said.'

'Oh, for pity's sake, you can't teach. You're too old.'

'I've been tutoring a young student who has majored in Shakespeare.'

Whack! That stopped Julia in her tracks. Her critical comments changed to genuine interest. 'Did you say Shakespeare?'

'I did, and as you're an expert on the Bard, I wondered if you might quiz her?'

'Don't be ridiculous. I'm far too old.'

'Now be fair, Mother. If anyone can find fault with my student, it's you.'

'I can't.'

'Yes you can. You're a genius when it comes to finding fault.'

'But I'm dying, and want to be miserable, and wallow in self-pity.

'That's copyright. I have that line.'

'What did you say?'

'Oh please Mother. You used to be so good at testing my Shakespeare.'

That was the clincher. Secretly she would love to be involved with anything to do with the Bard, but pretended to be making a huge sacrifice.

'All right. Bring her with you when you fetch my pills.'

'Actually she's here now.'

'What? Now?'

'She's outside. I'll have her recite for you over the phone.'

More grizzling and grumbling emanated from South Yarra.

'Well don't be long—my hair is getting tired.'

David went to his front door and called. He could have knocked on Thanh's door but had long sensed her grandparents, with whom he had shared nods but never spoken, regarded him as a cross between a snake-oil salesman and a pervert.

'Mistress? Art thou within?'

David waited. Then Thanh's door opened and she appeared. He gasped. Wearing a traditional Vietnamese red gown with high collar, exquisite beading, and matching headpiece, she accepted his hand and entered his flat.

Once inside, she turned to David and bowed. 'My Lord,' she said and smiled. He was dazzled.

Thank God I'm wearing these decent clothes, he thought.

'Mistress,' he replied and bowed.

He took her hand and led her close to the speaker phone. He put a finger to his sweet friends indicating she should be quiet. He whispered. 'I want you to recite some Shakespeare for my mother. Prithee, wilt thou?'

Thanh nodded but shook with nerves and excitement. She'd never performed before except for her teacher. David spoke to the examiner.

'Mother, may I introduce my Shakespearean student.'

Silence. Mother was uncertain. 'I can't hear a thing.'

David smiled. He only had eyes for Thanh but explained to his mother. 'Patience, Mother.'

Again he smiled at Thanh. Mother misunderstood his last sentence and assumed the student had been introduced.

'Oh, hello Patience,' she said.' The teacher and his student shared their amusement. 'Well get on with it. Let me hear your Shakespeare.'

David stepped back and gestured to Thanh to begin. This was a big occasion; Thanh's first "public" recitation. She took a deep breath, stood tall and recited.

'Spread thy close curtain, love-performing night,
That runaways' eyes may wink, and Romeo
Leap to these arms, untalked of and unseen.
When the night comes and everyone goes to sleep,
Romeo will leap into my arms, and no one will know.
Come, gentle night; come, loving, black-browed night;
Give me my Romeo; and, when I shall die,
Take him and cut him out in little stars,
And he will make the face of heaven so fine
That all the world will be in love with night.'

She looked at David. His heart thumped with pride. His eyes told her so as he spoke to the critic in South Yarra.

'Mother?'

'She's very good.'

More smiles between teacher and student. David spoke.

'Shakespeare was right, Mother. Love looks not with the eyes but with the mind.'

Julia gave a detailed assessment. 'She speaks quite well. I would say she lives near me in South Yarra.' The others were delighted. 'Does she go to Merton Hall?' More smiles in Footscray.

'That's quite remarkable, Mother. May I ask her to read for you again?'

'Well all right. But don't forget my heart tablets.'

'Perhaps we could both come and visit you?

Thanh looked at David and nodded. Her happiness overflowed. Mother, on the other hand, was shocked.

'Visit me?' She considered the suggestion, and most definitely wanted it to happen but suppressed her happiness. 'Well, that might be nice.'

'Yes, it would be nice. Thank you, Mother.'

Thanh wanted to express her gratitude. 'Thank thee, Mistress.'

Mother was chuffed. 'Thank *thee*. And fare thee well.'

David stood by the phone. 'I'll come and see you soon, Mother. Fare thee well.'

He hit the button, and the couple wore grins you could bottle. They joined hands and skipped in a circle. They stopped and beamed at one another.

'My God, Pickering, we did it.'

Thanh had yet to discover Mr Shaw's tale but right now she understood how months of study had produced spectacular results. However, David's health was the most important thing on Thanh's mind.

'To see thee smiling, my Lord ... tis wondrous.'

They faced one another and fell back into those early lessons where it was Shakespearean quotes at 20 paces. He started the ball rolling.

'Shall I compare thee to a summer's day?'

She relished the game. 'Thou art more lovely and more temperate.'

'I do love nothing in the world so well as you.'

Thanh came alive and meant what she said. 'Hereafter, I shall desire more love and knowledge of you.'

Shakespeare, it seemed, had written these lines exclusively for David and Thanh. 'Love is not love which alters when it alteration finds.'

'If music be the food of love, play on,' she replied.

He remembered they had a function to attend. He was to escort Thanh to her young man's family with him, David, the guest of honour. He indicated the door and offered his arm.

'Come Mistress, let us depart.'

She slipped her arm into his. 'My gracious Lord.'

'Now wilt there be dining at thy fiancé's dwelling?'

'Oh aye, my Lord.'

'Wilt there be some of thy finest Vietnamese cuisine?'

'Indeed, and which surely will visit thee with …'

They froze, faced one another and spoke as one.

'Shitty shitty bang bang.'

They laughed without restraint and began their journey.

Thanh's grandparents were unwell and unable or unwilling to attend the engagement party. As the elderly couple sat in their small flat, the sound of David and Thanh's laughter lingered long after the couple walked down the stairs.

18

THE TAXI PULLED UP outside the former Cadwallader residence. The family, well the parents, had moved out many moons ago, once their children had flown the nest. Actually *crapped* in the nest was a better description. The new family in residence was a like for like replacement. They were Caucasian, Australian, and middle class—a husband, wife and two teenage kids, although these kids were still on the rails.

The passenger in the cab struggled to alight and used up much of her cash in paying the fare. She had a 2 year old boy in tow, a baby daughter on her hip, and a suitcase containing their worldly possessions. The taxi departed, and the woman wiped the runny nose of her toddler son then rearranged the dummy in her daughter's mouth.

'This way,' said the mother, and walked up the drive. Nervous, she knocked on the door, and was surprised when a teenage girl appeared.

'Oh,' said the visiting mother. 'Who are you?'

'Who are you,' came the reply? The girl called into the house. 'Mum?'

A middle-aged woman appeared. 'Can I help you?'

'Hello. Yes, I used to live here. My name's Rosie. I didn't know my parents had moved. Have they sold the family home?'

'They certainly have, ages ago.'

Rosie was stuck. She didn't have a Plan B. 'Ah, could you tell me their new address, please?'

The homeowner spoke to her daughter. 'Get me that address book by the phone.' The young teen departed.

'I don't have either address,' said the woman. 'But I may have their solicitor's details.'

'Did you say *either* address,' asked Rosie?

'Yes, Mr and Mrs Cadwallader separated.' Shock and sadness struck the caller. The teenager returned with a book. The woman flicked over some pages. 'Here it is. Do you want to write it down?'

Rosie struggled. She'd just discovered the parents she hadn't spoken to for years were no longer a couple, and Rosie's family home belonged to another family. Rosie's daughter grizzled and her son pulled at her hand.

'Mummy,' he pleaded.

The woman stepped inside and came back with a pen. Rosie fossicked in her shoulder bag to unearth a piece of paper. The woman took pity on Rosie, and scribbled the details on a page in the back of her book, tore out the page, and handed it to Rosie.

'That's the solicitor our solicitor dealt with. They should be able to give you the address of where one or both of your parents are now living.'

Rosie gratefully took the paper then left. She was doing it tough. Little cash, two irritable kids aged 2 and under, and no idea how to get to the office of the unknown solicitor.

She made it down the drive, parked on the nature strip, and sat on her suitcase. From her son's small backpack, she extracted a bottle and some biscuits. She fed him. Her daughter needed a nappy change. What, here in the street? This adventure was getting to be way too hard.

One tear trickled down Rosie's face. Another sat primed to enter the fray. Her life was a mess.

She decided to walk to the nearest shops and find a public phone although who she would call was uncertain; the Salvation Army perhaps. Her decision to run away from her husband, his family and their church, looked like a giant mistake. She had good reason to flee but her life now was a case of jumping out of the frying pan and into the you-know-what. With suitcase and kids, she set off—slowly.

She hadn't gone half a block when a car tooted and pulled up beside her. Inside the vehicle were the mother and daughter she met a few minutes ago. The mother called. 'Hop in. We can drop you at the solicitor's office.'

Rosie burst into tears. At her lowest ebb, any act of charity became overwhelming.

The mother lied about having to go shopping. She felt sorry for Rosie and told her daughter they would find her and help. The car took Rosie to the address, and she couldn't thank the woman and her daughter enough.

The young mother with her kids and chattels entered the solicitor's office. A receptionist looked over her glasses.

'Can I help you?'

'Yes,' said Rosie juggling offspring. 'My name is Rosie Cadwallader, well it was, and I'm trying to locate my parents, David and Judith Cadwallader.'

The receptionist knew the name. 'Will you take a seat please?'

Rosie dumped her luggage, and tried to settle her children. A woman appeared and spoke.

'Rosie?'

The woman was Sue the solicitor, and soon Rosie and tribe were in the spacious office of their mother and grandmother's partner. Once settled, Rosie gave little explanation of her situation but finished with, 'Can you help me contact my parents?'

Sue gave a solicitor's smile which had several meanings. Being a savvy solicitor, she was good at eliciting information, and even better at concealing it.

'I can,' she said, 'but tell me, why are you looking for your parents? I understood you'd married and joined a church which has no contact with non-believers.'

Rosie sighed. She didn't want to recall unhappy times and besides, her kids grew ever more restless. Sue stood, excused herself, and then returned with the receptionist. She was a grandmother who regularly cared for her own toddlers, and now offered to mind the children. Rosie again felt an urge to cry.

Now childfree, she chose to reveal some basic facts. If this was the way to find her folks, then it was a price she was willing to pay.

'I've had difficulties with my husband and in-laws, and wanted a break. The only people I can ask for help are my parents. I had no idea they were separated.'

'Divorced,' said Sue.

Rosie gasped. 'I didn't know.'

'I know your mother tried a number of times to contact you but I gather you refused to answer her letters or return her phone calls.'

Rosie put her head in her hands. Shame and sadness washed over her. Decisions she made about her family, now came back to haunt her. Sue said nothing and allowed Rosie to recover. She did, a little.

'Do you have any news of my parents and brother? And please let it be good.'

Sue shrugged. 'Sadly your brother, like you, has lost contact with your parents but I believe has an issue with drugs.'

This time Rosie's tears were from sadness. 'And my father,' she asked?'

'I believe he lives in a small flat in Footscray.'

'Footscray,' said a surprised Rosie?

'Yes, I believe he lost all his savings in a fraudulent scheme run by your Uncle Robert, who is now in jail.'

Rosie sat stunned. How much bad news can there be? 'He lost *all* his money?'

Sue nodded. 'But there is some good news as he now has a new wife.'

Rosie shook her head in disbelief. 'My father is broke and lives in Footscray with a new wife?'

'I'm told she's Asian and about your age.'

Rosie was glad she didn't have her children with her as she might well have dropped them when told this news. Being whacked in the face with a large fish would have had less of an impact. Eventually she asked a pertinent question.

'May I ask how it is you know so much about my family?'

'That's easy. Your mother and I live together.'

Well, talk about saving the best or worst till last. Rosie stared at Sue who said nothing. She was good at poker was Sue.

The last two minutes for Rosie could well be described as eye-opening. Her brother was a junkie, her father was broke and living with an Asian child bride, and her mother had divorced her father and moved in with a woman, the one now talking to her. *Were the women lovers?*

For a fleeting moment, Rosie wished she had never left her husband.

'Would you like your father's address,' asked Sue?

'I would, please,' replied Rosie. 'And my mother's too, if that's all right.'

Sue wrote a certain Footscray address, and handed the note to Rosie. 'I think perhaps I should ask your mother about a suitable meeting time. I can tell her tonight that I met you and your children.'

'Her grandchildren,' said Rosie returning serve.

'Of course,' said Sue with half a smile.

Rosie got the picture. Sue was a solicitor, possibly a lover, and most definitely a gatekeeper.

If I want to meet my mother, I have to go through Sue.

Sue walked Rosie to Reception and smiled. 'Nice to meet you, Rosie,' she said and disappeared. The receptionist did a brilliant job with the kids.

'I think the little one needs a nappy change,' said the receptionist. 'There's a bench in the ladies' loo.'

Rosie decided the world had at least two types of humans, and Sue and her receptionist represented opposite ends of the spectrum.

After her baby was changed and chipper, Rosie asked for directions to Footscray.

'The station is just over Chapel Street, and from Flinders Street, you take the train to Footscray. Ask anyone at the stations.'

Rosie smiled, thanked the lady profusely then headed off to meet her long-lost pater; the man who was broke but apparently still able to pull the birds.

David's social outing with Thanh was a hit. It was to celebrate the engagement of Thanh and Huu. Linguistically there was a mix of Vietnamese, broken English and Elizabethan English.

Thanh's boyfriend's family treated David like royalty. He couldn't believe the affection, even adoration they showered upon him. Thanh had described David as a saint. And to top off the grand occasion, the food was magnificent, and the hospitality superb.

David's elevated status was all down to his student. She told the truth. She explained how her neighbour had, without pay, taught her to speak a beautiful form of English, and how he encouraged her, had helped and advised her enabling her to express her love for Huu.

The young man was over the moon having met such a wonderful girl, and joined his fiancé in wanting to thank and help David in any way he could.

With the celebrations over, David begged to leave announcing that he had to visit his mother who had recently had a fall. He bowed, thanked Huu's parents and grandparents, shook Huu's hand and kissed Thanh's hand.

He waved and started to leave but stopped when Thanh spoke. 'Forgive me, my Lord, but how art thou to travel to thy mother?'

'I will use the usual way, now that they call me Mr Public Transport.'

Thanh looked at Huu.

'If you will permit sir, I would be honoured to drive you there in my car.'

David was shocked at not just the offer but by the young man's sincerity. 'That's very kind of you but it's really not necessary.'

'Come, my Lord,' said Thanh, 'you have sounded the very base-string of humility, but now let us depart.'

David was swept up in the enthusiasm of the young couple. He was half led, half pushed and, looking back, saw the Huu family smiling and waving.

The car arrived in South Yarra with David thankful, and wishing them a safe return journey. For Thanh, that was never part of the plan. She and Huu would wait and drive him home when his visit was o'er. He was overcome with their kindness but then decided to try a little reciprocity.

'Prithee, come with me to meet my mother.'

Thanh was surprised. 'My Lord?'

'I insist. I know she would like to meet my student called Patience, and her young man.'

David insisted and soon it was smiles all round as the trio mounted the steps to Mother's apartment. She was expecting only her son, and her jaw headed south when he appeared, looking quite splendid, accompanied by two "foreigners" dressed in traditional and striking costumes.

'Mother,' declared David. 'May I present my Shakespearean student and her fiancée? This is Thanh and Huu.'

Thanh bowed and spoke, 'Greetings Mistress.' Julia was impressed. Huu repeated the procedure, and Julia contracted a rare malady—being tongue-tied.

'It's only a short visit, Mother, so may we come in,' asked David?

Julia's shock retreated a little and she soon had three guests in her sumptuous living room. The young couple sat in awe of their surroundings. David hogged the conversation with Mother finding it difficult to concentrate in her own home as her ability to whinge and complain became lost in the traffic.

David had counselled Thanh and Huu about when to leave and, upon his subtle signal, the young couple stood, bowed, graciously thanked their hostess and left. David showed them out then returned to his mater. She regained her expertise in being able to complain.

'I do not appreciate you bringing strangers to my home at all, and certainly not without notice.'

David smiled. 'Oh, come now Mother, you loved it.' She stiffened. 'And besides I know you wanted to meet the gold digger.'

He left the line hanging. Her face was a picture. 'Don't tell me she's the child bride?'

David nodded. 'That she is, and due to wed her young man. All I've ever done is teach her Elizabethan English.'

Mother was struck dumb. She found it incredibly difficult to offer congratulations or admit she'd made a mistake. Nothing new there. She settled for a grunt.

'And would you believe Thanh has asked me to give her away at the wedding.'

Julia mounted her high horse. 'What's wrong with her own father?'

David grimaced. 'Don't ask, Mother. It's a tragedy of epic proportions, something about the South China Sea being the largest cemetery in Vietnam.' She imagined horror. 'You should come to Thanh's wedding, Mother.

'Don't be ridiculous.'

He changed gears. 'Now, about you having a fall.'

'I'm fine.'

'I've spoken to Dr Pitt the Younger.'

'How dare you.'

'He's arranged for you to have a new emergency button which you must wear at all times, a wheelchair for when you go out in public ...'

'A wheelchair! Never!'

'... and for a visiting nurse to come several times a week.'

'Over my dead body.'

'Be careful what you wish for, Mother.' He grinned. She scowled. He bent and kissed her head.

'What's your game,' she snarled? 'It's usually your brother and his money-grubbing wife who deal in subterfuge and skulduggery.'

'No game, Mother; it's a plan to give you the best quality of life your money can afford.'

She grunted a second time. Deep down, she was delighted to have welcomed genuine visitors who were polite and interesting, not to mention dazzling, and to have a son who had taken steps to ensure she received the support she needed.

'I'll call you tomorrow, Mother. Fare thee well.'

He left, found Thanh and Huu waiting for him in the street, and then was chauffeured back to Footscray. Thanh remained with Huu in his car for a lovers' farewell while he thanked them again and climbed the stairs to his bolthole. His busy day was about to get busier.

Sue left work early. She wanted to give Judith the good news. Rosie's mother had returned to part time nursing, and was due to start a night shift later that day.

Judith was ironing her uniform and looked up in surprise when Sue came home.

'What are you doing here,' she asked, still ironing between buttons?'

'I have good news,' said Sue, 'and wanted to tell you in person.'

Judith stopped ironing, her curiosity piqued.

'Good news? Tell me.'

'I had a visit from your daughter and your grandchildren.'

'Rosie?' Judith nearly collapsed. 'Why? What for? How was she? Are the kids okay? Tell me.'

'Take it easy,' replied Sue, holding up a hand. 'I said it was good news.' She went to the fridge. 'I need a drink.'

'I'll get it,' said Judith pushing past her. 'Just tell me what happened.'

'Well, my receptionist came in and said there was a Rosie Cadwallader in Reception with a suitcase and two children.'

'A suitcase; why a suitcase?'

'Shhh,' said Sue accepting a glass of wine. 'Long story short, she's run away.'

Judith went from being shocked to being stunned. 'She's what?'

'Reading between the lines, hubby's a bastard, so Rosie grabbed the kids and did a runner.'

'Was she hurt? Were the kids okay? Sue, tell me.'

Again Sue used a hand to calm Judith. 'She looked fine. The kids were grizzling but that's what they do—or so I'm told.'

'But how did she find you? I've never told her anything about you.'

'The people who bought your house had my details.'

'Rosie went there?' Sue nodded. 'My God, she must be desperate. So where is she now? Did you tell her to come here?'

Sue shook her head. 'Not exactly.'

'Is that lawyer-speak for no?' Sue hesitated but Judith persisted. 'Well did you give her my phone number?'

Sue explained. 'I wasn't sure if you wanted to see her.'

Judith lost it. 'You weren't sure if I wanted to see my only daughter and my only grandchildren who I've never even met? They're my family, for God's sake, my flesh and blood.'

'I thought it might be better if you met on neutral ground.'

'Neutral ground! Are you devoid of feeling? My daughter's in serious trouble and you've helped her by pushing her and her two dependent children, back onto the street.'

Sue paused. 'Not quite.'

Judith twigged. She died inside. 'Oh no, oh no ... don't tell me. Don't tell me you gave her David's address.'

'She asked for it. What was I supposed to do? Quote some privacy law?'

'So not only are you heartless and stupid, you're cruel as well.'

Sue didn't take it personally. 'Look, Jude, you've had a shock, calm down. Have a drink.'

'The shock I've had is that the woman I thought I knew and loved has denied me the chance to see and possibly save my child and grandchildren. Do you know how much I've suffered because of my kids?'

'Of course I do. But look, it's good news. Rosie's come home.'

'Not to my home she hasn't.'

'You mean my home,' automatically corrected Sue.

Oops.

Judith filed that comment for future reference but lost none of her anger and frustration. 'And now you've handed them over to their father who lives in a Footscray shithole with his teenage concubine.' Judith screamed. 'Do you know what you've done?'

She collapsed on a chair and sobbed. Despite her mantra of "never explain, never apologise", Sue accepted the fact that, in this particular situation, she might, just might have goofed.

David left the lovers in Huu's car and climbed the stairs to his flat. He was happy for once. Happy since he couldn't remember when. He whistled the melody of the song his father taught him about the Sun having its hat on.

Half way up the stairs, he thought he heard singing. He did. Someone was singing the words of the song he whistled.

David's whistling froze mid-bar. He knew that voice. But it couldn't be. He raced up the second last flight of stairs then looked up and nearly died. There stood his daughter, his long-lost only daughter with two small children.

'Rosie,' he cried, and flew up the remaining stairs. He had a million questions but settled for a very difficult hug; difficult because there were two frightened children who saw their mother cry and smile and weep and kiss a strange man. After a long and emotional reunion, David stepped back to survey the bawling babes.

"Dad, this is your grandson, Adam.'

'Hello Adam,' said David, squatting, then wiping his eyes, still with his sleeve, and not knowing the etiquette for being a kind grandfather who didn't frighten the horses.

'And this is your granddaughter.'

David stood to greet the baby in his daughter's arms.

Please don't be called Eve, thought David. *I couldn't bear introducing my grandkids as Adam and Eve.*

'... Elizabeth.'

'Hello Elizabeth,' said David, scared he might frighten the little mite. He did, but not intentionally of course.

'She gets called Lizzie, at least by me,' said Rosie.

'Then Lizzie it is,' said Grandpa, as he gently placed a hand against a cheek of his daughter and granddaughter. 'Well, don't just stand here, come in, come in.'

He opened the still unlocked door and welcomed the visitors to his magnificent mansion. He didn't care that it was a shoebox. He didn't care that he had no money. He didn't give a fig that he had little to offer. All he cared about was that here and now his darling daughter and his gorgeous grandchildren, were alive and well and here with him.

'Sit, sit, sit, make yourself at home.' He took Rosie's suitcase and stood, looking at his visitors. His heart was under attack. He struggled to express his joy. Then he panicked. *Why is Rosie here?*

She told her story with courage. When she spoke about her husband being cruel, and being supported by his parents, she lost it. She cried and her sadness was contagious. Her kids cried, and their grandfather cried. It was the sobbing centre of Footscray.

'Well, my darling,' said David, ...' She interrupted.

'Dad, I have to say sorry for everything I said and did to you and Mum when I was young and selfish and stupid.'

'Hey, hey, hey, none of that. Remember what the great man said. *Love is an act of endless forgiveness, a tender look which becomes a habit.* All that matters now is that you're out of a difficult situation and back in the bosom of your family.' She couldn't speak but nodded her thanks. He indicated their surrounds. 'Although I admit it's not much of a bosom.' They both smiled, not much, but they smiled.

'And I'm sorry about you and Mum.'

David shrugged. 'Well, you know what the great man said.' He imitated Groucho. *Politics doesn't make strange bedfellows—marriage does.*' She wanted to cry some more. 'So you've met Sue the solicitor?'

Rosie nodded. 'She said that Uncle Robert stole all your money.'

David opened his hands. 'Easy come, easy go.' He wanted to change the subject. 'Enough of these happy tales of yore; so, what are your plans? Have you seen your mother? How can I help?'

'The solicitor wouldn't give me Mum's address. Are they living together?'

'So I'm told. But come on, what are you going to do?'

'I've no idea. I've got no plans. Dad, I just couldn't stand the abuse and cruelty anymore. I just ran. If I'd told Aaron I wanted to leave, he would have kicked me out, and kept the kids.'

Silence settled. Amidst the happiness of the reunion, reality kicked in and life was definitely no bed of roses.

'Okay,' said David, 'first things first. You and the kids are welcome to stay here forever and a day, but no longer.'

'Dad, we can't, there's no room.'

'Nonsense. You and the kids can have the bedroom. I've slept more on that settee than I care to remember. Then we'll sort out your situation; a day at a day, my darling girl, a day at a time.'

He stood and picked up the suitcase.

'Come and unpack and get yourself settled in the bedroom. I'll duck down the street and get some things for the kids. What do they need?'

'Dad, I'll do that.'

He pretended to be upset. 'Oh, we're not going to argue on the first day,' he groaned. She smiled. He patted his grandson. 'I've got some heavy babysitting time to make up.'

'Dad, I've never seen you looking so smart.'

He did a terrible twirl. 'I'm thinking about a new career as a male model. Wotcha reckon?'

'Is this because of your new lady friend?'

He stopped and realised. 'Ah, so Sue the solicitor is Sue the snitch. Yes, it's true. My new lady friend has turned me into a new man. Right, enough of this banter. You unpack and I'll get some baby food and be back in two shakes of a lamb's tail.'

He departed thinking all his Christmases had come at once. While David was shopping, someone knocked on his door, and Rosie went to answer it.

Matthew Cadwallader copied his sister, Rosie. His life hit a brick wall. But where Rosie looked for a solution, Matthew crashed. Rosie wanted to see her parents, Matthew didn't. Rosie wanted to do something with her life. Matthew wanted his next fix.

His drug addiction was out of control. Like so many addicts, he didn't think he was addicted, believed he could kick the habit if he wanted to, but worse, he didn't care. Denial and lies were often found in someone hooked on heroin. If David and Judith were suddenly transported to Heaven having discovered their daughter and grandkids, these same parents would have plummeted to Hell, had they discovered their son.

He was a dealer, a regular user and had recently moved into that danger zone; the one where addicts are likely to overdose. Matthew risked his life every time he injected.

Today was the day.

19

ROSIE PICKED UP LIZZIE and opened the door. There stood her mother and words were irrelevant. The women spoke the language of tears—fluently. Eventually they settled inside where Rosie introduced the grandchildren. She explained her father's absence, and gave a potted history of her troubled marriage.

'I can't tell you how happy I am to see you, my darling,' said Judith. 'I've cried myself to sleep so many times wondering if you were safe and well and happy.'

'Mum, please, I've apologised to Dad for my unforgiveable behaviour and want to say sorry to you as well.'

'Don't be silly.'

Rosie's tear supply dropped into the Empty range. 'Dad said the same thing.'

'I bet he added some saying by Shakespeare.'

'And Groucho Marx.'

'Typical.'

Before their conversation could continue, they heard the door being opened and a familiar voice, this time calling.

'Hell-o. Heeeeeer's Grandpa.'

He stepped into the room and froze. Judith sat on his settee nursing their granddaughter. 'Oh,' was all he said.'

'Hello Grandpa,' said Judith.

David became Groucho. 'I never forget a face, but in your case ...'

Judith and Rosie spoke with him. ' ... I'll be glad to make an exception.' They pretended they hated his humour but in this case they were almost pleased.

He put the shopping aside and tousled Adam's hair. It was all too much for the toddler who clung to his mother. David pulled a kitchen chair closer to the group and sat.

'Well then, here's a pretty kettle of fish.'

'Forgive me for barging into your home,' said Judith, 'but like you, I was desperate to see our family.'

David fired on all cylinders. 'Gentle madam, you never had a servant to whose trust your business was more welcome.'

Judith ignored the Bard. 'The last time I was here, ...'

'The only time,' he corrected her.

She grinned with her lips closed. 'I was impressed with your housekeeping. Now I'm even more impressed with your appearance.'

He indicated his garb. 'You like?'

'I do. I must congratulate your mail-order bride.'

'Too kind. Now enough of this vituperative gossip, let's make a plan to help Rosie and our gorgeous grandkids.'

'Please,' said Rosie, 'I don't want to be any trouble. I've caused you enough already.'

Judith stood and handed Lizzie to her mother. 'Why don't your Dad and I have a chat about how we can best get you sorted?'

David stood and became Groucho. 'Behind every successful man is a woman, behind her is his wife.' Judith's glare spoke volumes and he dropped the comedic role. Well, until the next gig. He indicated. 'The boudoir awaits, Madame.' She walked to the bedroom and he followed, winking at Rosie. She wanted to smile but felt terrible.

In the bedroom, Judith started in a whisper. 'She desperately needs help.' David put a finger to his lips and Judith dropped her volume. 'She needs security and protection.'

'Both of which are available right here,' whispered David.

Judith scoffed. 'Oh please, you can't be serious.'

'I suggest they stay here until there's a better alternative.'

'You can't put a family of four in a shoebox.'

'It won't be forever; just until we find somewhere appropriate.'

Judith stalled. She knew David made sense, and she couldn't match his offer.

'Did she tell you her husband has been violent?'

'She did. And he won't find her here, and if he does, I'll tell him I know jujitsu and three other Japanese words.'

Judith despaired. *Once a comedian, always a comedian.*

David probed. 'I assume Sue the solicitor won't betray her location.'

'Of course not,' snapped Judith.

He probed some more. 'So may one ask why your first-best friend didn't give Rosie your address?' Judith fell silent. David seized on her hesitation. 'Ah, so Sue the solicitor doesn't want the rug rats running ragged round the Rembrandt.'

David nailed it. Judith fought back.

'I think they should be in a hotel with space and proper facilities.'

He laughed. 'Oh come on, Judith. The best thing that's happened to both of us for years is having Rosie back, and meeting our grandkids. Let's not fight over who's got the better home or reads the funniest bedtime stories; not now, anyway.'

She looked at him and knew he was right. He continued.

'Besides, I'm a fulltime babysitter. Rosie can sort out her life while I take care of the kids. Even you once awarded me the Nappy Changer of the Year award.' She did, about 25 years ago. Judith knew he made sense. 'And you can visit every day, twice a day if you like.'

His offer was genuine and she knew it. She couldn't argue with his logic. She wanted to. She hated her situation. Her home was spacious and prestigious but Sue was adamant. 'No piddling, pooing pipsqueaks will ever cross my threshold!' She didn't use those specific words but that was her drift. Just as Judith was about to concede, they heard a knock on the door and a familiar voice calling.

'My Lord.'

Judith felt a rush of pleasure. Now she could embarrass David in front of Rosie, and race back up to the moral high ground.

'Dad,' called Rosie. 'Someone's at your door.'

The parents came out of the bedroom. Judith sat and picked up Adam. David went to the door.

Judith whispered. 'This is your father's child bride. I reckon he picked her out of a catalogue. I think her name is Tun.'

David led Thanh into the room. 'Mistress, prithee greet my family.' Thanh smiled and bowed. Rosie was stunned by Thanh's beauty and magnificent outfit. Judith was more impressed than the last time.

'My former wife, my daughter and my grandchildren,' said David with pride.

Thanh bowed again and greeted the guests. 'How now, mother and daughter and thy issue?'

The visitors were speechless. This woman looked a million dollars, was obviously in love with the resident, and spoke as if she lived 400 years ago in Merrie England.

David explained. 'My daughter and her children will be staying here for a while, and I wouldst greatly love thee if thou wouldst look to caring for yon issue.'

'Oh my Lord, I wouldst take my office as thou hast bade me.'

Judith cringed and had an urge to scream, particularly as Rosie seemed infatuated with the "Mistress". When Thanh held out a hand towards Adam, the world stopped spinning.

The toddler looked at the strange woman then moved to her holding out his hand. Thanh won another heart. Judith's mood slipped into the black zone.

My grandson ignores me and takes a shine to the bimbo. $#@^&!

Thanh reminded David they needed to rehearse tomorrow then made her apologies having to care for her grandparents. She bowed again, and David escorted her to the door. He returned and Judith stood to leave.

'I think congratulations are in order. You've picked a winner, my Lord. No chance of a wedding, I suppose?'

'Yes, it's all planned and ready to go.' The women imitated goldfish. 'That's what Thanh was talking about, the wedding rehearsal.' He exhaled. 'I'll be honest. I'm deadset nervous just thinking about standing up in public with that beautiful young bride.'

Judith copped a body blow. He saw they were stunned and had an idea.

'Why don't you come, all of you?' He indicated his suit. 'I'll be wearing my new bag of fruit.'

Rosie was the first to recover. 'I hope you and Thanh will be very happy, Dad.'

'I'm sure we will.' He grinned at Judith.

It was difficult for her to speak. 'Yes, I hope you and Thanh will be happy.' There was no *very* from Judith.

David loved this. He particularly enjoyed Judith's suffering, but didn't prolong her woe. 'And I hope Thanh and her husband will be even happier.'

He enjoyed watching their faces. The women could never tell when he was serious, and his last statement confused both of them. He milked the moment.

'Oh my goodness, you didn't think Thanh and I were ... oh my lordy lord, you *did* think that.'

'Of course not,' scoffed Judith. Rosie became speechless.

He teased. 'Oh come on, admit it. You thought boring old fart David had miraculously pulled a drop-dead gorgeous mail-order trophy wife.'

The women were shell shocked. 'No, ladies, I'm not the groom, I'm the stand-in father of the bride. I'll be giving Thanh away.'

Judith suffered. Her smorgasbord of emotions threatened her sanity. She'd experienced joy, jealousy, confusion and now humiliation. She kissed Rosie and her grandchildren.

'I'll ring you tomorrow, darling, and we'll arrange a picnic for you and the kids.'

'And Dad,' asked Rosie?'

David grinned like a Cheshire cat. Judith stormed out speaking through gritted teeth. 'Yes, and your father.'

'Bye,' called David and waved. He turned to his family. 'Right then, hands up those who like spaghetti?'

Father and daughter raised their hands with Adam a millisecond later. The party began and David's smile became Texas-like.

Rosie and the kids settled into David's flat, and everyone adored their new home. Being cramped for space meant nothing when happiness ruled the roost. David and Thanh shared the babysitting duties while Rosie went out and did the rounds of Centrelink.

Sue gained a few Brownie points by working pro bono on Rosie's behalf. Judith's passion to help Rosie meant Sue's conscience kicked in, and she started preparations for Rosie to establish separation and custody rights in dealing with her alleged abusive husband. The application would state that Rosie should have custody of the children with husband Aaron having limited access, and always under supervision. Sue was told to play hardball and she did.

Husband Aaron and his parents were ropeable. Rosie, that scarlet woman, had abandoned her husband, kidnapped his children, abandoned her faith, and must be punished. The paternal grandparents knew how to bring up children in the way of the Lord.

Bullshit.

Far worse, apparently the godless David and the lesbian Judith were taking it in turns to corrupt two young souls. And when news arrived that a Buddhist, albeit no longer practising, was allowed to babysit their grandchildren, well, outrage didn't even come close to expressing their rage.

To make matters worse, Aaron's lawyer was no match for Sue the solicitor. She might have been a heartless bitch who hated children invading her spotless home, but she treated Rosie's case as if it were before the High Court. Legally, the Cadwalladers were streets ahead.

With her wedding day fast approaching, Thanh worried about her grandparents. Her grandfather's health kept declining. Her grandmother faced a quandary. She was pleased her granddaughter was to marry a fine young Vietnamese man but Grandmother wanted the cash Thanh's sewing brought to the family. Sadly the old woman missed the boat with social change.

David went to the final wedding rehearsal and loved it but these days he couldn't wait to get home. Rosie and her kids were the light of his life. Young Adam couldn't decide if he loved Pop or Thanh more. Poor old Judith limped along a distant third.

The night before the wedding, with the kids asleep, in the dimly lit flat, David and Rosie chatted over coffee. He was curious.

'Do you think your mother will come to the wedding?'

Rosie felt sad. 'What I think, Dad, is that my mother has a big house, a good job, money, a wealthy partner and access to her grandkids but is still unhappy.'

'Well if Sue the solicitor wasn't such a snob, you and the kids could be staying in that big house.'

'Maybe, but I wouldn't be happier than I am right now.'

David was touched. 'Thanks, my girl.'

They sipped in silence.

'Dad?'

'That's me.'

Why don't you talk about Matt?'

He didn't answer, well not for a while.

'Because every time I think about him, a bit of my heart shrivels up and dies, and by talking about him, two bits of my heart shrivel up and die.'

'I'm sorry, Dad, I didn't mean to upset you.'

'Of course you didn't mean to.'

She knew this conversation was tough for her father but she really wanted to talk about her brother.

'Do you think he's dead?'

David's head dropped and in the darkened room, he wept. Rosie didn't know he was crying until he sucked in a big breath and gasped. She put down her coffee and moved to his side. She took his mug and placed it on the coffee table beside the thick tome of *The Complete Works of William Shakespeare*. She hugged him and he cried the more.

Finally he settled, and she snuggled into him and stroked his arm. He managed to speak.

'Every night, provided I'm sober, I talk to him. I ask him how he's going, has he got a girlfriend? Does he think the Bombers will win the flag?' David blew his nose on a clean handkerchief. Clean was good so domestically, things had definitely improved.

'What does he tell you?'

'That he loves your Mum and me and you and I know, if he knew he was an uncle, he would tell me how much he loves Adam and Lizzie.'

Rosie cried now. How could she not? Prayer was not an option. Rosie had lost her faith and David never had any.

They might have sat there for ages had not Adam found his voice.

'Grandpa,' he called. The couple on the settee got active.

'I think I'm jealous,' said Rosie. 'Who you gunna call? Grandpa!'

He laughed and lost some of his Matthew misery as he trotted off to see his grandson.

The wedding day turned out a ripper. Guests didn't need a coat or umbrella but sunglasses were all the rage. Thanh and Huu had chosen to be married in a civil ceremony by the Maribyrnong River. It was a small guest list. Thanh had only two members of her family Down Under and sadly they remained at home. Grandfather couldn't even get out of bed. His wife's dedication and stubbornness kept the old man out of hospital.

Huu had many family members and friends while Thanh's side was represented by David and Rosie and her kids. Little Adam had the time of his life and headed the list of Thanh admirers.

Just as the service was about to begin, and David's nerves hit fever pitch as he prepared to walk Thanh down the path, a familiar voice was heard.

'Just a minute,' called the late arrival. Everyone turned to see Julia "racing" to join the party. She sat in a wheelchair with a smartly dressed young man driving the machine.

David and Thanh looked at one another, Rosie giggled, and the company smiled.

Once Julia was in position, she looked at her son. 'Fight valiantly today!' she said. 'Live, love and let be.'

The company murmured, the music started and David escorted Thanh to marry her true love. The ceremony was simple, short and stuffed full of love and happiness. Huu thought he'd won the lottery. His family were over the moon. Thanh couldn't believe her good fortune standing between the two men she loved more than anyone in the world, and Rosie and her grandmother were bursting with pride admiring the "father" of the bride.

The food at the wedding breakfast would have won praise in a top restaurant. Thanh was a superb cook but Huu was the one with the contacts, and his friends created a sumptuous feast. The Cadwallader Caucasians adored the Vietnamese cuisine. Wee Adam had never given his taste buds such a workout. His great-grandmother did something remarkable—Julia enjoyed herself.

David sat next to her and made a confession between courses number 3 and 4. 'Thank you for coming, Mother. It meant a lot to Thanh and Huu.'

'But not to you?'

'No, it meant even more to me. Thank you.' He leant in and kissed his mother's cheek. She showed no outward reaction but internally, she felt grand. 'Now don't forget, Mother, it's the weekly visit for Rosie and the kids and me tomorrow.'

'I haven't forgotten. And I need to speak to you about my will.'

David lost control of his chopsticks, and his spring roll performed a forward roll.

20

MATTHEW NEEDED A HIT. His heroin addiction was so entrenched he lost his bargaining skills as a dealer. He got ripped-off on a regular basis. He used too much thus having less to sell. With less money he couldn't afford what he needed. He turned to crime, petty stuff for starters. The downward spiral got busy. He raced past warning signs and lost all sense of reality.

He shared an abandoned warehouse in Brunswick and had to go "out of town" for the gear. He crouched in a Richmond laneway, tightened the belt around his arm, and probed for a vein. He jabbed the syringe and sent a bad batch of heroin into his bloodstream.

Psychologically he felt fantastic. Physically he felt like crap. He collapsed.

Good Samaritans were constantly in demand in North Richmond when it came to addicts overdosing. Residents had long demanded a safe injecting room. They were sick of the needles and other paraphernalia in their gardens, and sick of the comatose bodies blocking their vehicle or pedestrian access.

One caring resident saw Matthew slumped in the laneway and phoned an ambulance. Luck's a fortune. One was nearby attending to another heroin overdose patient. The ambos knew the routine and could perform it blindfolded.

A shot of naloxone could have an almost instant impact. Matthew got expert attention and a free ride to St Vincent's public hospital. The staff in Emergency had seen this type of patient more times than they could remember.

Matthew was lucky. He was minutes from death. Had the ambulance not been called, or not been close at hand, he would have become another statistic in the column headed *Death by Misadventure—Drug Overdose.*

He lay in bed with tubes and monitoring equipment attached to his drug-addled body. Arguably the worst part of this tragic situation was that his family knew nothing.

Would they want to know?

It was a trip and a half from Footscray to South Yarra by public transport. Rosie's life improved out of sight having a babysitter, carer and entertainer in Grandpa David. He and Adam got on like a house on fire, and Lizzie found it easy to love her Pop.

Julia would never admit it but her first great-grandchildren were just that—great. She asked them to call her Julia which meant nothing to Lizzie and a mouthful for Adam. 'Joolya,' was the best he could manage.

The matriarch had sent out to the Toorak Village patisserie and some of the best afternoon-tea fare in the world was on show.

Adam adored the space of Joolya's abode and could have been reprimanded for running from room to room. What a contrast. Had Adam behaved like so in Sue the solicitor's abode, she would have called the cops, whereas great-grandma Julia positively encouraged the little tacker. David and Rosie couldn't believe the generosity being displayed by the old girl.

The surprises kept coming when, with the kids both having a nap, Julia announced she had something to say.

'I'll go and sit with the kids, Gran,' said Rosie.

'No you won't,' replied Julia. 'This involves you and your father.'

Oh dear, this sounded serious.

'Are you okay, Mum,' asked David?

'Well according to my doctor, who is one of the rudest men I've ever met, I'm in rude health. I told him that only a rude man could make a rude diagnosis.'

David and Rosie looked at one another.

'I'm not getting any younger, and so I've changed my will.'

'Now you know what the great man said, Mother.' He became Groucho. 'I intend to live forever, or die trying.'

She ignored his performance. 'I will leave my entire estate to you and your brother.'

That was it. She waited for a response. David was confused.

'But that's your old will, Mother.'

'How you two divide it up between your children, if at all, and now even your grandchildren, is up to you.'

'Thank you, Mother. Rest assured my brother and I will look after all your grandchildren and great-grandchildren.'

'The change in my new will changes the order in which my assets are liquidated and the proceeds shared.'

That was new. The others became fascinated. She continued.

'The apartment will still be sold upon my death but I've made a new arrangement and had it noted by my lawyer.'

'I see,' said David, not seeing at all. Rosie was clueless.

'I've been busy of late arranging my affairs. On Friday, I'm moving to a ridiculously expensive retirement home, just down the road, so vacant possession of this apartment begins this weekend.'

Her son and granddaughter sat stunned. 'You're moving,' asked a confused David?'

'Keep up, keep up,' urged Mother. 'I'll pay for your removalists this week.'

That sentence hung in the air and refused to move. Julia was a drama queen par excellence. She looked at them then delivered the knockout punch.

'Oh wake up, sleepy head. This apartment is to be your home until I die. And by you, I mean you two and Adam and Lizzie.'

David and Rosie looked at one another. Rosie started to cry. David was speechless. His mother was not famous for her generosity.

'Your brother went ballistic when I told him, and apparently his wife spontaneously combusted.'

David and Rosie couldn't help but smile.

'I don't know what to say, Mother. That's extremely generous.'

Rosie went to her grandmother and hugged and kissed her.

David shook his head. 'This weekend?'

'Are you deaf,' asked Julia?

Rosie copied her father in head shaking. What could they say?

'Now I expect you to look after the place,' said Julia. The others were still struck dumb. 'No extra guests. Judith may visit but not her lady friend. And no sleepovers. Is that understood?'

'Yes Gran,' said Rosie.

'Yes Mother,' said David.

'Your brother may never speak to you again, and you'll need a restraining order for his wife.'

The smiles became grins. Even Julia enjoyed her own joke.

'Oh, but there is one exception to the rule about extra guests. Matthew will always be welcome.'

Boy, did that fire an arrow into a couple of hearts.

David whispered. 'Thank you, ...' He wanted to say "Mother" but his voice cracked.

Lizzie started to cry in what would soon be her new bedroom, and that woke Adam. Rosie headed off to attend to her brood. David didn't know what to say or do. He finally began to think straight.

'What about packing, Mother. What about ...'

'It's all under control. All the furniture, my books, knick-knacks and things stay. I'll leave most of my clothes, and Rosie can have what she wants. The rest you will give to charity but don't take them to a shop in South Yarra or Toorak. I couldn't bear to be having coffee in the Village and see my French suits being paraded by some new money cheapskate.'

David smiled. His mother was nothing if not a character.

That weekend it all happened. Judith waited until her former mother-in-law had departed—they never got on—and then made her way to South Yarra. She helped Rosie set up the bedroom for the grandchildren, and then Rosie's room as well. Judith had been shopping and stocked the kitchen cupboards with all manner of goodies for the little uns.

Sue the solicitor had forced Judith's son-in-law to hand over all the toys and clothes belonging to the kids, which Rosie had left on the day she fled the marital home.

Sue had advised Aaron's solicitor that his estranged wife had taken photos of the bruises Aaron had caused when being violent to his wife. Aaron justified that under the "wives submit to your husband" malarkey. There were no photos but Aaron and his furious parents were not to know that. Sue had the children's goods collected, after which a carrier rang the doorbell on the South Yarra street.

Rosie and the kids rejoiced when the pile of goodies arrived. Sue the solicitor had her uses.

Back in downtown Footscray, David packed his worldly possessions. He missed Thanh. Not only were her lessons complete, so too was her time as his next door neighbour. She and hubby Huu were on their honeymoon—nowhere near an ocean—and upon their return, would live in a flat in Kensington. Of course she would visit her grandparents but David was moving and wouldn't be next door.

In the middle of his packing, he picked up the book that started it all—*The Complete Works of William Shakespeare*. David sat on his settee and opened the tome. He remembered their first encounter when Thanh rushed in to his flat speaking fluent Vietnamese or, to David, fluent gibberish. Happy days.

Suddenly loud knocking sounded on his door. For a moment, David thought it was Thanh. It sounded just like her knock all those months ago. He went to the door and suffered a case of déjà vu.

Thanh's grandmother, speaking Vietnamese, said almost exactly what Thanh had said when she first met David. But instead of the word *grandfather*, it was *husband*. David didn't need a translator. The elderly woman took David's hand and dragged him across the landing and into her flat. Thanh's grandfather lay on the floor. David knelt and felt panic. The old man made strange sounds. Was this the death rattle? David looked around and couldn't see a phone.

'Telephone,' he said miming using a phone. The old woman shook her head. Trying to ease the woman's distress, David rushed to his apartment, and called an ambulance. He raced back and gently lifted the old man onto the settee.

He was alive but unconscious. David did what he thought was the right thing. The old woman kept speaking in her native tongue. David went through a range of charades and felt overjoyed when the ambulance siren sounded. He repeated his routine from his previous performance.

'Up here,' he called to the ambulance crew. When they arrived, David explained. 'The old woman only speaks Vietnamese.'

Once they began treating Grandfather, they gave David the thumbs up. He told them he was next door then bowed to the old woman and made his exit. Just as he entered his flat, he felt something on his arm. Madame Nguyen had followed David. He looked at her as she bowed and offered thanks. David smiled and watched as the woman hurried back to her husband.

'That was nice,' he said, 'and on my final day. Talk about the wheel turning full circle.'

He returned to packing, thinking about his two experiences helping Thanh's grandfather. Another knock sounded on his door. Not as insistent as before but still with a touch of strength. Hoping it wasn't the ambulance crew to tell him the old man had died, he opened the door.

'David Cadwallader,' asked the man?

'Possibly,' replied David.

The man was mid-40s, bald, powerful-looking and Asian, probably Vietnamese. David wondered if he was a criminal involved with drugs.

The man called himself Quan with David unsure if that was a pseudonym. He sat in Thanh's armchair.

'I got your name from a friend of a friend.'

'I see,' said David, not seeing at all.

'I'll be straight with you David. Can I call you David?'

'Please do, Quan.'

'I believe you have a son who has a drug problem.' David was hooked. 'I'm involved with a drug rehabilitation programme. It's privately funded, and nothing to do with government, NGOs, churches or charities. Am I right about your son?'

Alarm bells rang in David's head. *Is this a scam? Is he from the police? Is he a religious weirdo? How does he know about Matthew?*

'Yes, you're right.'

'I believe his name is Matthew.' David nodded. The mood was serious. 'What do you want?'

Quan took a deep breath. 'I want to help your son. Let me explain what we do.'

'Who or what are we?'

'There are two wealthy Vietnamese businessmen here in Melbourne. They're linked because each had a child who died from a heroin overdose. These men have funded a private project to help Vietnamese drug addicts beat their addiction.'

David found the man and his story fascinating.

'You must know my son is not Vietnamese.'

'Please, let me finish.' David fell silent. He had no urge to throw in a Groucho quote. 'We operate a unique, unofficial, and illegal but effective treatment. As you may know, many addicts complete their rehabilitation, quit heroin then return to society and live a normal life. But, sadly, for a few, something happens and they go back to drugs, and, all too often wreck their life or even end it.'

David had vivid memories of Matthew going to rehab, getting clean and then relapsing. 'I know about that,' he said. 'But why is your system illegal?'

'We kidnap the addict.'

David gasped. 'You kidnap them? What, take them off the street?'

'Off the street, from their home, from a laneway where they've just shot up, anywhere.'

'What about the police?'

'We fly under the radar and the cops rarely get wind of us, but if ever they do, they look the other way. Why wouldn't they?'

'Why indeed,' said David?

'We're successful and every addict we reform means the cops have less crimes to solve and hospitals have less emergencies.'

David said *fewer crimes and fewer emergencies* under his breath. 'When you say successful, how successful?'

'Put it this way, our success rate is much better than the official rehab places.'

'Why? What do you do that the others don't?'

Quan hesitated. 'That's like asking the Colonel for his recipe with its secret herbs and spices. We keep our methods under wraps just like our venues and benefactors.'

Quan stopped speaking allowing David to process the information. Finally David asked the obvious question.

'So I have to ask about why you're here? You must know my son's Caucasian.'

'We do and if your son gets involved, he'll be the first non-Vietnamese to do so.'

David pondered. 'I'm impressed but all this begs the question, why?'

'We got a request from one of our own. This person said you'd done a power of good within the Vietnamese community, that you'd had a hard time of late and deserved a break.'

'I can only think of one person who might have said that.'

'And pretty persuasive they were too. We've never helped a drug addict who wasn't Vietnamese.'

'When you say "they", I assume you mean she, and by name, Thanh Nguyen, now Thanh Phan.'

'You might think that, David, but I couldn't possibly comment.'

'You sound like a cop or someone who watches upmarket TV.'

Quan grinned. 'As I said, David, ...' They spoke together.

'I couldn't possibly comment.'

Silence commenced. David had a long list of questions and started.

'How much will it cost?'

'There is no cost.'

Of all the shocks David had received in the last few minutes, this was the biggest. He remembered the money he and Judith paid for weeks of treatment in some rehab place interstate.

'Nothing?'

'Nothing. As I told you, the operation is funded by two wealthy Vietnamese businessmen who came to this country with nothing, who worked hard and became successful, and I mean very successful as law-abiding citizens, and it's their money that funds the business.'

'So are you offering this service to my son?'

'Well it'd be pretty cruel of me to tell you all this unless your son was not offered the opportunity.'

'You offer it to the addicts? I thought you said they were kidnapped.'

'They are. Sorry, as the Americans say, I misspoke. We approach the parents. If they agree, we go ahead. We don't tell them if their child has been taken. We don't tell them if the addict completes the course. We just return them back to society and hope they stay clean. And as I said, most of them do.'

A long and silent pause ensued.

'I don't know what to say,' said an emotional David.

'*Yes* would do.'

'And you ask permission from both parents?'

'We do.'

'Is it possible to not involve my ex-wife?'

'Why?'

'I'm sure she'd approve of the project but she's invested a lot of blood, sweat and tears into helping our son, and if she knew about this and it failed, I think the disappointment might just be too much.'

'But not for you?'

'Well you've told me so the option of not being aware isn't available.'

The visitor pondered David's request. 'Sounds like you still love your ex-wife.'

David smiled. 'Let's just say I take the "first, do not harm" bit to heart.'

Quan nodded. He wanted to help this man. 'We'll it's crunch time, David. It's a silly question but do you want us to help Matthew?'

'You're right; it is a silly question. Where do I sign?'

Quan stood. 'No signature.'

David's shock continued. 'No signature?'

'No paperwork, no records, nothing; remember we fly under the radar.'

David stood and offered his hand which Quan grasped. It was a handshake on the high side of firm. 'Thank you, Quan. I only have words to express my appreciation, and sometimes even they fail. Your kindness makes me weep.' On cue his tears arrived. 'Of course I hope you are successful, but just for trying, I will forever be in your debt.'

'We'll do our best.'

David wouldn't let go of Quan's hand, and repeated the words of the Bard. 'I can no other answer make, but, thanks, and thanks.'

Finally Quan's hand was freed and, without speaking, he turned and left. When Quan reached the door, David spoke.

'I suppose I'll never see you again.'

Quan hesitated, didn't turn then walked out of David's life forever.

It took David and Rosie and the kids a week to get the hang of living in a "slightly" changed environment on the other side of the tracks. It was carpet versus no carpet, three loos versus one, a study and playroom and a huge sitting room versus one cramped lounge—and much more. The furniture was all class, and the kitchen appliances created an adventure playground when whipping up meals for the kids and the grown-ups.

Judith arrived on a regular basis and she and David found a new type of relationship. She buried her anger, and he half-buried his sense of failure. They took their grandkids on treats allowing Rosie to hit the books as she went back to school to acquire the qualifications she needed to become a fashion designer—something for which she had a real flair.

It was David and Rosie's six month anniversary in "Joolya's shack". Up the road, she did okay in her upmarket residence, and loved showing off her great-grandchildren when David brought them to visit—quite often too. So to mark the anniversary, David and Rosie planned a special meal.

'I'll make the main course, Dad, and you can make dessert,' said Rosie.

'You mean I'm in charge of opening the tin of stewed fruit and the ice-cream,' replied her father.

Adam heard the magic word and screamed. His grandfather launched into a song he'd taught the kids. Adam was good with the last line. 'You scream, I scream, we all scream for ice-cream.' Even Lizzie had started her speaking with *Mummy, Poppy* and now *ice-cream*.

That afternoon, David, the babysitter, took the children for a walk with Lizzie in her stroller. He perambulated in the park, allowing Lizzie to "walk" while helping her balance with a harness. Adam seemed intent on becoming the next David Attenborough finding leaves, twigs and ants. David examined Adam's latest exhibit when he heard a special voice.

'Greetings, my Lord.'

He looked up to see a beaming former student. 'Mistress,' he exclaimed and Adam turned and came running. Lizzie was not sure but quickly joined the happy reunion. They moved to a park bench where Thanh sat beside David who nursed Lizzie. Adam wanted to sit on Thanh's lap.

'Sit here, Adam,' said David placing his grandson between the two adults. David had enjoyed Thanh's regular visits but it had been several weeks since they last met.

'How art thou, Mistress, and thy husband?'

'Well, my Lord, and full of good cheer.'

'Dost I be forward and enquire of thy condition?'

Thanh laughed. 'Thou may, my Lord and yea, I am in the childing condition.'

David beamed, Adam tried to show Thanh his latest leaf, and Lizzie bounced on her grandfather's knee. He thought it appropriate to hear Thanh's great news at the time when he enjoyed the boisterous behaviour of two toddlers.

'Congratulations. And please convey the same to thy husband.'

Thanh had something she wished to say but found it difficult. 'My Lord, if my child is a son, Huu and I have chosen to call him David.'

She looked at him with excitement and love in her heart. She didn't know how he would react but longed for his response. He didn't respond, at least not externally. Thanh sensed his lack of words meant his emotions had caught fire. His mouth went dry. He couldn't speak.

'Adam looked up and questioned his carer. 'Why are you crying, Grandpa?'

David made light of his condition. 'I am not crying. Grandpa is happy.' He tickled his grandson. 'Happy, do you hear?'

Adam shrieked, hopped down and ran around the grass. Lizzie wanted to join him. She waddled but would soon be able to chase her brother.

David squeezed Thanh's hand and whispered, 'Thank you ... thank you.'

Once upon a time in Footscray, they couldn't stop talking. Right now, words were unimportant. Both had come a long way and found a rich and ever expanding love. He thought it selfish but dearly wanted Thanh to have a boy.

'I am glad you hath come today. I hath been keen to thank you for talking to a man about my son.'

'Your son, my Lord?'

'You cannot deny thy kindness. I cannot tell how happy you have made me; not just because my son may get help, but because you have done this for me.'

'I am repaying thy kindness, my Lord.'

They looked at one another. She said those words before, at a time when she tried to lift his spirits. Both had moved on since then, and still their love grew ever stronger. He had a new home and his "new" family. She had a husband and a child to be. If male, his name would be David.

Thanh declined his invitation to come back to the apartment and stood to leave. Seeing her condition, David only wanted to help. They kissed and the children gave Thanh the sweetest of farewells. They waved and she waved and then she was gone.

'When is Thanh coming to our house, Grandpa,' asked Adam?

'Soon,' he replied. 'And when she comes to our house she may bring a special present, a baby.'

'A baby,' exclaimed Lizzie.

'What's its name,' asked the curious Adam.

David pretended to be thinking. 'I know. It might be David.'

Adam looked at his grandfather, his little brain working overtime. 'That's your name, Grandpa.'

David laughed. He didn't see Thanh hidden behind a tree observing her favourite teacher and his family. She felt good, nay, wondrous.

David told the children they were going home. Lizzie demanded to walk but Grandpa insisted she travel in style. No way would Adam travel in any stroller. They set off and Adam played with his big round ball. He threw it and it rolled away. He ran to pick it up but a man stopped it and gave it to the boy.

'Say thank you, Adam,' said David, looking at his grandson.

'Thank you,' said the youngster.

The man smiled and David nodded his appreciation. He started to push the stroller then stopped and stared at the stranger, who spoke.

'Hello Dad.'

The Detective Joanna Best Mysteries

www.cenfoxbooks.com

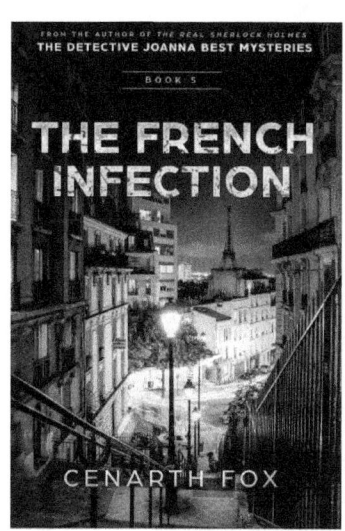

www.ingramcontent.com/pod-product-compliance
Lightning Source LLC
Chambersburg PA
CBHW071112100726
47908CB00008B/2347